THE COLLAPSE:
FATE'S VULTURES

BEG FOR MERCY

JAMI GRAY

Copyright © December 2021 by Jami Gray
All rights reserved.
Beg for Mercy - The Collapse: Fate's Vultures - Book 2
Revised Publication: March 2022
Celtic Moon Press
ISBN: 978-1-948884-54-9 (ebook)
ISBN: 978-1-948884-55-6 (print)

Cover Art: Deranged Doctor Design
www.derangeddoctordesign.com

Initial Publication: April 2018
Escape Publishing - HarperCollins Australia
ISBN: 978-1-4892-519-8 (ebook)

what readers say...

also by jami gray

PSY-IV TEAMS (ongoing)

Hunted by the Past

Touched by Fate

Marked by Obsession

Fractured by Deceit

Linked by Deception

ARCANE TRANSPORTER (complete)

Ignition Point - novella

Grave Cargo

Risky Goods

Lethal Contents

THE KYN KRONICLES (ongoing)

Shadow's Edge

Shadow's Soul

Shadow's Moon

Shadow's Curse

Shadow's Dream

Shadow's Fall

FATE'S VULTURES (complete)

Lying in Ruins

Beg for Mercy

Caught in the Aftermath

Fear the Reaper

BOX SETS

PSY-IV Teams Box Set I (Books 1-3)

acknowledgments

As always, this whole writing schtick would never work without the unending support of the males of my heart, Ben, Ian, and Brendan.

I can never say thank you enough to my readers because the whole writing thing wouldn't be as much fun without you. Who else, other than the crazy writer behind it, is going to get as excited about these stories as you all?

And to be sure those stories work, my gratitude to those who offer hours of advice instead of barricading themselves inside when I head their way—my cohorts in the wacky world of writing: Camille, DeAnna, and Dave, plus the talented support of Brooke, Kate, and Johanna from Escape.

This one is for Donna Jo, Robin, Kristin, Kim, Amber, Monica, and Angie, a group of women who take on life's messy challenges with an enviable grace that leaves me humbled. You women kick serious ass!

one

A breeze trickled through the heated air trapped inside the shop's dim interior and the barest shadow inched along the wall, its presence drifting through the sunlight stretched across the pitted floor. It wasn't much of a disturbance, but it was enough to make Havoc pause, his dark bottle of home-brew suspended halfway to his drier-than-the-desert-outside mouth.

He continued to watch the furtive movement from the corner of his eye, unwilling to reveal his awareness of the interloper. As the shadow slipped along the rusted interior wall of the local ammunition dealer's shop, his recently lax muscles coiled in anticipation and the bottle's edge hovered over his lip.

Another breeze caught the ragged edges of the head scarf and caused a traitorous ripple. The deeper inside the shadow crept, the more human shape it became. A slight shift in stance pulled the loose material tight, just long enough to determine a slender set of feminine curves under the baggy cargo pants and oversized, dust-stained layered shirts.

Havoc took a slow blink to keep the sandy grit that floated

on the air from making a permanent home on his eyeballs. Faint shouts drifted through the shop's opening off the rutted street, but a strange, unwelcome curiosity held him in place. The shouts came closer, carrying the heavily accented voices inside. An old rage roused, but with the ease of practice, Havoc locked it down and kept watching, wondering.

The female tried to sink into the shrinking shadows. He should probably tell her that it wouldn't do shit all, but his brain was determined to warn him off. *Nothing good would come from getting involved.*

Whatever sent her scurrying into the dubious protection of the shop, wasn't his damn business. He wasn't here to get involved in other people's troubles, he was here for one thing —to reload his brass, a necessity when ammunition was difficult to acquire. A project, the shop owner, Boomer, was currently assisting with in the backroom.

As if Havoc's thoughts were a primer, Boomer's rough voice shot through the shop. "You need to be more particular about your salvaging, my man. Some of this brass is for shit."

It was almost comical how fast the female's head snapped around. Her dark, heavily lashed eyes hit and held his, and despite the crappy lighting he caught the flash of grim determination edged with defiant fury before it was quickly banked into a predatory stillness.

The impact landed a sucker punch to his gut, and that single look blew his resolve about getting involved to shit. Silently cursing as he held the wary woman's gaze, he took a sip of his beer, set the bottle on the table's top, and answered Boomer, "Most brass nowadays is shit."

That elicited a bark of laughter from the back room. "True."

Outside a heated exchange erupted, Spanish curses flew like horseflies on shit, and the woman's head whipped back toward the street.

Bad move, darlin'.

Utilizing on her momentary lapse of attention, Havoc slipped around the table and closed in, ignoring the snarled curse from the devil on his shoulder. He trapped her smaller body against the wall with his heavier frame, wrapped one hand around her wrist and forced it between the wall and her hip, locking it in place. Undaunted, she lashed out with her blade, but he blocked her intended strike, and with a sharp twist, had her well and truly caught.

As close as they were he couldn't miss the feel of the sinuous lines of muscle under the loose clothing or the unyielding fury raging in the brown, green-shot depths of her eyes under the grimy head scarf that covered the rest of her features.

The voices outside got closer. He put his lips to her ear and did his best not to react to the not-unpleasant, faint scent of dust and sweat that drifted from her. "Crate to the left, over by the table, see it?"

He pulled back just enough to watch her search his face.

Wary confusion laced with a healthy dose of self-preservation nudged the fury in her brown eyes aside. Cautiously, as if waiting for him to bite, she looked to the shipping crate that back against the wall. Her gaze came back to him, and she gave a slow nod.

"You get in and stay quiet." Once he had another nod, he released her empty hand, dragged her over, and then flipped the lid up. The box was empty since Boomer had just inventoried his delivery. He tugged on her wrist, ignoring the blade in her fist. "Get in."

Another sharp burst of Spanish erupted from outside and she flinched, her eyes darting to the door before coming back to him. A muscle in her jaw jumped and she followed his instructions. She got in the box and tucked into a small ball.

With both hands on the lid, he stared down at her, the

devil on his shoulder still ranting curses. "Don't make me regret this, hear?"

She dipped her chin once.

He dropped the lid in place, shifted the crate so it hunkered between the wall and the table, and then sat on top of it for good measure. The sturdy wood creaked under his weight but held. He leaned his back against the wall, sprawled his legs under the table, and reclaimed his beer.

Time to confirm who the hell was chasing her. He lifted the bottle and took a drink as his answer stepped into the doorway, blocking the sunlight.

Fucking great. Didn't it just figure that when he decided to step in it, he seriously stepped in it.

As the trio stepped deeper inside, there was no mistaking them for anyone else. From their dust coated boots to their faded jeans, and the knife laden, leather bandoliers strapped over sweat-stained t-shirts, and all of that topped off with the telltale Stetsons.

Yep, Cartel scum.

The scourge of depravation known as the Cartels ruled the southern territory that stretched from the drowned remains of Los Angeles through the dust-scoured bones of Phoenix, and down into the ravaged remains of El Paso and San Antonio. It was unusual, but not completely strange, for them to be this far north.

The lead dumbass of the three-man pack puffed out his barrel chest in a weak attempt to make Havoc quake in his boots. "You see a woman, *boracho*?"

Havoc squelched his sneer and checked his contempt. Taking his time, he set his bottle on the table, leaned back, and dropped one hand below the table's edge and closer to his blades. "I've seen a lot of women. You looking for something particular?"

The blowhard snapped his fingers. At his signal, the two

sidekicks jumped, then spread out to rifle through the haphazard boxes and shelves that cluttered the shop. Their careless search toppled boxes to the floor and the dull din of falling objects filled the shop.

Bad move, cabrons.

Not wanting to ruin the impending entertainment, Havoc kept mute and took another swig, hiding his mirthless grin behind his bottle.

Before the metallic echoes could fade away, they were replaced by the distinctive ratchet of a shotgun. "What the fuck are you doin' in my shop, asswipes?"

The brainless twins stopped, their gazes skittering from a grim-faced Boomer, who stood behind the long counter cradling a classic Benelli, to their red-faced leader, who was obviously unsure of what to do next.

The head honcho stepped forward with studied casualness, a smarmy smile emerging under the trimmed mustache. "We're not looking for trouble, just a woman."

Unable to resist, Havoc decided to poke the snake and drawled, "Seems they're one and the same."

His comment earned a narrow-eyed glare before the Cartel's man turned his attention back to the bigger threat. "Have you seen her?"

"I'm a munitions shop, not a whorehouse." Boomer motioned the Benelli towards the door. "Want a woman? Head down a couple streets, turn left and ask for Margo's. She'll be more than happy to take your order." The shotgun leveled and held steady. "Get out."

The leader lifted his hands in surrender and cocked his head in acknowledgement. "Perhaps a woman would do you good, old man. You seem a little tense."

One of the idiots behind him snickered. Boomer's hard gaze flicked to the offender and the snicker choked out. Then Boomer's attention returned to Mustache man. He smiled and it wasn't pretty, flashing his teeth, what few remained, stained by years of tobacco chewing. "I prefer to release my tensions with target practice, hombre."

"*Cálmate*, my man. We're leaving." Mustache's dark eyes slid away and drifted over Havoc. He gave another one of those mocking smiles and accompanying nods, before he turned on his heel, uttered a sharp command in Spanish, and then strode out, his dogs on his heels.

Under the table Havoc's hand flexed near the hilt of the throwing blade tucked at his thigh. It took an ugly amount of restraint to not send the beautiful knife deep between the man's shoulder blades. Just on principle. Instead, he lifted the bottle and drained it in one long swallow.

Boomer and Havoc remained still and silent as they listened to the Cartel trio move away down the street. Finally, Boomer sighed, pressed the Benelli's firing pin release lever and set the shotgun on the counter. "What in the Sam Hill was that about, Havoc?"

Havoc didn't answer, not because he didn't trust Boomer, but because he did. Well, as much as you could trust anyone anymore. His gut was all about keeping this situation as low key as possible. No sense in tempting that capricious bitch, Fate.

At his silence, Boomer's eyes narrowed, and he shook his head slowly. "I know that look."

Havoc raised his brows and adopted an innocent expression. "What look?"

Boomer snorted. "Don't bullshit a bullshitter, boy." He picked up the weapon and set it on his shoulder. "Fine, I don't wanna know." He turned back to his reloading area. "Your brass will be ready in about twenty." Then he disappeared through the ratty curtains strung up between the thin back wall.

It wasn't long before Boomer's stool scraped against the

floor, the distinctive noise unmistakable, as he resumed his task. Minutes ticked by as Havoc debated his next move. Not that there were many to pick from because once he tucked the woman in the box, they were pretty damn limited. First things first, he and his newly acquired shadow needed to slip away.

He sighed. His partner, Vex, was going to have his balls for getting in this mess.

He nabbed his empty bottle, stood, and made his way behind the counter. He tossed the empty into the recycle box of other fallen glass soldiers, the chiming crash echoing through the shop.

He opened the small, ancient cooler tucked in the corner, grabbed the water jug, and a relatively clean glass from the counter. "Boomer?" Taking his cue from the responding grunt, Havoc continued as he poured, "Mind if I make use of your escape hatch?"

"Feel free," the other man called back. "Just don't bring any trouble back to my doorstep."

"Not planning on it," Havoc muttered as he put the water jug back in the cooler. He picked up the filled glass and paused just outside the curtains. "Thanks."

He got another grunt for his gratitude. He shook his head and went back to his surprise package. Although it wasn't the height of summer, it was still warm enough that being crammed into a box would be far from comfortable.

He crouched and lifted the lid. Sure enough, what little skin not covered by the scarf now carried a rosy hue and a sheen of sweat. He held out the water. "Here."

Dirt-grimed hands gripped the box's edge as she pulled herself up, and those eyes locked on him with a prey's wariness.

Smart girl.

He noted the ragged, torn nails and the fact that some of the rust-colored grime was blood.

With a bit of maneuvering, she managed to sit tailor style in the box and pulled the tail end of the scarf free, revealing an intriguing face. Heavily lashed, wide eyes sat under dark brows and reflected a strength belied by the delicate jaw line. There were a few small nicks mixed with the freckles that marred the warm, honey-touched tones of her skin.

Hers wasn't a breath-stealing beauty, but one that snuck in and wrapped temptation's hand around his dick.

Cautiously, without looking away, she reached out for the glass, her fingers brushing his as she took it. The water rocked as she lifted it to her nose and took a delicate inhale.

He stifled his grin. "No poison."

Her eyes flashed just before her lashes dropped, but she brought the cup to her chapped lips and drained it. Once it was empty, she handed it back, but she caught her lower lip with her teeth as her gaze followed the empty glass. Then, as if realizing what that revealed, her gaze jerked back to him.

But it was too late. That one move told him she was hitting the end of her reserves. Which meant one glass of water would do jack to quench her thirst. Time to see if she was mute or obstinate. He took the cup from her and waited.

The monotonous tick of a clock on the back wall counted the seconds as their staring contest became a silent battle of wills. He was beginning to wonder if they would be here for the rest of the afternoon when she finally sighed. "What?"

Fierce satisfaction that she broke first flared and made him an asshole. *But he was an asshole who won the first skirmish, so who the fuck cared.* "Want another?"

Her head tilted and her husky voice remained flat. "Is it going cost me?"

"Nah, the water's free." He straightened and knowing any offer of help would be rebuffed, he left her to make her way out of the box.

He went back to the cooler and refilled the glass, giving her his back. It might not be his smartest move, but he wanted to see if she'd run or stay. He wasn't sure which he'd prefer.

When he turned back, he found her standing on the other side of the counter. He pushed the glass over and waited until she picked it up and brought it to her lips before adding, "But if you want a way to get around the dick weasel on your ass, gotta know why you're running."

Instead of answering, she took another healthy swallow, downing about half the contents. She set the glass back on the counter. "Thanks for the water."

She turned to leave but Havoc wasn't done. He caught her arm and despite her rather impressive snarl, he held her in place and warned, "You step outside that door, you'll be dead before sunset."

Quick as a snake, she grabbed his finger and yanked it back. It stung, not as much as she intended, but he granted her request for freedom. She leaned in, her eyes narrowed. "You don't know me well enough to make that prediction."

Her stubbornness triggered an unfamiliar anger and turned his smile nasty and evil. "You, no, but the Cartels? Yeah, babe, I guaran-fucking-tee, they'll have your throat slit and your pretty tongue playing necktie before the moon rises." He shook off her hold and stepped back. "But you're right, I don't know you from jack, so good luck.

two

Mercy wanted to snatch up the half-filled glass and brain the man staring at her with such contempt. But that was the exhaustion and dehydration talking. Contrary to the obvious opinion of the bruiser staring her down, she wasn't an idiot. A fact proven when she managed to stay one step ahead of those hunting her and survive as long as she had, both of which were minor miracles. If she wanted her luck to continue, she needed a game changer.

One like the giant in front of her. And considering his obvious disgust for the Cartels, he was a better option than the alternative trolling the street outside. Plus ditching his ass shouldn't be hard. *Use 'em and leave 'em,* a personal motto that worked wonders as far as she was concerned.

She folded her arms over her chest, rolled the damned dice, and prayed for anything but snake eyes. "Does it matter why they're on my ass?"

The big man studied her and then shrugged his thick shoulders. "Probably not, but color me curious."

Yeah, he didn't strike her as the curious type. *Or the forgiving type either.* Given the harsh angles of his face revealed by the pulled back dark hair, the equally dark eyes, and the coiled danger, all wrapped in a six-foot brawler frame, he was probably the strike first, ask questions later type.

She heeded her instincts because time had proven their reliability, and shared. "They think I killed someone."

Instead of the expected shock he rubbed a hand over the shadowed scruff lining his jaw, his coffee-colored eyes drifting from her head to her toes and back, and his expression remained inscrutable as if waiting for her to say something more.

His silent perusal threw her off balance, and shockingly, ignited an unexpected heat. She frowned, a little shaken when a long-forgotten hunger coiled low and spread like wildfire.

What the hell was wrong with her?

She stuffed her bat-shit crazy reaction into a dark corner to be bitch slapped later. If there was a later.

Finished with His once over complete, his hand stilled at the dark trimmed beard covering his chin and he raised his brows, the right one bisected by a small, curved scar, his eyes lit with some unknown amusement. "Did you?"

She had a sinking feeling what was amusing him was her. Her frustration gained another layer, and she gritted her teeth. She considered taking her chances and hitting the street solo-style, but survival instinct kept her feet locked in place. Determined to break his unsettling scrutiny and regain control of this unravelling situation, she muttered, "I didn't."

"Uh-huh." A long second went by before he shook his head, pushed away from the counter, and stalked closer, leaving only a handful of inches to separate them. "Whoever you didn't kill had to be someone damn important for them to chase you this far north."

Her pulse gave a heavy thump as he crowded her, his tantalizing scent curling around her. Her nerves stretched to a wary snapping point as unwanted reactions swarmed. Somehow, she managed to keep her mouth shut and her hands to herself. *Damn adrenaline rush!*

"Know I shouldn't, but I'm going to," he muttered under his breath as he rubbed the back of his neck. He dropped his hand and glared at her. "Before I stretch my neck out, I have to know how much of a pain you're going to be."

Her bark of laughter caught them both by surprise and she hoped she was the only one who heard the crumbling, brittle edge of despair buried in it. "It might kill us both."

Her brutally honest answer earned a fierce grin which tripped her pulse even as she questioned his intelligence.

"Maybe, but that answer makes me believe it might be worth it."

Not the reaction she expected, but she'd take it. "You're nuts."

"Aren't we all?"

Since the civilized world and Mother Nature decided to throw normal off the careening disaster-ridden train seventy plus years ago and hurl straight into crazy-town without brakes, Mercy was pretty sure everyone qualified as crazy nowadays. It was just a matter of deciding which kind of crazy you wanted to be.

While the devil on her shoulder urged her to lead the man in front of her on a merry chase, she couldn't escape the grim voice of her conscience that warned against dragging another soul into the shitstorm she was floundering in. "Safer if you walk away."

"Safer for who?" he pressed, his earlier humor wiped away by a startling seriousness.

"You." She was too tired to play games. She needed ... God, she had no idea what she needed. *An escape route? A do over? A fucking miracle? Hell, she'd take any of the three at this point.*

"Why?"

His relentless inquisition had her amending her earlier opinion on his curiosity. She could give him part of the truth, enough to see if he would back off or shift his ass in gear. *And what a fine ass it is*, a voice she long thought gone piped up with wicked intent. She fought back the burn in her cheeks ignited by that last rogue thought and laid it out. "Like you said, they wouldn't be this far up my ass if it wasn't someone big."

He gave her a long, slow blink. "So, who was it?"

Her mouth got stuck on the name, but she finally choked out, "Tavi Suárez."

Every one of those impressive muscles coiled and the air around him turned ominously heavy with menace. Wisdom dictated she should back away. Slowly. Since she was more inclined to curl up and snuggle with that dangerous heat, she mentally flipped wisdom the finger.

"Tavi." The name emerged on a low hiss and fell between them like spoiled meat. "That would be Guillermo's youngest."

Her interest sharpened, and so did her worry. If he knew enough about the Suárez's to identify who was who in one of the five ruling Cartel families, it made her question her instincts. It was her turn to study him. Despite his inked and battle-scarred body (and those intricate designs bore quite the collection of knife and bullet wounds), he wasn't just some hardened road rider. Nope, if she heeded her gut, honed by years of unrelenting experience, there was much more to him. So much more she wondered if he was more dangerous than what chased her.

"You know who pulled the trigger?" His low voice question curled around her.

Cautiously, she nodded. Not that she had proof, but yeah, she knew.

He waited, a frown darkening his face when she didn't elaborate. "Not in the mood for guessing games, babe."

Her hands curled into fists at his throwaway endearment. The combination of heat, lack of food, water, and no rest left her head aching and her thoughts scattered. Which in turn made her snarly. "Felix, or as you called him, dick weasel."

He remained unfazed by her bark. "I take it he's not some random Cartel solider."

"Not even close." And that's all she would give him because there was a difference between changing the game and throwing the game. And with one more move left to make, she was determined to hold her cards close.

Another indeterminable minute passed as he studied her, his thoughts locked behind a stony façade. Finally, he came to some internal decision and straightened. "Right. Let's go."

Stunned by his abrupt change in demeanor, she watched him head towards the opening in the back wall without looking back.

He stopped, pulled back the faded drape with one hand, and threw over his shoulder, "Move your ass, darlin'. Clock's ticking."

Grappling with the unexpected break, she sucked in a breath and muttered, "I'm not your darling." Then she followed in his wake and refastened the scarf covering her face. When she stepped into the small back room, habit kept her close to the walls where the shadows lingered, making it easier to hide.

The shop's owner was hunched over a table with his back to them. He didn't bother looking up as he dropped another bullet into the small leather pouch to his right, the dull clink indicating it was one of many. "Finishing up a few more, then they're all yours."

"Thanks, Boomer." Her would-be rescuer stopped behind him and squeezed his shoulder. "Keep those for next time."

Then the big guy pocketed the leather pouch. "Heading out, see you around."

Boomer didn't turn or look up from his worktable, deliberately ignoring her, and her bruiser. "Watch your back, Havoc."

Havoc? The name raised the hairs along her arms. She knew that name, but between her headache and exhaustion she was having a difficult time placing it. She tucked it away for later and waited just inside the back-room's entry as she watched Havoc move to the metal gun cabinet taking up most of the right wall.

He pulled open the doors, crouched down, and lifted something that gave a soft sigh. He shot her a look over his shoulder. "Ready?"

To get out of here? Yep.

She no longer cared why he was offering, because the more distance she could put between her and Felix the better. She went to Havoc's side, unsurprised to find an opening where the cabinet's floor used to be. *A tunnel, nice.*

Way back when things initially went to shit, everyone got a brutal lesson in looking out for themselves, and as such, escape routes became routine additions to living spaces. Here in the southwest, it also helped to have an alternate route available when the massive dust storms hit. She crouched next to Havoc and tried to guess how far down it went.

As if hearing her thoughts, his voice rumbled by her shoulder, "About a nine-foot drop. Doable?"

Please, even half dead she could manage that. Add in the hanging ladder and this was a freakin' breeze. Without answering, she slipped into the hole, kept a grip on the opening's edge until her legs hung down, then bypassed the ladder as she dropped, landing with bent knees and a soft thud. She rubbed at the bruising bite from the hilt of the blade strapped to her thigh and scooted out of the way.

Havoc's long legs dropped down, and then he was at her side, reaching around her to grab the thick rope dangling from the trapdoor. He pulled it closed and sealed them in darkness.

The heavy scrape of metal over wood indicated the cabinet was being shoved back into place, and a tiny shower of dust and gravel followed. Then came the soft scratch of another sound followed by the warm glow of solar camp light that pushed the darkness back.

The illumination gave Havoc's face a devilish cast. "Hope you can handle tight spaces."

Behind the thin protection of her scarf, she grinned. "Not an issue."

His brow furrowed and before she could utter a protest, he tugged the tail end of her scarf free.

"What the hell?"

He batted her hands away. "You're not going to need it."

She propped one hand on her hip and used the other to circle her face. "Hello, disguise?"

His lips twitched, but he turned and tossed the scarf to the far corner. "We'll get you another one."

"Right," she huffed. "Because they're so easy to come by. We'll just swing by the store and pick one up, shall we?"

He turned back to her. "You always this much of a smart ass, babe?"

"It's Mercy," she corrected tartly. "And no, I can get much, much worse, if you'd like."

"Great, just what I needed." He lifted the lamp until two openings, one to the left and one to the right, were revealed. "Well, Mercy—" he stressed her name, "—let's get."

He stepped around her, and in the confined space, she could not only feel him, but caught his faint scent of honey-laced wood smoke. It kind of reminded her of winter torched mesquite. She wrinkled her nose, shook off her momentary whimsy and followed the intriguing, yet compelling man as he bent his head, curved his shoulders, and moved into the tunnel.

The tunnel was impressive, especially considering the soil here in the high desert was a bitch to dig through. Of course, necessity was the mother of all stubbornness.

Once upon a time, huge cities sprawled across what once was the United States, technology ruled over physical labor, and the necessity of escape routes were only for those with less than legal intentions. Civilization's fairy tale started unraveling when weather patterns went from predictable to savage, forcing humanity to retreat further into overcrowded cities for protection.

That, of course, opened the pandemic floodgates of viral infections which further thinned out humanity's numbers. Toss in shriveling food and medical supplies and it wasn't long before the economic cracks widened into canyons and known civilization slipped into the darkness, taking another huge chunk of the population with it.

All these years later there wasn't much left of the old world besides rusted out remnants of what used to be. A few bigger cities still stood, New Seattle up north, Mendocino further south, and Boulder to the east, but they were mini-kingdoms where gangs ruled at the whim of powerful individuals and survival meant keeping your head down.

Towns and communities still dotted the landscape, but they weren't exactly opening their gates with a welcoming smile. Some were created by those with like-minded beliefs, while others gathered under the protective shadows of larger groups.

Which was the case here in Page. When things started tumbling downhill, the Native American tribes banded together into a nation of many and became the Free People. They considered themselves the last line of protection between man and Mother Nature. Here in the Southwest the Free

People held the water rights in a ruthless fist, and since water was crucial to survival regardless of who you were or how you lived, the Free People were a force to be reckoned with.

A fact Mercy was banking her life on.

Ahead of her the tunnel curved and Havoc disappeared, taking the soft glow of light with him. Snapped out of her wandering thoughts, she scurried forward and found him hanging the lamp on an iron spike impaled in the stony wall. He raised his arms and twisted, stretching out his spine.

She leaned a shoulder against the tunnel's entrance and enjoyed the view because it was one any breathing female could truly appreciate. The man was seriously built—thick shoulders supported by a heavily muscled chest that led to the flat planes of a stomach even the t-shirt couldn't disguise. The material was tucked in at trim waist that led to long, long legs. Legs that ended in thick-soled boots which were currently standing right in front of her. She raised her gaze to his as fire scalded her cheeks.

He studied her, giving nothing away. "You're not going to pass out on me, are you?"

"I'm fine." Deciding it was best to redirect his attention from her sleep-deprived weirdness, she shifted to peek around him. If she calculated right, their tunnel route managed to cover a couple of blocks. "Where to next?"

"Up."

From her position, the shadows were murky, which made it hard to see much of anything outside the light. "Up?"

He walked over to the far side and tilted his head back, his focus on the tunnel's ceiling. He leapt up, hand extended, and when he landed, another rope ladder unraveled. He turned back to her and kept one hand on the dancing ladder. "Ladies first."

She recognized his invite for the dare it was, but it didn't stop her from joining him. Once she was standing in front of him, she held his gaze, reached under her oversized shirt, freed the knife strapped to her thigh, and drew it out.

His eyes narrowed as the light played over the blade, but other than that, he continued to watch her.

With a provocative smile, because she found teasing this dangerous man exhilarating, she brought the blade to her lips and used her teeth to hold it in place. Granted, it was not the best way to transport a sharp blade, but it left her hands free for the climb and meant one less bruise to carry.

The ladder stopped about waist level, so she took a small hop and grabbed the rungs a little higher up. Despite the protest of her exhausted limbs, she pulled her body up in one smooth move.

When her foot hit a lower rung, a large hand curled over her ankle, and drew her attention to man behind her. "Should be quiet above but watch your back."

Since her mouth was full, she blew air out of her nose and nodded. She had cleared a couple of rungs when the ladder swayed under her with the addition of Havoc's weight. Once it steadied, she continued, feeling his presence behind her.

When the wooden trapdoor came into view, she crowded close until she could curve her shoulders and upper spine against the surface. Havoc's arms wrapped around her waist as he pulled his big body behind hers. She braced her hips and ass against his chest, let go of the rope and used her arms and shoulders to lift the trapdoor.

Cool air rushed in and dried the sweat on her face, while airy fingers curled under the heavy braid of her hair. Her nose wrinkled as a strange combination of skunk, coppery rotten eggs, and the faint burn of gas hit. She kept one hand on the edge of the trap door as she climbed out.

She held it as she scrambled out of the tunnel and carefully set the hinged door on the ground. She straightened, transferred her blade to a hand and looked around.

Late afternoon sun drifted through holes dotting a metal roof overhead. Tiny rays of light poked among the looming stacks of corroded steel and other unidentifiable objects.

She took a moment to settle her blade back into the sheath strapped to her thigh and when Havoc joined her, asked, "Where are we?"

"Old steel yard." Havoc stepped around her and wound his way through the metal maze. "Come here."

She followed him to a set of dilapidated lockers.

He yanked one of the locker doors open.

She winced at the screeched protest and her gaze jumped around for any incoming visitors. Quiet answered. Correction, the soft whisper of an occasional breeze whistled, but there were no other sounds of life. Comforting, but a bit disconcerting.

She craned her neck and spotted a set of metal stairs one stiff breeze from collapse leading up to a platform. She wandered a few feet in the other direction, peered around another stack of beams and realized why Havoc didn't need to be sneaky. The place was deserted. The towering structure consisted of three walls with a massive opening at the far end.

Havoc's grunt brought her back to his side. He emerged from a locker with a faded baseball hat as he hitched a faded blue, grease-stained shirt over one big shoulder. He tossed the hat to her.

She caught it one-handed, then held it between her finger and thumb, and raised her eyebrows. "Let me guess, my disguise?"

He crowed her, took it out of her hand, wrapped her braid around the back of her head and pulled the cap on until the brim almost touched her nose. "No need to get fancy. They're looking for a woman in a headscarf, not a dust rat." He pulled the shirt down and held it out.

She eyed the bedraggled material in his hand and had to

admit he had a point. No matter the town, street rats were basically invisible. *Dammit.* She sighed, shrugged out of her oversized shirt, wadded it up, and tossed it in one of the lockers. Her grimy, baggy t-shirt followed, and left her in a faded, fitted olive tank and her cargos.

She reached for the shirt, but Havoc kept it just out of reach, a small smirk on his lips. She glared and demanded, "Hand it over."

"Don't rush me." He held the shirt out, forcing her to reach up to take it, his eyes riveted on her and practically leaving scorch marks on her skin.

Heat that had nothing to do with the temperature outside and everything to do with the illicit images his intense scrutiny created, whipped through her, leaving her aroused and aching. She shrugged into the stinky shirt and tried to ignore the weight of his gaze and her body's errant reaction.

Of course, stripped as she was, he couldn't miss the bruises and cuts that ranged over her arms and disappeared under the tank. Or the layer of dirt and dried blood that added an authenticity to the street urchin disguise. Both of which shifted his attention from bothersome to worrisome.

Sure enough, she caught his soft curse followed by, "Holy shit, woman."

Her innards squirmed with an unexpected surge of embarrassment that left her voice sharp. "Why?"

At her surly question, his gaze snapped to her face. "Why what?"

She tipped her chin up and nailed him with a glare, hoping it hid her other, more disconcerting reactions. "Why are you helping me?"

"An inherent need to serve my fellow man?" If she hadn't been watching, she would have missed the slight twitch of his lip. "Or woman, in this case."

His flippant response sparked her severely frayed temper

and she couldn't stop her frustrated growl. "Truth, Havoc."

That wiped his amusement away and left his face hard. "Truth?" He backed her against the lockers and braced his hands on either side of her head, the metal groaning under the pressure. His head lowered until her eyes almost crossed trying to keep him in focus. His voice was so low, it vibrated through her, eliciting shivers that had nothing to do with anything as mundane as temper. "You're offering me something I want."

Wicked images of what a man like Havoc could possibly want from her exploded through her brain and she couldn't seem to catch her breath. "I don't remember offering you shit."

"Oh, but you did." Something cruel and ruthless slid through his dark gaze, a hint of something she recognized. "A chance to fuck with the Cartels crosses my path, I will gleefully take it and make it my bitch."

Even as every warning bell she owned rang its heart out, savage anticipation curled through her veins. Maybe running here hadn't been quite as futile as she believed. Maybe, just maybe, this man would be the key to fixing her problem.

Or make it worse.

She ignored the insidious voice, buried her excitement at an unexpected opportunity and focused on the second part of his answer. Time to clue him in as to who he'd be working with—emphasis on with. "Try making me your bitch and your dick won't be good for much."

Instead of his anger, she got a disturbing smile, one that sent adrenaline streaking through her veins even as it seduced. "Is that a challenge?"

She flattened her palms against his chest and leaned in. "Nope." She lifted her gaze, and let him see it all—her calculation, her desire, and her mercenary soul. Without breaking eye contact, she rose on tiptoe until their lips brushed in the lightest touch. "A warning."

three

As evening settled in, Havoc slipped through the maze of Page's back streets and narrow alleyways that twisted through the eclectic mix of structures created from salvaged materials and wondered what the hell he was doing. Rescuing this woman was asking for trouble. Her entanglement with the Cartels alone guaranteed it would go down as one of his worse decisions. Yet, he couldn't find it in himself to give a damn. Especially since he carried a soul deep addiction to causing as much damage as possible to anything touched by the Cartel.

He slid between two dust-covered miners heading to either a bar or home and glanced over his shoulder at the source of the constant hum in the back of his head. Mercy moved with deceptive ease as she dodge the other pedestrians, her attention constantly monitoring her surroundings, as she stayed on his ass.

He turned forward and reluctantly admitted it wasn't just the prospect of screwing with the Cartels that made him want to keep her, as if she as a damn lost, rabid puppy.

A puppy that would as soon rip your throat out as kiss you, asshole.

The harsh rejoinder did jack on changing his mind though. There was something about her that whispered to the deepest, darkest depths of his non-existent soul. As unsettling as that realization was, he couldn't deny she intrigued the hell out of him. How she managed to go from lost waif to dangerous temptress in the blink of an eye was a mystery, and it had been a long time since any woman managed to prick his curiosity.

A flailing ball of human limbs exploded from a nearby doorway and rolled across his path interrupting his grim thoughts. He pulled up short and felt Mercy jerk to a stop behind him. The worn path lining the front of the shops cleared as people gave a wide berth to the two drunken idiots, who continued to whale on each other amidst slurred curses and unintelligible grunts.

It wasn't long before a bull of a man filled the doorway, stepped forward, and dumped a pail of questionable liquid on the drunks. "Don't come back, either."

The smell of vinegar filled the air as the uncoordinated mass of limbs slowed and broke apart into two bleary-eyed men. Dirty water dripped over their faces as they sat up and blinked stupidly at the big man. "Sorry, Lee," mumbled the one who wasn't weaving.

The half-assed apology earned a disgusted look and head shake. "Both of you, go home. Sleep it off." When neither drunk moved, he barked, "Now!"

The two idiots scrambled up into a stumbling zigzag. Havoc figured they'd be face down further up the street in no time.

Lee turned and caught sight of Havoc, his fierce expression replaced by a wide grin. "Havoc, my man, been waiting for you."

"Looks like the night started early, Lee."

A puff of air escaped Lee's pursed lips and he shook his head. "Those two idiots do this at least once a month. If it ain't a girl, it's over some imagined insult. Good for entertainment, shit for business." He motioned toward the doorway with the now empty pail. "I sent food up a bit ago, but if you need more, holler."

"Thanks." Havoc stepped inside, followed by Mercy's mute presence. Lee's was the best place for a hot meal, not to mention decent booze, but what Havoc needed right now was the small apartment tucked upstairs. "Might have to take you up on that."

Lee strode through scattered tables, most of which were empty, unlike the stools ranged along the long bar top.

Once inside and off the street, the tension that rode Havoc's shoulders eased. He ignored the few individuals who looked their way and kept his body between Mercy and the curious.

Near a door leading to the back, Lee stopped and pushed it open with one big hand. Havoc heeded the silent invite and when he stepped through the entry, Lee followed him into the privacy of the kitchen. "Not one to be nosy," the pub owner said. "But if you're heading up the canyon, keep your eyes open. Things ain't right up there."

Havoc's stomach did a slow roll at the obvious worry in Lee's voice and face. "How so?"

Lee set the empty pail in the corner and washed his hands in a stained sink, his back to Havoc. "Someone's determined to take out the dam. So far, it's just been a bunch of half-assed attempts that ain't done much. Sun-crazed idiots if you ask me."

He grabbed a cloth towel from the shelf above, turned around, and dried his hands. "Those boys I threw out?" He jerked his chin up and waited for Havoc's nod. "They work up there for the Free People. Their argument started over who'd be stupid enough to screw with the dam and face the People's wrath." Lee tossed the towel on the counter. "Whatever's going on up there, it's getting worse. Messing with the water supply ain't real bright."

No, it wasn't, but intelligence never ranked as a prerequisite for those who lusted after power. Havoc added this latest craptastic news to his slow growing pile of clusterfucks. "Appreciate the head's up."

Lee dipped his head in acknowledgement. "Got to get back to it." He headed to the front and paused to clasp Havoc on the shoulder. "Kitchen'll stay open another few hours, yeah?"

"Yeah, thanks." Havoc rubbed his chin, his thoughts unable to find traction without more information. Information he wouldn't get until tomorrow so no sense in gnawing on it now.

He turned and found Mercy studying him. Before she could voice any of the questions bubbling in her eyes, he said, "Come on, we're heading up."

He led the way up the narrow back stairs, the wooden steps uttering soft groans under his boots. They reached the top and stepped into a short hall covered in well-worn carpet, the wood floorboards showing through in spots. Two doors sat on either side of the hall. He rapped his knuckles against the one on the right and a lock clicked before the door was thrown open.

"What the hell, Havoc?" The impatient question was asked by his partner and massive pain in his ass, Vex. The evil woman, who missed his height by a couple of inches, stood in the doorway blocking his entry with her arm braced against the doorjamb. "You bailed hours ago." Her gaze slipped past him, narrowed, and came back, shooting sparks. "Tell me you aren't bringing back a piece of ass to tap."

"For fuck's sake, Vex." He pushed against the door until she stepped back, then nabbed Mercy's wrist before she could slip away. "Stop." He dragged her close and then propelled her into the room as an irritated Vex watched on. "Get inside."

He added a firm nudge between her stiff shoulders to emphasize his order. As soon as Mercy cleared the door, she spun around, put her back to the room and faced him and Vex, her hand slipping under the stained shirt.

He pointed a finger at her knowing she was probably going for her damn knife and growled, "Don't even." He turned to Vex, who had opened her mouth and added, "You either."

Undaunted, Vex stuck her tongue out before moving out of the way so he could close and lock the door. Behind him, he could feel the two women eyeing each other, like two rabid dogs. It was there in the screaming tension choking the room.

Fucking great.

Bringing Mercy here was his only option, but given Vex's inability to interact with, well, anyone, if he got through this without either female drawing blood, he would consider it a win. He faced the door, closed his eyes, and took a second to question his sanity.

Not much rattled him, but trapped in a small space with two deadly women? He wasn't stupid. He should lock them inside and sleep in the hall. Instead, he sucked it up and turned to the inevitable clash. "Vex, Mercy. Mercy, Vex."

The two women went into a stare down, which he broke by walking between them. "No bloodshed," he warned uselessly. "There's a child present." He skirted one of two beds and aimed for the table by the far window. There wasn't much more to the room than the basic amenities, but it was clean.

On the table's other side sat a young, dark-haired boy who held two playing cards and warily watched him approach.

Despite his youthful appearance, his eyes were stained with newly acquired soul-scarring experience.

Old sorrow rose at that haunted look, but Havoc smothered it before it could spread. He checked the three cards that lay face up in the middle of the table—a king of hearts, a five of spades, and a six of diamonds—and then settled in an empty chair. "Hey, Katori, she teaching you poker?"

Katori gave him a slow nod before Mercy's terse voice cut through the room. "Vex and Havoc."

Havoc picked up Vex's discarded hand—a pair of fours—and waited, knowing his little runaway had finally put two and two together. *Sure enough...*

"I'm going to take a wild guess and say you're the same Vex and Havoc belonging to Fate's Vultures."

His lips twitched at her aggrieved tone.

Vex did a slow clap. "Brilliant deduction."

"Right." Mercy's voice was tight. "I'm out of here."

"Not so fast, sugar." Confident that Vex would ensure Mercy didn't make a break for it, Havoc didn't look up from his cards as Katori dealt the turn, adding an ace of clubs to the dealer's hand.

Hmm...

Havoc added another (was that a jellybean?) to the growing pile and waited while Katori ponied up with a few candied pieces of his own. When Havoc finally looked up, Vex was barring Mercy's intended escape by leaning back against the door, her arms crossed and her patented crazy grin firmly in place.

Vex eyed Mercy. "You that anxious to die tonight?" Her question was heavy with sardonic amusement.

Not exactly sharing the other woman's sense of humor, Mercy snapped, "Not particularly." She stepped back enough to watch him and Vex and palmed the knife at her thigh. "But

I've got enough odds against me, don't need to stack the deck."

Havoc's attention was drawn from the women when the boy reached for the dealer's pile and added a fourth card to the river. A two of diamonds. *Damn.* "Fold," he murmured as he pushed his pair off to the side.

Katori flipped over a queen and king, his eyes brightening as he nudged his king next to the dealer's to claim the high pair.

"Nice." Havoc pushed the pot of candy to the kid.

On the other side of the room the women amped up, Vex taking the lead. "Oh look, she plays with knives." There was the soft hiss of metal leaving leather and then, "Wanna see if mine is longer?"

"Enough." God save him from female pissing matches. He didn't bother to raise his voice, instead he relied on the whip of command. He half-turned in his seat, and rested one arm on the chair's back, the other on the table. "You're about to keel over." He pinned Mercy with a practiced look he normally reserved for Vex and her equally irritating twin brother, Ruin. "You need rest, food and probably a shower. Not necessarily in that order." He then turned his glare on Vex. "You, go down and grab a couple more plates from Lee. You want to sharpen your tongue on someone, pick on some idiot downstairs."

He got identical stubborn chin tilts in response. After years of dealing with Vex, he maintained silence and waited them out. Sure enough, it took maybe half a minute for Vex to shoot him a finger, turn, and slam out of the room.

One down, one to go.

He turned to Mercy and saw her composure slowly unravel. It was there in the tremor of the hand wrapped around her knife that she tried to hide, and the white lines etched near her bruised eyes and chapped lips. Quiet stretched into a humming tension, then her gaze flicked to Katori, and her shoulders dropped, not much, but enough. The knife disappeared.

"We scored an attached bathroom." He tilted his head to the towel-draped door behind her. "Water's a bit limited but should be enough to get most of the dust off."

He eyed the stained shirt hanging on her slumped frame, got up, went to the bed nearest the door, and pulled his travel bag from under it. He set it on the rumpled blanket, dug around until he found a fairly clean t-shirt, then tossed it to the bleary-eyed woman. "Here, clothes until we can find something that fits."

She caught it and stood there, staring at him.

"What?"

She tilted her head at Katori. "That the reason you're heading up the canyon tomorrow?"

So, she hadn't missed Lee's comment. "Shower, then we'll talk while you eat."

She stood there, most likely cataloguing her options, and nibbled on her bottom lip. Finally, she heaved a sigh and her head twitched to the side. "Fine, but I'm having you take the first bite."

He fought to keep an unexpected grin from his face. "More likely she'll spit in it," he told Katori.

The boy dropped his head to hide his small grin.

A soft snarl escaped Mercy before she choked it off. "Definitely making you take the first bite." With that, she turned on her heel and disappeared in the bathroom.

four

Mercy emerged from the bathroom minus a few pounds of grime and drowning in the massive t-shirt that smelled like Havoc. The mouth-watering scent of roasted meat hit her so hard her stomach emitted an audible growl and seized. She fought back her embarrassment as she clenched her teeth until the ache in her belly receded.

"How long since you ate?" Havoc's rumbled question snapped her momentary paralysis.

How long had it been? Her brain turned his question over slowly, like it was trudging through honey. It had to have been before she hit the sand-scoured remains of Phoenix, definitely. "Couple of days."

She turned, hooked the damp towel over the door, and avoided his too-knowing gaze. Thankfully, Havoc's t-shirt was big enough that her movements didn't flash her ass. Not that she was complaining. Nothing beat being clean. As it was, she almost felt normal. As if that particular thought was a trigger, her vision swam, her head went light, and she braced a hand on the door, determined to ride it out.

"Come dig in before you pass out." Havoc took another

bite from his half-filled plate.

The world slowly stopped spinning and finally leveled out, but she took her sweet ass time to turn and face him. She propped a hand on her hip and asked, "You order everyone around?"

"All the damn time," Vex answered cheerfully from the bed where she was played cards with the kid.

More concerned with Havoc's lethal partner, Mercy missed his name earlier, but from the boy's features—pitch black braid, dark eyes, razor blade of a nose and burnished skin —he belonged to the Free People. Which added weight to her earlier guess that Havoc intended to head up the canyon. She wanted to drill the frustrating man with questions, but her stomach voiced another loud demand, so she took her place at the table.

She sat in front of the plate piled high with two slices of cornbread, shredded meat smothered in sauce, a mini pile of steaming corn, and devoted serious dedication to dulling the edge of her hunger. Two red apples rested next to a pitcher of water. All in all, it was a veritable feast.

As she ate, she couldn't help but note the earlier tension was gone. In its place was a strange calm, broken by Vex's teasing as she wagered against the quiet child and the occasional utensil that scraped against the stoneware plates. She made a satisfactory dent in the meat, finished about half the corn, and devoured both pieces of cornbread before she had to stop and breathe. Uncomfortably full, she sat back, cradled her third glass of water, and waited for Havoc to begin his inevitable interrogation.

Havoc tilted his head towards the bed. "Vex found some clothes."

Mercy shifted in her seat and spotted a pair of jeans, a burnt orange t-shirt and what she thought might be a vest. "Thanks?"

Vex waved her off. "One of Margo's girls donated them." She cut a sly glance Mercy's way and drawled, "In case you're interested, your scumbag stalkers are being well distracted by the girls. Guess you're not more important than getting l—"

"Child," Havoc cut in. "Ears."

The child in question ducked his head, but not before Mercy caught a hint of a smile.

"Please." Vex discarded a card before replacing it. "Katori's ears can handle it. He's not a kid, he's a warrior."

Katori's head snapped up, his gaze meeting Vex's. She held it until a restrained pride broke through his normal stoic expression.

The exchange, simple though it was, sparked Mercy's curiosity. There was a story there, a big one. Probably the same story that would explain the boy's presence with two members of Fate's Vultures because they were far from her first babysitting choice.

Last she heard, the notorious band of nomadic vigilantes with a growing reputation of brutal justice was working for, or with, Crane, head of the Central territories. Problem was no one could decide on the "for" or "with" part of the rumors.

Since Havoc didn't appear to be in a rush to ask her questions, she set her glass aside, leaned forward, and folded her arms on the table. It was time to find out what she was dealing with. "So, Fate's Vultures?"

Havoc pushed his empty plate away and shifted his chair so he could stretch out his legs. "Yep."

"Hmm." She made the noncommittal sound and waited for him to take the bait.

Sure enough he folded. "Hmm, what?"

Determined to uncover a diamond of a reason to stick around, she dug her proverbial shovel into the dirt. First, she needed to unearth why Katori was keeping company with the two, especially since her mind could swing down some pretty dark paths. "Thought you all were more inclined to finish trouble than start it."

Havoc sank further into the chair, folded his hands over his stomach, and watched her through half-closed eyes. "What makes you think we're starting anything?"

By sheer force of will, Mercy refrained from rolling her eyes. Instead, certain she could make her point in one word, she asked, "Babysitting?"

"Don't you love when our reputation proceeds us?" Vex chimed in from her position on the bed.

"What?" Havoc didn't acknowledge Vex, but kept his attention focused on Mercy. "You think we kidnapped him?"

Katori's spine went ramrod straight. The revealing movement caused a corresponding tension to coil around her, a fact that wasn't helped by the added pressure of Vex's glare.

Kidnapping was definitely involved somewhere.

"And we, what?" Havoc continued, his heavily sarcastic tone scathing. "Decided to stay within striking distance of his people?" His lip curled into a sneer, and he shook his head. "Underestimating my intelligence, a bit, aren't you, babe?"

His mocking tone raked over her nerves but strangely eased her tension and concerns. "Still trying to decide how much is smarts and how much is luck, sugar." Although she had to concede his point. The Vultures were far from stupid, so playing kidnapper was a far-fetched theory, but it did give her another direction to pursue. "Retrieval."

Catching the subtle tightening around his eyes, she pressed her luck. "You're taking him home. Something that will get the Vultures, or maybe Crane, in good with the People." A smart move on whoever's part because you could never have too many alliances. After all, wasn't she ultimately banking on the same theory?

Havoc exchanged an unreadable look with Vex before he turned to Mercy. "Why does it matter to you?"

Because maybe she could ride that wave of goodwill for her own benefit, but she wasn't ready to share that answer. Instead, she shrugged. "Just curious."

"So am I." His ominous tone stole every drop of moisture from her mouth.

As casually as possible she reached for her glass, took a sip of water, and never broke eye contact. Not even when a foreboding light burned in the depths of his eyes.

"What's your deal, Mercy?" His question carried a hard edge. "How'd you end up with a front row seat to a killing?"

She hiked a negligent shoulder and offered, "Luck?"

An amused snort came from the observer on the bed, but Havoc's eyes narrowed. "How long do you think you can stay ahead of the Cartels?"

Partial truth would garner better results than continuing her game of twenty questions, so she kept her tone bland. "Long enough for you to take me up the canyon."

There was nothing nice or happy about the smile he aimed her way. "And why would I do that?"

"Because you think I can f—" She switched her phrasing for their younger audience, and turned his words back on him, "... cause problems for the Cartels."

His smile died.

"What the hell is she talking about, Havoc?" There was no more amusement in Vex's voice, in fact it was downright arctic as she sat up and threw her legs off the bed.

Havoc raised a warning hand, palm toward Vex, holding off her obviously unwanted opinion and held Mercy's gaze without flinching. "Am I wrong?"

No dammit, he wasn't. But she wasn't backing down now. "Are you taking me with you?"

"Havoc!" Vex nearly vibrated with fury from her perch on the edge of the bed. "You go play with the Cartels now and Reaper will have your balls."

Havoc ignored Vex's threat, and got to his feet. He brace his hands on the table, leaned in, and put his face inches away from Mercy's. "Give me a reason or I leave your ass here."

Her temper overrode caution. "Think I won't follow?"

"Think you won't get far," he countered,

A fissure of unease struck her. He had a valid point. The Free People took guarding their territory to a lethal level, but these two could not only get her where she needed to go but help her shake the Cartels' dogs loose.

Two birds and one stone and all that.

She shifted through what she could safely share because she couldn't afford to screw up this chance. Her mind spun then caught on different approach. "Answer something for me."

He studied her intently, then slowly nodded.

"Do you know which came first? The kidnapping or the troubles at the dam?"

His face tightened and his lips thinned with anger, but it wasn't his voice that answered. It was Katori's. "There weren't any problems at the dam before the Raiders took me."

The boy's unexpected answer tore her attention from Havoc. Her instincts wove the pieces together, the nightmares haunting the boy's too-old eyes, Vex's comment about him being a warrior, and his mention of Raiders. It all came together in a cruel, heart-breaking realization.

Katori's simple explanation could have been reduced to one word—Raiders. Vicious and ruthless, they were the dregs of what was left of humanity. They crawled among the desert ruins of Las Vegas that they called home and preyed on anything with a heartbeat. They were notorious traffickers, and they weren't picky about their merchandise—weapons, drugs, humans, if it could be bought or traded, they'd take it.

Sympathy spiraled up, but mindful of the root cause of the shadows in his eyes, she knew it wouldn't be appreciated.

She searched for a more polite version of the question she needed to ask to determine if she was on the right path with her burgeoning suspicions. "How long have you been gone?"

His gaze skittered to Vex, who answered, "Roughly two months."

Dammit, the timing was off. Maybe Katori's kidnapping wasn't linked to her reason for being here. Which meant she was back to where she started with Havoc. Still, she needed an in with the Free People and this was probably her best chance.

She turned to Havoc and made a devil's bargain. "Take me with you and I promise to help you screw with the Cartels."

He straightened and folded his arms over his chest, his face unreadable. "Tell me why."

With no room to dodge, she admitted, "I need to speak to Istaqa."

At the name of the Free People's leader, Katori's head jerked around, and a fierce frown darkened his face. "Why?"

Unable to ignore the boy, she answered, "To warn him."

"About?" This time it was Havoc who asked.

"He's being targeted." She closed her eyes briefly and used her hand to brush her answer away. "Not him specifically." She opened blurry eyes, her thoughts jumbled by exhaustion. "But the dam."

"Yeah, got that from Lee's comments." A healthy dose of skepticism rode Havoc's

voice.

"Except I know who's behind it." Information she had no intention of sharing with anyone but Istaqa. "Whatever is happening now, it's a smokescreen meant to keep his attention off what's coming."

Unmoved by her rather dramatic statement, he drawled, "And what's that?"

She held his gaze with hers and stated, "War."

five

Darkness and early morning were spending some quality time together when Mercy rolled over yet again and tried to get comfortable. She lay on her side and blinked into the darkness, her mind at war. After days of running and trying to cover her ass, the irony of having a soft bed for said ass, but not being able to sleep, wasn't lost on her.

It wasn't the only ironic thing in her life right now.

In her line of work being accused of murder was nothing new, but being accused of a murder she didn't actually commit? Yep, that was totally ironic.

Of course, there were those who knew her, who'd say attributing a dead body to her name, justifiable or not, was damn sloppy. She couldn't argue, not when she'd been trained better than that.

Memories strode close but she turned away, determined to deal with her current situation, not one years beyond help. She was given a job, one she handled just fine until Felix decided to screw her over.

It shouldn't have been difficult. Slip into the Suárez family, ferret out who they recently tumbled into bed with, and bring back the proof. Things had sailed along beautifully until Felix got a bug up his ass.

Lord love a right-hand man who coveted the criminal crown. One way or the other, they always fucked things up at the worst possible time.

When Felix took out Tavi, he not only put an end to Mercy's infiltration plans but screwed her chance to obtain the proof she needed on the Cartels' new partners. The only upside to Felix setting her up as his patsy? Running across the Suárez's plans against the Free People.

Unfortunately, after months spent embedded with the Cartel family, she wondered who the real mastermind was behind the plans—the Cartels, their partner, or Felix?

Not that it mattered. She gone under with crystal clear orders—get in, get the proof, get out. There was nothing in those orders about warning the Free People, but considering their role in the unstable world order, there was too much at stake not to warn them.

It didn't help that her boss was very explicit about her steering clear of the Vultures. Vex wasn't far off about their reputation. They were the common person's last hope for justice and the stories bandied far and wide held a re-occurring theme—facing the Vultures' judgement generally didn't end well.

While she wasn't looking for a judgement call, she couldn't accomplish her assignment if she didn't take the opportunity presented to hook up with them.

Choices, choices, choices.

She wasn't one to follow orders blindly, because in her line of work knowing which side to land on was a critical skill. The issue was what her boss would do when she picked said side?

He had two options, understand her choice, or leave her bleeding out in some godforsaken alley (and there were so many to choose from nowadays). Either way, at least her conscience would be happy.

Hell, it was better to die at his hands versus the myriad of other unpleasant options waiting in the wings. It would be quicker too, that's for damn sure.

She rolled to her other side and did her best to ignore the fact she was sharing a bed with Havoc. Not an easy feat. He took up more than his fair share, plus the man was a furnace. Even now, as she basically clung to the bed's edge with her back to him, his heat wrapped around her, and triggered reactions she knew meant trouble.

How sad was it that when she finally found a male worth a minute, she didn't have one to give?

She freely admitted she had a type, one Havoc fit to a T— lethally dangerous. Yeah, he was quiet, had an irritating habit of using stupid nicknames and spouting off orders, but she caught glimpses of the predator under the mask. He not only fascinated her but made her want to poke at him until she earned a reaction.

A heavy arm curved around her waist and drew her back against his hard body. Temptation stretched awake with a purr, and without her permission her body softened, tucking her curves against his solid frame. Every nerve ending fired with shocking speed. Stunned by the wildfire reaction, she closed her eyes and indulged her feminine side in the delicious burn for an interminable treacherous minute.

It was beyond stupid, but it had been so long since she felt a man's arms wrap around her without there being an ulterior motive. *Was it so wrong to take a selfish moment out of time and enjoy it?*

She stifled a groan, forced her lashes up, and wrapped her hand around his thick wrist. For sanity's sake, it was best to remove temptation. Maybe she should sleep on the floor. Her muscles tightened as she began to lift his arm.

"Settle, babe." The husky words brushed over her ear and sent chills cascading over her spine. Then the evil bastard pressed a soft kiss just behind her ear.

White-hot desire curled low and spiraled outward, leaving her unbound breasts aching, nipples peaked, and her legs shifting restlessly. Her hand tightened on his wrist, but she couldn't get it to move any further. His name escaped on a breath. "Havoc."

His lips kept moving and her breath stalled in her lungs as he nipped a wicked path along her neck. It was followed by a long, slow swipe of tongue. "What?"

"Knock it off." She was amazed she could get the words out considering she couldn't find any oxygen.

His arm tightened and then he rolled her to her back and tucked her under him. Their legs tangled and her hands gripped his shoulders as he loomed above her.

His bare shoulders.

Unable to resist, she petted him, brushing her hands over his equally naked chest, and savoring the feel of heated skin over sculpted muscle. He was a veritable treasure trove of decadent sensations.

His head lowered and he nipped her chin. "You going to keep thinking so loud?"

She blinked as his question rattled around her desire-induced haze. "Hmm?"

Despite the low light, she caught his wicked, wicked smile just before he took her lips.

There was nothing sweet about his kiss. He dove in and took no prisoners. His taste exploded in a carnal combination of heat and spice and swept their surroundings away in a wash of white-hot hunger. His tongue tangled with hers in a seductive battle where submitting still counted as a win.

She sank her nails into his skin and arched up, trying to get closer. On some level she registered his fingers digging into her ass, lifting her until the hard press of his cock made her thoughts scatter and drove her need higher. His mouth muffled her moan as she sank her fingers into his hair in a desperate bid for more of his intoxicating taste, more of his heat until they burned to ash.

A soft snuffle from the other bed snapped her out of her looming sexual oblivion and served as a harsh reminder they were far from alone. She jerked against him, and he gentled his kiss, taking them both back from the crumbling edge of control.

One last nip to her lower lip, and he raised his head. "We head out soon and you need sleep."

Really? Sleep? With her body on fire? "Like that's going to happen," she groused, careful to keep it to a whisper, since she didn't want an audience.

He leaned in and buried his face against the curve of her neck, muffling his quiet chuckle.

The hands at her hips flexed and then slowly released. He raised his head until his lips were by her ear. "But it got you out of your head, didn't it?" He shifted up to see her face.

Unwilling to admit it had, she glared back.

He grinned, then shifted the two of them until she was once again on her side, his arm around her waist, while he tucked in behind her. "Sleep while you can, Mercy."

She let out a soft *humpf* and glared into the darkness as her humming body slowly slipped into sleep.

six

Havoc slowed his bike as they drove down the rutted trail that led into the canyon the Free People called home. His neck itched in a sure sign that the sentries were tracking the progress of their little group. Eventually those same sentries would show themselves, but for now they appeared to be content with just watching.

Havoc, Mercy, Vex and Katori managed to leave Page without running into anyone. Thanks to the flat rocky land surrounding Antelope Lake, the first part of their trip was a breeze despite both his and Vex's bikes carrying double. Still, it had taken longer than the normal couple of hours to hit the familiar arid landscape that left no way to sneak up on the Free People's territory.

Mercy rode behind him with the ease of familiarity that had him wondering why she ended up in Page on foot. Stealing a bike would not be a challenge for her, not unless she hadn't been able to get her hands on one. And that was a high possibility since reliable transportation out here was critical.

The red rock walls rose from the flat desert floor and funneled their trail into a curve. The small hands at his waist shifted their grip, his cock twitched, and last night's kiss took front and center. Behind the bandana covering his nose and mouth from the dust, his lips curved in anticipation. Now that he had a taste, he intended to go back for more.

Soon.

First things first, he needed to deliver Katori back to his people and get some face time with the Free People's leader, preferably without his newly acquired troublemaker tagging along. He was reluctant to broker the meeting Mercy wanted until he knew what she was bringing to the table. Maybe he could get Vex to keep her busy?

Good fucking luck with that, snickered the devilish bastard in his head.

The walls stretched deep into the canyon and should the sentries tracking them from the top of the cliff's edge choose could become a fatal funnel. He backed off his throttle and caught the echo as Vex did the same. Before the sentries could raise the rifles, he knew they carried, he lifted his hand in a signal known only to a few.

Moments later he got the okay to continue their approach.

They took another turn, then another, when a growing rumble of engines announced new arrivals. Two bikes paced them, then pulled ahead. Havoc didn't bother to check for third positioning behind them as he followed their welcoming committee into the canyon's heart.

Another half mile passed, then he heard Mercy's sharply indrawn breath. Navajo City emerged before them. Prior to the Collapse, water rushed through this and other surrounding canyons to feed a man-made Lake Powell. When the Free People decided to invoke their century's long water rights, they restructured the dams to corral the vital resource, and created Antelope Lake.

Then they rebuilt their home in the dried-out canyons. These cliff dwellings bore little resemblance to the ancient, simple rock hewn cave he ran across while traveling the west territories. Instead, they were a graceful combination of ancient techniques, clever architecture, and renewable resources.

Colorful awnings mixed with more sustainable coverings that resembled small garden plots lined the canyon walls. Both options offered shade and protection, a necessity here, especially during the brutal summer months. Narrow footpaths zigzagged across the rock face, but at the canyon's floor, sprawled a thriving marketplace.

The Free People weren't isolationists, not by a long shot, but they were cautious. For good reason. When the world went to hell and it became obvious that man was more concerned about saving his own ass than salvaging the world he lived in, the Native American people set aside tribal differences and became a unified force intent on protecting what natural resources they could.

In a progressive move that positioned them ahead of general society, they banded together in various regions and took control of critical natural resources—dams, wind turbines and solar fields. Some even managed to save large stretches of crops and grazing lands.

In this area they controlled the water that supplied most of the west coast. The Free People stood apart from the reigning power players—the Cartels to the south, the Rocky Mountain queen, Lilith, to the east, and the Emperor of the West Coast, Michael—because they were the protectors of resources that didn't recognize territories.

And that's why Havoc was here now.

Fate's Vultures had recently found themselves in reluctant control of the neutral territory that sat smack in the middle of Michael and Lilith's domains. The area stretched from what used to be Idaho, through Utah and bumped up against the Free People in northern Arizona. It also included the safest (and he used that word loosely) supply routes between the two major territories.

Initially, the Vultures worked for Crane, the man who controlled the Central territories, but after he was killed and his second, Simon, got himself strung up and tortured by Raiders, Reaper had been shoved into the driver's seat by Simon. He told the Vulture's leader that it was temporary, just until he got back on his feet, but Havoc thought Simon had never wanted the damn position in the first place. Which meant that instead of the Vultures riding free and clear of any responsibilities, they found themselves anchored by a handful of potential problems that left them mired in a looming storm of power struggles.

Mercy's comments last night indicated that part of the story had not yet made it to the rumor mill, and Havoc was in no rush to enlighten her. Because no matter how much of a temptation she was, he only had her word about her situation with the Cartels. And Vex was right on one thing, if Havoc added trouble with the Cartels to their current pile of shit, despite their years long friendship, Reaper would kill him.

Havoc followed their escorts into a smaller canyon as they headed for a garage crouched at the boxed end. The two front riders pulled into the wide lot of the low-slung building and rolled to a stop.

Havoc and Vex did the same. The rumble of engines died away and it took a few seconds for the dull ringing in his ears to fade. He braced his feet against the hard packed ground and waited to be approached.

Mercy's hands at his waist disappeared. He reached back and squeezed her knee in silent warning. To his right, Vex braced her bike and waited, keeping Katori behind both her and Havoc.

An older man stepped into the garage's wide doorway and wiped his hands on a stained rag as he greeted the two escorts with a nod. His barrel chest stretched the black t-shirt, faded jeans covered his thick legs, and a dirt brown cowboy hat perched on his shaggy brown hair, shadowing his face. He walked forward. "Welcome."

Havoc pulled his bandana down until it hung around his neck. "Hey, Ed, you still running the garage?"

The older man's step hitched. "Havoc? Is that you, boy?" He nudged the brim of his hat back to reveal a weathered face lined with a salt and pepper bristle. "Damn, man, it's been what?" He tucked the rag in a back pocket. "Four, five years?"

"Hop off," Havoc directed Mercy, and as soon as her feet hit the ground, he kicked his bike's stand down. "Closer to five I think," he told Ed as he swung off his bike, clasped arms with Ed and did the shoulder pound exchange before stepping back.

While Ed's smile was real, it carried visible strain. "You staying longer this time?"

Havoc shook his head. "Day, maybe two at most."

"Like the damn wind, you are, boy." His attention left Havoc and touched on Mercy, who unwound her face covering and left it hanging from her shoulders. "Ma'am."

She dropped her head in acknowledgement.

When Ed turned to Vex, he caught sight of the boy behind her, and his skin paled. "Katori?" The boy's name emerged in a guttural shock.

The boy scrambled off Vex's bike and flew to the older man, who darted around Havoc's bike to meet him.

The impact was audible as Ed crouched down and wrapped his arms around the smaller frame. "Oh, thank God!" The rest of his words were muffled against Katori's slender frame.

Havoc gave them a minute and turned to the stunned sentries. "One of you might want to let Istaqa know," he offered.

The one on the left gave a sharp nod and took off.

Ed finally released Katori so he could straighten. However, he kept ahold of the boy's hand as he turned to Havoc. "I have a million questions."

"No doubt, but not a fan of repeating things, so can you hold them until we see Istaqa?" Mindful of the situation, Havoc kept his question as gentle as possible.

Ed nodded. "Let's get your bikes inside so we can head up."

"Sounds good."

Ed turned and led them to the garage, Katori close to his side. The rest of them followed, ignoring the occasional face swipe as Katori tried to hide his tears. Instead, Ed told the boy, "Forgive me, Katori, but I'm not sure I can let go of you quite yet."

"'S okay," Katori mumbled, earning a smile from the garage owner.

They stashed the bikes in minutes, then followed Ed up the narrow, winding passageway. It wasn't long before the rush of running footsteps pounded closer. Despite having an idea of who was headed their way, Havoc moved closer to Ed and Katori, while Vex and Mercy took his back.

A figure burst around a corner, rushing down the path without slowing. Katori pulled free of Ed's hold and dashed ahead. He barreled into the man on a cry. "Dad!"

"Katori!" Tall, lean, and imposing, the male dropped to his knees in the middle of the passageway and drew his son close.

A male and female rushed up behind him, and both skidded to a stop at the scene before them. The female's eyes turned suspiciously bright, while a slow smile spread over the male's face. Ed slowed to a stop and let the father and son have their minute.

Havoc came up beside him, their shoulders brushing as

they watched the emotional reunion. "How's he been?" Havoc kept the question between them.

"How'd you think?" Ed folded his arms over his chest. "Trying to keep him in check has been difficult. If you hadn't sent that message, I'm not sure anyone would've been able to stop him from heading out much longer."

Yeah, that's what Havoc had been afraid of, because years ago Katori's father had brutally lost his wife. To then have his son go missing was bound to drive a man to madness, a kind of madness Havoc was intimately familiar with. That kind of emotion didn't give a damn about anything, except striking out at those who took what wasn't theirs.

In this case, he was grateful that Katori made home relatively safe and sound, because if the leader of the Free People went on a revenge-filled rampage now, when so much was shaky as sin, it would be an unimaginable nightmare.

Havoc waited a few more minutes before he stepped forward. When Istaqa's dark head lifted, he said, "I hate to interrupt, but we need to talk."

The other man dropped his chin in acknowledgement and rose to his feet, never letting go of his son. Once on his feet, he cleared Havoc's six-foot frame by a bare inch. He held out his hand, and when Havoc took it, pulled him in, Katori stuck between them. "Thank you." Istaqa's gratitude carried a rough edge.

Havoc drew back, held the guarded brown gaze, and kept his voice low. "No thanks needed."

That got a twitch of lip and some of the lines on the scruff-lined face eased. "Well, then, welcome home."

The words hit with unexpected strength and stirred emotions Havoc didn't want to identify. He shifted back and Istaqa's attention went to the two women standing quietly behind him.

Istaqa turned to Havoc and raised his brow. "I'm assuming

the Valkyrie is Vex, but the shadow at her side doesn't quite match what I've heard of your Vultures."

Havoc angled until he see the women, and motioned them forward. "Vex, Mercy, meet Katori's father, Istaqa."

Mercy nodded, but Vex folded her arms, cocked her head, and flashed the leader of the Free People her crazy ass grin. "You got a hell of a son there."

Istaqa brushed a hand over Katori's head as a small smile full of quiet pride pierced his stoic expression. "Yes, I'm extremely lucky." Pleasantries completed, he turned to Havoc. "Give me a few hours to get Katori settled, then we can meet. Agreed?"

Havoc nodded, understanding Istaqa wanted privacy to talk to his son. Besides, it was closing on midday and after hours riding through dust, the delay would be appreciated. "Your place?"

"You remember the way?"

Havoc nodded again and ignored the weight of unasked questions from the females behind him. There was time enough to get into that later when they didn't have an audience.

Istaqa took Katori over to the woman who now wore a big grin. They spoke and then she held out her hand. Havoc caught the worried glance Katori sent his dad and his jaw tightened. It would be a long time before that kid felt safe, even here in his home.

Istaqa's shoulders tightened, but it was the only outward sign that he hadn't missed his son's look. He lifted his chin in reassurance. "Go on, son, I'll be right behind you."

Katori took the woman's hand and followed her back up the path as she chatted away.

Havoc stepped up to Istaqa's side as the other man kept his gaze on his departing son and fisted his hands at his side.

"You better have names for me, Havoc." The harsh

demand came out in a low voice, but Istaqa didn't wait for a response, before stalking after his son, the young male guard on his heels.

"Come on, boy," Ed called softly. "Let's go find you three some lunch. Have a feeling I'm going to have to wait a bit for answers." He waited just beyond Vex and Mercy, for Havoc to turn back to him. "I'm sure Nora will be over the moon that you're back."

At Ed's comment, Havoc winced, turned around and came face to face with Vex and Mercy, who now blocked his path.

Vex made a soft hum as speculation washed over her face. "Nora?" she repeated.

He shot her a finger with the futile hope it would curb her curiosity. Futile being the operative word.

"You've got some explainin' to do, partner," Vex drawled, her voice low.

Mercy stood on her other side, eyes narrowed and her expression bland. Like nosy bookends, the two women stared at him with undeniable curiosity that he intended to ignore. He strode forward, unsurprised when they shifted to let him pass between them.

He cursed Ed to hell and back. "Not now."

"But soon," Vex pushed as she dogged his heels.

He shot a disgruntled glower at the strangely silent Mercy who was keeping pace on his other side. "What?"

She arched a brow. "What what?"

Please God, let there be some home-brew at the market. Because it would be the only way he would make it through lunch since the two women existed to drive him fucking nuts. He caught up to Ed and grumbled, "Thanks a lot, old man."

Knowing damn good and well the pot he stirred, Ed chuckled.

seven

Mercy watched Ed head back to the counter for seconds, her mouth full of spicy meat, cheese, lettuce, salsa and hard corn shell, and wondered if she could get away with ordering another taco or two. Nora's was an open-air eatery, a small building lined with a long counter that hid the bustling kitchen behind it.

She, Havoc, Vex and Ed sat on the edge of a collection of picnic tables situated under thick awnings. The lunch crowd was slow to thin, and privacy was a joke but from where she sat, she could see who was approached without getting an ache in her neck.

Vex, who sat next to her, pushed away an empty plate with a few surviving grains of rice mingled with straggler pinto beans. Sunlight danced off the delicate metal lacework claw covering her right hand and left Mercy blinking away tiny starbursts. Decorative and lethal, it was a beautiful, but strange weapon, obviously created by a talented artist.

Vex leaned forward, causing the string of colorful beads that lined one of her thin braids to dance together in a soft clicking chorus and rested her chin on her hand. She tapped one metal tipped finger against her cheek and aimed her gaze at Havoc, who sat across from her. "So?"

He used the last of a flour tortilla to capture his refried beans, took a bite and chewed slowly as he met her gaze, his face impassive.

Undaunted, Vex continued. "Nora seemed happy to see you."

Mercy's stomach soured at Vex's not-so-subtle jibe, and her previously delicious bite turned into tasteless mush.

Not her business.

The stern reminder did little to ease her unwarranted jealousy. She set down the last bit of unfinished taco and glared at her plate as her appetite went up in a puff of smoke.

Dammit.

Just because Havoc razed her world to ash with a simple kiss, didn't give her a right to play the jealous bitch with one of Havoc's women. And no matter how low-key Nora played it, there was no missing the subtle signs that marked Nora as one of his women and delighted Vex to no end.

Upon their arrival, Ed led them up to the counter and called out a greeting. Mercy, busy checking out the handwritten menu propped against the side of the building, hadn't seen Nora at first. But when the woman turned and spotted Havoc, her entire face lit up, taking the strikingly strong features to the edge of beauty.

That stunning and telling change definitely caught Mercy's attention.

Nora wasted no time slipping out front and wrapping her arms around Havoc with an ease of intimate familiarity. Even that hadn't bothered Mercy—much. It was when Havoc returned the hug, the hard lines of his face softening, that the green-eyed serpent struck with viper quickness, and left behind poisonous images of what created their closeness.

Mercy's unexpected ache of want threw her normal live-

and-let-live worldview for a loop. She wasn't naive enough to believe sharing a simple thing as a kiss with a man like Havoc equaled some kind of commitment.

Hell no.

Not only did he have the whole silent and brooding thing down pat, but he was surrounded by a tangible distance, an emotional fissure no bridge could cross. All of which acted like catnip for the female half of the population.

Even on her, though Mercy knew better. She wasn't the kind of woman a man would let close. Not unless he liked to live on the edge of uncertainty because her lifestyle was hell on relationships. But when she witnessed that poignant exchange, none of that had mattered, and it left her to wonder which of her impulses would win out—sinking her blade in between Havoc's shoulders or ignoring the couple altogether.

Fortunately for her, she managed to hold strong and stalk to the counter on the pretext of ordering lunch.

Blessedly ignorant of Mercy's upheaval, Vex wasn't backing down. "Thought for a moment we'd have to give you two some privacy."

That got a reaction. Havoc's face darkened, from anger or embarrassment, Mercy couldn't tell. However, she voted for anger since he didn't strike her as someone easily embarrassed. That guess was further reinforced when he growled, "Drop it."

The thin layer of Vex's amusement disappeared as if it never existed. In its place was the Vulture behind the merciless reputation. "What the fuck, Havoc? You have history here."

Based on how pissed Vex was, it was a history he obviously hadn't shared with his partner. Question after so-not-her-business question churned through Mercy's mind.

Havoc held his partner's glare and snapped, "We all have history somewhere, Vex."

Vex took his hit, but her eyes narrowed as she came back

swinging. "Not talking about the woman. The other history." Her gaze deliberately swept over their surroundings, silently making her point before returning to him. "That one seems pretty damn important, *partner*."

Mercy managed not to wince at the caustic whip Vex added to the last word. She nabbed a chip from the basket holding at the table's center and continued to watch the entertaining exchange.

Havoc didn't back down, if anything, he just doubled down. "The definition of history is that it happened a long fucking time ago. It has nothing to do with now."

Unwilling, or unable, to conceded, Vex groused, "Still, would've been nice to know it existed before we got hit with your welcome home party."

Nibbling on her chip, Mercy tried to decide if it was jealousy or frustration fueling Vex's attack. It wasn't the same sickening mix of jealousy and frustration that crawled through Mercy because it carried a different flavor. It fascinated her, this relationship the two Vultures had, almost as if Havoc was the big brother and Vex the bratty ass, lethal little sister.

Havoc studied Vex, then he sighed and lost some of his prickly defensiveness. "My past, my *private* past," he stressed, "was why Reaper sent Katori with us. Better for someone they trust to bring back Istaqa's son, than someone they've only heard about."

Vex's eyes flashed, and her hand curled into a fist against the table's top, hiding the beautiful but deadly honed tips. "So, Reaper knows?"

Havoc held her glare. "Yeah, it's the reason why he and I started riding together in the first place."

Confusion crowded out Vex's angry expression. "But I thought you two started riding together because—"

He cut her off with a look. Vex's mouth snapped shut and

as Ed came back with a cup of coffee and a muffin, she shook her head. "Fine, we'll pick this up later."

"Or not at all," Havoc muttered.

Mercy washed her chip down with water and stifled her impatience at Ed's untimely interruption. *Just when things were getting interesting.*

Ed sat next to Havoc. "Guess you'll be here at least the night?"

"Yeah."

The older man nodded. "Well, then I've got two empty rooms above the garage, if you need a place to crash."

"Appreciate it."

"You're a quiet one."

It took a moment for Mercy to register that Ed's comment was directed at her. She gave the old man a bland smile. "Not much to add."

"Hmm." He took a sip of his coffee and studied her over the rim, his hazel eyes sharp despite the weathered wrinkles surrounding them. He set his cup down, then turned back to Havoc. "Warning, boy, Nora's gonna offer you a bed for the night."

Vex's glared made a comeback and Mercy hid her pitching stomach with a smirk.

Havoc dropped his head and ran a hand over his neck. "Dammit, Ed, why do you have to stir shit up?"

That earned a bark of laughter. "She don't need much encouragement." Still chuckling, he shook his head, amusement adding a mischievous light in his eyes. Obviously taking pity on Havoc's pained expression, he soothed, "I'm just giving you grief. She'll leave you alone, no worries. She hooked up with Able."

"Able?"

"Yeah, he took over his dad's herd few years back."

The two men began a discussion about sheep and people

Mercy had no interest in. As her unexpected bout of jealousy waned, her attention drifted to their surroundings.

The lunch crowd had thinned considerably, but a few customers lingered. A young couple talked quietly on the other side as they leaned towards each other over their food. The woman occasionally turned to keep an eye on a pair of youngsters playing nearby. A trio of teens messed around at another table, their loud laughter earning dirty looks from a pair of older women.

Out of habit Mercy's scanned the other tables, because even though the most dangerous threat was back in Page, she was aware that when Felix set her ass up, he did it right. Proof of that being the Cartels had wasted no time in getting the word out that they wanted to get their hands on her, which led to a close call in Phoenix that had nothing to do with Felix and everything to do with the Cartels' generosity for her carcass. Like swarming rats, there were plenty of bounty hunters, mercenaries, and other nasty individuals who wouldn't hesitate to work with the Cartels. Unfortunately, Felix happened to be the one currently in the lead.

At a table toward the front, a group of farmers engaged in an amusing conversation based on the bursts of laughter. Over to the side, a man was slouched over his table, his head resting on folded arms, and his hat pulled low, keeping his face in shadow. His siesta was interrupted when a young man walked up, kicked the boot-heel sticking out from under the table, and jerked Nap Guy upright. There was no time to catch a glimpse of his face because his friend placed his hands on the table and leaned down to talk to him, blocking her view.

She moved on to the three generations of women sitting a table away—grandmother, mother, daughter—a safe assumption since they shared the same eyes and chin. The two older women quietly ate and chatted, while the daughter appeared slightly bored as she checked out the teens on the other side of the counter.

All in all, a fairly non-lethal lunch crowd.

A racket erupted from the far end of the street. Vex shot to her feet, Ed and Havoc half turned their chairs, and she did the same. All of them eyeing a cloud of dust that rose in the air, and drifted closer on a rush of noise, a crush of yells, hooves, baas, and bells.

"Ah dammit!" Ed took one last gulp of coffee, untangled himself from the bench, and pushed to his feet. "Looks like Ben's flock is making a run for it again."

Mercy slowly rose as Havoc did the same on the table's other side. As the noise and dust tumbled closer, the lingering lunch customers started their exodus. In a vain attempt to avoid the incoming grit, she pulled the tail end of her headscarf to cover her nose and mouth, then turned to follow the others.

"Get a move on, people!" Ed shouted, then he slapped Havoc's shoulder and pointed to the side of the eatery. "Head that way, we'll circle around back."

The last of the patrons sprung up and bailed just as the leading edge of sheep bled into the tables and divided the lunch crowd. The dust got thicker, the noise rose to deafening, and the pleasant lunch area was soon turned into a haze-filled pit of chaos. Their table was closer to the building's far edge, so the woolly bodies lapped their space like a sea of bleating obstacles.

Mercy scrambled backwards but didn't get far as a large hand grabbed her wrist and pulled her along. Trapped in Havoc's unrelenting grip she stumbled in his wake and slammed a hip on a table's edge with bruising force. She kept her feet, but the next wool-infested surge shoved her against Havoc's back for a second time. Not keen on bloodying her

nose every few seconds, she yanked her wrist free and transferred her hand to his waistband.

After navigating a series of turns that took them clear from
the choking dust and crazed wooly terrorists, Havoc slowed and
eventually stopped. Mercy uncurled her hold on his waistband
and looked around. A cloud of dust hovered just beyond the
awning and roofs, the noise level was now a dull buzz, and they
appeared to be on the backside of the market and free of sheep.

Ed took off his hat and slapped it against his thigh,
knocking off dust. "Damn kid knows better than to bring
those thick-witted cotton heads down through main street."

Next to him, Vex bent over with her hands on her knees as
she coughed, spit, and used the tail end of her shirt to wipe her
face. She straightened, her face marred by rust colored streaks.
"Never thought I'd have to worry about death by sheep."

Mercy, in the midst of unwrapping her face, dropped her
head to hide her grin at the other woman's appearance. She
tried to brush the red dust off her pants, but it was tenacious.

Proving she didn't miss much, Vex growled, "What?"

Mercy took a moment before lifting her head as she tried
not to laugh, but her lips still twitched when she motioned to
Vex and said, "You missed a spot."

"C'mon." Ed resettled his hat. "We'll use the back paths
and avoid that mess out front." He gave Vex a smile and a
wink. "We'll make a stop so you can wash up."

AN HOUR LATER, Mercy stood on the far side of a
breathtaking room as far from Havoc and Vex as she could get,
as they waited on Istaqa. Normally the unique home with its
rooms carved out of the canyon walls, complete with cleverly

disguised solar windows that offered sweeping views, would captivate her, but not right now.

Now she was struggling to contain her resentment thanks to her earlier argument with Havoc. All it took to blow her temper was one causal comment. The stubborn bastard wanted to leave her behind with some lame promise she could meet with Istaqa tomorrow. The words, *"fuck that"*, and *"they had a deal"* were bandied about with *"trust your ass as far as I can toss it"*, and *"not vouching for a murderer"*.

Throughout the entire exchange, Vex watched and waited with an amused grin. Only when Mercy threatened to ditch his overbearing ass and find her own way to Istaqa, did Havoc give in.

Now they were here, waiting for Istaqa to join them, and no one was talking, which was fine with her. What she had to say needed to be said to Istaqa, not to the condescending, thickheaded ass parked in the chair behind her, staring holes in her back.

She leaned a shoulder against the wall's edge where it met the window and stared down into the canyon's floor. From this vantage point, she could see the majority of the market-place sprawled below where a couple of sheep still wandered through the streets. It was moving into late afternoon with the sun beginning its descent, and the canyon walls deflecting its rays.

She caught movement at one of the entryways in the glass's reflective surface and watched Istaqa and another man stepped into the room. The second male's attention zeroed in on her, and the weight of it crawled over her spine.

Had they crossed paths at some point?

He didn't look familiar, and she was good with faces. He continued to stare and her discomfort grew. As difficult as it was, she maintained her casual pose and refused to turn around.

"Havoc." Istaqa moved to the bigger man, who rose to meet him. They did the male arm grasp thing again. When they separated, Istaqa turned to Vex, who was stretched along the length of a couch. "Vex, apologies for my shortness earlier."

"None needed." Vex swung her legs around and sat up.

Then it was Mercy's turn. She turned away from the window, met Istaqa's sharp gaze, and waited for him to speak first.

He tilted his head, his smile polite and his face hard. "And you are?"

"Mercy." Her name alone wouldn't satisfy him. Hell, most of what she could share with him wouldn't endear her, but it was a chance she had to take.

His politeness took on an unmistakable chill. "You're not a Vulture and you're not sharing Havoc's bed."

His blunt assessment brought a cynical curl to her lips. "No to the first, and not any time soon, to the second."

Vex snorted at her answer and Havoc heaved an audible sigh.

Their reactions earned a surface thaw from Istaqa. "You are here, why?"

"Made a deal with Havoc." Her smile tightened and she flicked a glare at the source of her irritation. "His part was to get me face time with you."

Istaqa looked at Havoc, who shrugged. Istaqa turned back to her, eyebrow raised, and genuine interest edged out the ice. "Before I ask the next obvious question, I'm curious as to what you offered him, considering he understands how much I value my privacy."

That was a given, considering just how difficult it was to get time with the leader of the Free People. Which was why she used Havoc to get it. Like a lodestone to iron, her gaze went to Havoc. Despite his unreadable expression remnants of their earlier argument stared back. But he wasn't the only one pissed and knowing it would be taken for the challenge it was, she turned to Istaqa and laid it out. "He wants to screw with the Cartels, and he needs me to do it."

That wiped away Istaqa's amusement and replaced it with something she didn't understand. He looked to Havoc. "Again, my friend?"

Havoc's expression didn't change but his shoulders rose in a negligent shrug. "Not like you're thinking. She ran into Boomer's, dragging a couple of roaches behind her. Decided helping her meant pissing them off. Win-win."

Istaqa folded his arms and his brow creased as he studied the other man, clearly not buying it. "For you maybe, but I don't need them infesting my house." Some serious eye contact went down between the two, before he shook his head and turned the spotlight back to her. "Why do you want to speak to me?"

Her nerves tightened and her fingertips tingled because this was it. Either Istaqa believed her and helped, or he kicked her out and left her on her own with the Cartels. One gave her a slim chance at survival, the other guaranteed a dirt nap. She took a breath and jumped. "Your dam's set to blow sky high. I can help you stop it. In exchange, you get me a meet with Guillermo Suárez."

eight

Mercy's pronouncement hit the room with sonic force. Stunned, Havoc sat there and absorbed the shock. He wondered if his ears were playing tricks on him. Never mind the part about the dam, she wanted a meet with the head of the Suárez family? *Was she suicidal?*

Istaqa must have had the same question because he stepped right into her, fists clenched at his side, his expression filled with fury, and spat, "Say again?"

Havoc shot to his feet but didn't move toward Mercy because it was clear she didn't need his help.

She tilted her head back to maintain eye contact with Istaqa but held her position. The woman had had balls, rock solid ones, as she faced the Free People's formidable leader with a rigid spine. "If you check your dam, I can guarantee you'll find it's been seeded with explosives."

Clearly unimpressed by her undaunted façade, Istaqa stared her down as tension curled around him like a cat. "Say I send men to check your claim and they come up empty."

She didn't flinch under the hard whip of accusation in his voice. "Then I'd suggest upping your security because from what I can tell, things were already set in motion before I left. Which means if they aren't already here, it's only a matter of time before they show up."

Istaqa's jaw flexed as calculation and suspicion darkened his already furious expression. "And you know this how exactly?"

Mercy's defiant edge softened proving she was far from stupid, because if she was still breathing, Istaqa was listening. "You have paper and a pencil?"

Istaqa eyed her carefully after her unexpected question. Finally, he came to some internal decision and motioned to the man who stood silently off to the side. Heeding that signal, the guard disappeared. Mercy and Istaqa continued their stare down until the man returned with the requested materials. He laid them on the low-slung table in front of the couch behind Istaqa, straightened, and stood watch at the table's edge, as Istaqa stepped aside to let Mercy pass. The implied threat was clear.

Freed from Istaqa's gaze, Mercy knelt by the table and started sketching as she talked. "I was sent to the Cartels to find out who they're currently in bed with. While there, I happened to stumble across detailed plans on Antelope Lake's dam."

Her hand flew over the paper as she sketched. An image of the dam in question came together in recognizable lines. "From what I could piece together, the plan is to keep you off balance with a series of nuisance hits before they go all-out. Then, when you've been run ragged, they'll sweep in and destroy the dam."

It was beyond stupid and fell right into self-destructive to destroy the system that harbored the water lifeline so what were they missing? Havoc looked to Istaqa and shared a frown with him. "What the hell do they think they'll gain by taking out the dam?"

Without looking up from her sketch, Mercy answered, "It takes out your greatest bargaining power."

Istaqa's eyes narrowed, his brows lowered, and he shook his head in disbelief. "They'd be better served trying to take control of the dam itself."

"I think that option was considered." Mercy continued to mark the explosives' locations on her sketch. "But when they realized that taking your forces head-on was suicidal, they went with the distract-and-destroy route."

"That's bullshit." Vex sat on the edge of the couch, feet on the ground, elbows on her knees, and unconcealed suspicion colored her face.

Havoc couldn't blame her for calling out Mercy, because the same storm of suspicion was brewing in his mind. Mercy's theory made no sense, especially in light of the information the Vultures intended to share with Istaqa. Information Mercy didn't have.

Correction shouldn't have.

Mercy paused, met Vex's stare and asked, "Is it?" Then turned back to her sketch.

Vex looked to Istaqa and Havoc, her annoyance not quite covering the worry underneath. "Cartels are many things, but stupid isn't one of them."

Mercy shook her head, but instead of arguing the other woman's statement, she asked, "Do you know the history of the Colorado River?"

It was Istaqa, arms crossed over his chest and a frowned aimed at Mercy's bent head, who answered. "Before the Collapse, the Colorado was the main water supply for the west coast and its power was harnessed by a series of dams. After things went to hell, the Free People reclaimed Hoover and Glen Canyon dams, regaining control of our water rights. To ensure others wouldn't continue to abuse Nature's bounty, we adjusted the series of dams to sustain what was left of the Colorado and Antelope Lake was born."

Mercy's mouth gained a sardonic curl. "By 'adjusting' the river's route, the Free People became a power player while ensuring their survival."

Istaqa's voice tightened, but he continued with the history lesson. "Water doesn't recognize territories or politics. If those around us want access, they abide by our treaties, or they're cut off."

And, Havoc silently conceded, that threat was why Katori's kidnapping by the Raiders had come out of left field. To survive in the southwest, you needed access to water, water controlled by the Free People. Mess with the Free People, and you were left high and dry—literally.

But if there was a will there was a way, and Havoc could see exactly where Mercy was leading them. "If the Cartels remove the dams, the lake will flood through the old canyons. Not only will that redirect the water into the old channels, but it would wipe out Navajo City."

"Which means," Mercy finally put down her pencil and twisted her spine so she could see Havoc and Istaqa. "With one fell swoop, the Free People would be left scrambling to contain the damage at the dam and the fallout of losing a shit ton of your people." Her voice softened. "By the time you got a handle on things, it would be too late."

Istaqa muttered a foul curse, spun on his heel, and paced towards the window.

As rocks settled in his gut, Havoc watched his old friend digest Mercy's information. If she was telling the truth, she had unknowingly handed over some missing puzzle pieces to an emerging power struggle. One the Vultures had recently been drawn into. Now it appeared to be Istaqa's turn.

Istaqa stared down into the canyon as his fists curled and

uncurled at his side. When he spoke, his voice was harsh. "And re-containment? Did they have a plan for that?"

Mercy's answer was slow in coming. "Not that I found but it doesn't mean there isn't something in place."

"You came in through Phoenix, right?" Vex's question reclaimed Mercy's attention.

Mercy turned to Vex and nodded. "Didn't see much, I was too busy running and dodging." She looked down at the paper in front of her, frowned, erased a line, and redrew it. "I think the intent isn't to claim the water, but to get you out of the way."

Ugly speculation slithered through Havoc. "The way for what?"

"Whose way?" Istaqa's question rode over Havoc's.

"Not the who you're thinking," she answered Istaqa while conveniently ignoring Havoc's question. Before he could call her on it, she stood up, paper in hand and faced Istaqa. "The Cartels are sneaky ass bastards, but they aren't suicidal. Taking out the dam would basically be a declaration of war, and from what I saw while I was down there, that's the last thing they want." She handed the sketch to Havoc. "I think this plan belongs to one singular greedy bastard, not the Cartels."

Havoc followed her unspoken clues. "Felix?"

Her throat bobbed as she swallowed, but she gave him a shallow nod. "I think he's the one who's in bed with the mystery partner, and not with the Cartels' blessing."

Each time she opened her mouth, she added another pebble to the impending mountain of problems that threatened to bury them all. It made him want to shake her, instead he gritted out, "But you have no proof."

"No." Soft though it was, her answer was filled with grim acceptance. "Right now, it's all hypothetical."

Without proof it came down to her word. No matter how much she tempted him, or how much her information aligned with what he already knew, it didn't change the questionable nature of her motives. She was an unknown player in an already unstable game.

Their safest move would be to eliminate her and that was a solution Istaqa was well within his rights to demand. Not only would it erase whatever threat she posed, but it would remove the trouble chasing her. He handed Mercy's sketch to his friend and found dark resolve staring back.

Not fucking happening.

The instinctive denial for a woman he barely knew ripped through him, rocking his normal dispassionate demeanor. A strange mix of frustration, panic and fury coiled in his gut.

He turned away and his gaze locked with hers. Did she have a clue what the ramifications of her revelations meant? The position she put herself in? Hell, the position she put him and Vex in? If Istaqa wanted, he could demand judgement from the Vultures, the kind of judgement that would leave Mercy bleeding or worse.

A flash of apprehension swept through her tenacious gaze and disappeared.

Yeah, she knew.

But she wasn't done. "I didn't put it together until Felix took out Tavi." A sharp inhale came from where Istaqa stood, but she didn't look away from Havoc. "He wants Suárez's seat at the Cartel table, bad."

Istaqa stepped away from the window. "Bad enough to kill his boss's son."

She looked at him, her expression bland. "Yep."

He studied the sketch while silence descended. When he looked up, his face was unreadable. "If this proves true, why are you sharing?"

She slid a glance to Havoc, and he caught the sly spark in her eyes. No doubt the little troublemaker was considering using his earlier words about the goodness of her heart. He gave a sharp head shake to warn her off. Istaqa was too close to the edge as is, and if he was being honest, so was he.

She heaved a tiny sigh and played nice. "I need to contact Guillermo Suárez and make him an offer he won't refuse."

Istaqa watched her like a hawk. "And that offer is?"

"Proof that Felix killed his son and intends to betray him, and not just with this attack."

Unmoved, Istaqa's voice remained rock solid. "How do you plan on getting that kind of proof?"

Yeah, Havoc had the same damn question. What did she think would happen? She'd drag Felix down south, deliver him to Suárez, and he would just spill his guts? Not a chance in hell because Felix was more apt to slit his own wrists before Mercy could get him in front of the Cartels, who would waste no time gutting him. Either way, Mercy's proof was damn near unattainable.

Except none of that seemed to faze Mercy and her reply was calm. "I help stop the attack on the dam, then you act as my intermediary with Suárez. Once I have his agreement, I'll turn the tables on Felix and get the proof Suárez needs. If I'm right, you'll avoid starting someone else's war with the Cartels." She paused and held Istaqa's gaze. "I give you my word, I can do this."

Endless moments ticked by before Istaqa broke the tension. "You don't ask for much, do you?" Havoc wasn't surprised when his friend motioned his guard over and handed him Mercy's sketch. For the safety of the Free People, Istaqa couldn't afford not to verify her claims. "Send a team to check." He got a nod back and waited until the man left before he turned back to Mercy. "I suggest you get comfortable, because I'm not done with you."

Seemingly unconcerned, she shrugged, then walked over to one of the oversized chairs and curled up.

Havoc took advantage of the conversational lull as Istaqa

began to pace in front of the oversized window, his hands clasped behind his back. He retook his seat, sat back, and stretched out his legs, crossing his boots at the ankle. Then, even knowing her answer, he asked Mercy the one question that burned in his gut. "Going to share who you're working for?"

"Nope." She didn't even twitch. "Sorry."

He knew his smile was far from friendly when he said, "No, you're not."

Istaqa stopped, leaned a hip against Havoc's chair, and considered her. When he spoke, his voice carried a ruthless chill. "I'm sure we can change that."

Mercy's husky laugh hit Havoc hard. It scraped over his half-dead heart and slipped lower, the challenge tempting the predator within.

Unaware of his reaction, she drawled, "I'm sure you could, but it would be a waste of time and energy."

The darker side of Havoc didn't agree. "I don't know, it might make me feel better."

Istaqa grunted in agreement.

She quirked a brow. "Would it make you two feel better if I promise that my boss has no ulterior motives against Fate's Vultures or the Free People?"

Vex's boots hit the table as she propped up her feet and put her hands behind her head. "Got proof?" When everyone looked at her, she shrugged. "What? Seems to be the going rate lately."

"If that's the case, then I'm in debt up to my eyebrows." Mercy muttered.

"You know exactly how to wipe the books clear," Havoc said.

"Yeah, not going to happen, big guy." She eyed him for a moment, clearly navigating some thin internal line, and then sighed. "My boss thinks I'm still embedded with the Suárez's, he has no idea my mission's been blown to hell. The decision to come to you with this was mine and mine alone."

And based on the worry darkening her gaze and the nervous tug on her pants, it was a decision she still struggled with. Havoc steepled his fingers and adjusted his perception of her. "You're covering your ass?"

"Yep." There was no hesitation and zero shame in her answer. Her restless movement stopped, and was wiped away by a sharp, intense focus. "I still need to find out who's stroking whose dick down south, and if I can help avoid a massive cluster by sharing information with Istaqa, all the better."

Her explanation revealed a tangled core of ruthless practicality and compassionate honor, something he could appreciate.

"How long were you with the Cartels?" Istaqa asked seemingly out of left field. Except knowing the man as he did, Havoc could guess where this was headed.

Wariness colored her face. "Two months, give or take a few days."

"Were they involved with taking my son?"

"The Cartels?" Her gaze jumped to Havoc's then leapt back to Istaqa, her answer cautious. "No."

"Your answer isn't inspiring confidence, babe," Havoc pointed out.

Her shoulders lifted, but her tension turned it awkward and stiff. "Katori said he was kidnapped by the Raiders."

"But you wondered," Vex cut in. "When you first saw him with us, you wondered."

Mercy gave her a short nod. "The timing fit."

"You said 'distract and destroy'." Tension poured off Istaqa, but he tempered his tone as the worried father struggled with the ruthless leader. "You think my son's kidnapping was the distract part of the plan?"

Compassion seeped around the edges of Mercy's expression. "Look, the Cartel's wouldn't spit on a Raider if their ass was on fire. I can't see the two working together."

"But according to you, Felix is behind the dam attack." Havoc leaned forward, braced his elbows on his knees, and pinned her in place with his gaze. "Would he work with the Raiders to ensure Istaqa was distracted?"

Instead of offering a quick answer, she took her time and considered his question. "No. Where the Cartels' would stand back and watch a Raider burn, Felix is the type to light the match." Her eyes narrowed with speculation as she followed his lead. "But he is an opportunistic bastard."

Havoc looked to Vex and saw a reflection of grim understanding. "You thinking what I'm thinking?"

Her amber eyes lit by a cold rage, his partner nodded. "Felix's mystery partner is the same douche nozzle as Reznik's."

"Who's Reznik?"

Istaqa took a seat on the couch next to Vex and answered Mercy before Havoc could, his voice flat and hard. "Reznik hired the Raiders to take my son."

"Okay, that makes him a top-of-the-line idiot but doesn't explain who he is." Mercy's confusion was clear. "What the hell does he gain by pissing you off? Better yet, how'd he afford the Raiders? They don't exactly work cheap."

Vex held Havoc's gaze. "Might as well share. Who knows, she might come in handy." When he frowned, she pushed. "That's why we're here, yeah?"

He conceded her point, turned to Mercy, and studied her carefully. "Reznik was an up-and-coming crime lord in New Seattle."

Some unknown emotion flashed too fast to follow in her eyes, and her brows rose. "Was?"

"Yep, was." Vex didn't hide her satisfaction. "My brother's woman gutted him." She and Istaqa shared a fist bump.

Mercy's confused frown got deeper. "I don't get it. Why would a New Seattle crime lord target the Free People?"

Havoc decided to put a few cards on the table. "He wouldn't, not on his own." Then he sweetened the pot. "Reznik wasn't acting alone, he had help. Powerful help."

nine

Shock rocketed through Mercy, but years of deeply ingrained training kept it hidden from the three individuals who eyed her like a juicy piece of meat. It wasn't hard to connect the dots they offered her. "You think whoever Felix is working with, was working with this Reznik person."

No one answered since it wasn't a question.

She considered their theory. The list of those who could pull off such an intricate plan was short, but two names stuck out. Michael, head of the Northwest Territories, and Lilith, the ruling queen of the Rocky Mountain Territories.

The trio's silent implication hit Mercy with stunning force and left her stomach pitching with a combination of fury and excitement. She buried the first and reeled in the second. Her heart pounded as one name raced to the front of her mental line up.

Michael.

Not only did he hold the number one spot on her boss's lethal to-do list, but hers as well. She hauled on the reins of her raging emotions, and forced the name back into the locked vault of her heart. She couldn't get her hopes up, not yet. She swallowed against her dry throat and asked, "Do you have a name?"

"Wrong question," Vex chided, her tone scathing.

"No, it's the only question," Mercy snapped back, her patience dangling by the merest thread. "If we go with the theory that the Cartels are unaware of Felix's actions, and the Vultures are working for—" she caught Havoc's mouth opening and corrected herself, cutting him off, "—with Crane, and Istaqa wouldn't kidnap his own son, that leaves two others with the means and motive to utilize resources like the Raiders and Felix."

"We know it's not Lilith." Havoc's comment was low.

She whipped her head around and narrowed her eyes. "How?"

"Because," Istaqa said. "The Vultures and Lilith have an agreement."

She absorbed that shocking bit of news and shot back, "What kind of agreement? Like what they have with Crane?"

"If we tell you, we'll have to kill you," drawled Vex. "So please ask again."

Annoying bitch. Oh, what Mercy wouldn't give to take Vex up on her offer, if, for no other reason, than to wipe that smirk off her face.

Thankfully Istaqa spoke before she could do something epically stupid. "Perhaps a better term is a partnership, one where we all benefit."

Which sounded exactly like an alliance. "'We'?" she asked Istaqa.

His chin lifted and his dark gaze didn't waver. "As they saved my son, I'm considering it."

"Ain't that a relief." Vex rolled her eyes. "And here I thought our visit would be a total waste of time."

Mercy's mind spun through what was said and what wasn't, but she didn't miss the frown Havoc shot at Vex.

"Since when have the Vultures decided to enter the damn power game?" When the two Vultures in question turned to her, she elaborated. "I thought you were all about protecting the little guy and getting justice. Besides, doesn't Crane keep you busy enough? Last I checked, Lilith and the Free People had no need of the Vultures."

Havoc's face was impassive. "Shit changed."

I'll say. "Must have been some serious shit then." She rethought her sarcastic approach when Havoc's expression darkened, but since she was trying to keep her head above the flood of bad news, he'd just have to deal.

"Understatement of the year," muttered Vex.

Havoc's dark gaze took on an unsettling intensity as he shared with Mercy. "After the Raiders killed Crane, we were asked to step in and hold the Central territories until his second was back on his feet."

Killed Crane? Hold the Central territories? It took a second for the impact of his latest bomb to hit. "Wait! Crane's dead?" When no answered, she sprung from her chair, dragged her hands through her hair, and started to pace. Trying to reshape the world as she knew it left her head feeling like it was set to implode.

"Raiders took him out in a blitz attack on Pebble Creek." Vex's answer stopped Mercy in her tracks. She turned and looked to the other woman

Vex stared back, her face serious with no trace of her earlier snark and tapped one metal tipped finger against her knee.

Mercy slowly pivoted. "Raiders hit Pebble Creek?" Okay, she might sound like a mimic, but the shocks just kept coming. *Damn, she missed a lot while she was down south.*

"Yep." Vex's finger continued its rhythmic pattern but picked up speed. "Then they tried to take out Simon, which didn't end well for them."

There was a flash of emotion Vex failed to hide, which told

Mercy Simon meant something to her. Since he also appeared to be Crane's second, she tucked away the name for later consideration and concentrated on the bigger issue. "Pebble Creek is way out of their normal striking range."

"It is," Havoc confirmed. "But they were acting on Reznik's orders."

She stopped behind the chair she'd been sitting in and gripped the back. "Why?"

"Revenge." Istaqa sat in the corner, his arm outstretched along the couch's back, and his ankle on his knee, in what should be a relaxed pose, but an air of dark fury hovered around him. "Crane intercepted the Raiders and rescued Katori and the other children taken by the Raiders. That screwed with Reznik's plans, which pissed him off, so he moved his agenda up and sent the Raiders to take Crane out."

Moved his agenda up? What? Like there was more to killing Crane than a temper tantrum?

Mercy began to weave together the information being shared. What would a crime lord out of New Seattle gain by going after Crane? Hell, why team up with the unreliable craziness of Raiders?

Then logic took over. Raiders were the perfect fodder. Throw them at your problem and their stink would be thick enough to hide the true threat.

So why Crane?

The answer was simple. The supply routes. Crane's control was as vital to territories' survival as the Free People's control of the water. To check her assumptions, she asked, "Then what? This Reznik would sweep in and take control of the supply routes?"

"Got it in one," rumbled Havoc.

Holy shit, what a mess.

But she couldn't deny it made a sickening sort of sense. Control the supply routes and you kept a stranglehold on the population scattered outside the city's control. Same deal with the water supply. So, if you held both, you could sit pretty damn high on the power ladder.

Her gut cramped. *Shitdamnfuck, what a bowel-twisting cluster!*

It took a few moments to get her brain back on track, then she blew out a shaky breath. It was her turn to ask, "Do you have proof?"

Vex's smile was more a baring of teeth, but it was Havoc who answered. "What do you think?"

What did she think? If their theory on who might be playing partner in crime and pulling the strings on puppets like Reznik and Felix was correct, there wasn't a chance in hell they had proof.

Michael was legendary when it came to covering his ass. Something she had first-hand knowledge of. But, holy hell, if they were right, the key to settling a long overdue debt was well within her reach.

Too damn bad her boss had tied her freakin' hands.

Except she couldn't help but notice that Istaqa and the Vultures appeared more worried about protecting their people than exacting revenge or acquiring power. Which left her with a difficult decision.

Once upon a time, she chose a life based upon that same sense of protective justice, until time and circumstances twisted it into unrecognizable knots. Now she had a chance to not only get her vengeance but reclaim some of her tarnished honor.

But at what price?

She licked her lips, met Istaqa's gaze, and opened her mouth. Before she could say a word, the guard from earlier re-entered, and he wasn't alone.

Istaqa rose to his feet with a fluid grace and made his way across the room to stand in front of his man. He stared down at the man who hung between two stern faced guards. "I see you brought me back something, Daniel."

Havoc and Vex joined Mercy as they watched the unfolding drama.

Daniel gave his leader a grim smile which caused the cut on his lip to re-open. His gaze touched on her before going back to his leader. "We found explosives where she indicated. I've got teams disarming them as we speak." He motioned to the man hanging between the two other men. "We caught this bastard and three of his friends setting the last one in place."

The man could barely stay upright, but Istaqa yanked his head back with a cruel grip in his hair. The captive groaned and tried to focus through swollen eyes. Istaqa studied the bruised and battered face, then turned towards Mercy, angling the captive's head so she could see his face. "Do you recognize him?"

She studied the beaten features and ran them through her mental album. When nothing about him scratched her memory, she shook her head.

Istaqa's mouth thinned, he ripped his hand free, and then turned to Daniel. "The other three?"

"Dead."

"Shame," Istaqa murmured with an obvious lack of sincerity. "At least this one is breathing. Take him to interrogation."

Daniel gave a sharp nod then issued a few short orders, that had the guards taking the captive away. Daniel stayed behind but kept eyeing Mercy with speculation. Normally, she wouldn't hesitate to call him out on that kind of attention, but not now when she was on overload, trying to process what the Vultures and Istaqa had thrown at her.

"I'm going to have a chat with our latest guest. "Istaqa dismissed her and spoke directly to Havoc. "She's your responsibility. We'll finish this when I'm done." Then he turned to

Vex. "In light of our new relationship, would you like to join me, Vex?"

Predatory eagerness filled Vex's smile as she flowed to her feet and went to Istaqa's side. "Aww, I love a man who knows how to show a girl a good time."

"Istaqa." Mercy called out. Vex and Istaqa looked back. Mercy stepped forward, only to be brought up short by Havoc's hand on her shoulder. With a low, frustrated hiss, she wrenched free of his grip and stalked over to Istaqa. "You have your proof I wasn't lying."

It was stupid to push, but she couldn't shake free of the looming sense of doom. They might have stopped the dam's destruction, but it didn't mean they got all the players. With the way her luck was going, the possibility that a rat was currently scrambling back to Page, eager to report to Felix, was damn high.

Istaqa's face hardened and his response was clipped. "No, what I have is proof someone is targeting the dam. Before I agree to call Suárez, I want to ensure he's not the bastard behind this."

She gritted her teeth against the tide of impatience and frustration and gritted out, "The longer you take, the more time Felix has to slip away."

Istaqa left Vex and closed in, his voice cutting through her with the ease of a well-honed blade. "Then you better hope our bomber breaks easy." He held her gaze as she fought her desire to snap back. As she struggled not to scream in frustration at his thick headed, arrogant attitude, he turned, gave her his back, and stalked from the room.

Vex flashed an evil grin. "Don't worry. I like breaking things." She gave them a finger wave, light flashing off the lethal tips, and disappeared after Istaqa.

ten

"You going to pout all night?" Havoc asked as he nabbed a bottle of brew and took a long drink.

Mercy continued to ignore him, and kept her gaze focused on the group playing pool in the far corner of the room. Once Istaqa and Vex left, Havoc had dragged her out of Istaqa's house, down into the canyon, and sat her ass at a table in the local tavern, RedRock.

An untouched bottle sat on the table in front of her, sweating. She could feel the weight of Havoc's gaze, but she refused to meet it because thick skulled, arrogant males were currently topping her shit list.

When he kicked her foot under the table, her gaze snapped to his. She bit her tongue to keep from ripping him a new one. Undaunted, he leaned forward, and pitched his voice low so their conversation stayed between them. "Did you expect it to be that easy?"

Unable to keep her frustration at bay any longer, she unclenched her teeth and snarled, "I expected him to show a bit more intelligence."

Havoc's nostrils flared, but his tone didn't change. "Just

because you provided good intel, doesn't negate the fact you're an unknown."

"An unknown who just saved his ass," she shot back, but she grudgingly acknowledged his logic.

"An unknown with an unknown agenda working for an unknown boss." He tapped his bottle to hers. "Not a lot of foundation to build trust on, babe." He lifted his bottle to his lips.

She ignored the internal wince at his well-aimed shot. "Some are built on less."

She dropped her gaze, snatched up her bottle, and took a drink. Yeah, okay, she got it, but it didn't stop the warning itch that dug into the base of her skull.

Obviously taking pity on her, Havoc shared, "Right now, he can't afford a wrong move." He set his bottle down, leaned back, and absently twisted it in small circles with one hand as he considered her. "Solution's simple."

If not for the incoming shit storm, it would be so easy for her to get caught up in the chocolate depths of his eyes. She shook her head at the sappy thought, sat back, and folded her arms over her chest, Weariness tugged at her, but rationality nailed her with a cold kick of logic.

She knew what he wanted. "If you're right and it was up to me, I'd share in a heartbeat." And God knew she wanted to, so damn bad that she actually considered willfully ignoring the promises she had made. It was so tempting, especially since she could barely stay one step ahead of the danger nipping at her heels. But she couldn't.

She rubbed a hand over the dull ache setting up shop at her temples. What she needed was access to a phone. If she could just talk to her boss and catch him up on what was happening here, she might be able to take this whole thing to the next level without breaking her word. But she'd bet every piece of luck that the only phone available was locked up somewhere in Istaqa's home.

Havoc watched her with lazy regard, and she hoped her thoughts were buried deep enough to escape his detection. His lips twitched. A sharp crack followed by cheers came from the pool game in the corner. She turned just in time to catch a round of high fives being exchanged.

When she turned back to Havoc, he spoke. "I have to wonder."

When he said nothing more, she arched an eyebrow. "About?"

He stretched his legs and set his heels on the seat next to her, trapping her. "You barely batted an eyelash when we laid everything out for you."

She cocked her head to the side, uncertain where he was going with this. "Wasn't hard to follow the lines you all drew." She lifted her bottle and took another drink, enjoying the bite of bitterness.

Havoc waited until she had a mouthful before asking with deceptive casualness, "You working for Michael?"

She choked as her beer went down the wrong way, burning through her nose and making her eyes water. When she got herself back under control, she rasped, "Hell, no. I'd rather leave the bastard gutted in a ditch than work with him." As soon as the words left her mouth, she wanted to curse at what they revealed, but she refused to call them back. She didn't mind lying to get a job done, but Havoc wasn't a job and lying to him felt wrong. But keeping things from him, that she could justify, for now.

Interest lit his eyes, but it was the only change in his relaxed position. "Sounds like a story there. Going to share?"

Now he wanted to bond?

Deciding he wasn't the only one who could dig up the past, she took her turn at the shovel. "Sure, if you share yours."

A muscle twitched along his jaw. "I'm not the one who needs to shore up their foundation."

"Don't you?" She couldn't resist needling him even though in their brief time together, she found in a strangely unique way that she did trust him. Oh, she didn't expect him to lay his life down for her, but if he said he'd help her, he would. Still, years of hard-earned experience made it difficult to admit as much.

"I saved your curvy ass, even brought you to Istaqa. Plus, you don't strike me as a woman who would let a man touch her the way you let me touch you last night, not unless she trusted him at some level." The curve of his lips paired with the heat in his gaze created a dangerously carnal dare that left her pulse pounding. "So, I'd say my foundation is pretty damn solid right now." The evil, evil man didn't cut her any slack. "Wouldn't you agree?"

Her hand tightened on her bottle as an answering tide of lust left her hot and achy. Her tongue swept over her bottom lip and her voice was rough. "Maybe." Despite the hunger swimming under her skin, she refused to back down. "Doesn't mean it will survive when the storm hits."

He threw back his head and laughed, an honest to God laugh. It transformed his face and turned all the hard edges into something mesmerizing. Caught in the wonder of it, she was startled when he sat up, wrapped a curiously gently hand around the back of her neck and hauled her forward. The table's edge pressed under her breasts, but the discomfort disappeared as his lips closed over hers. His tongue swept in to tangle with hers in an unhurried rush as if he had all the time in the world.

Unable to resist the seductive dance, she joined in. The tart bite of the brew added a cool edge to his dark taste, and she took his intoxicating flavor deep. Her mind tumbled as it tried to place the elusive combination, some mix of heat and spice. It raced through her veins and sparked a voracious hunger. When he delicately bit down on her lower lip, a soft moan escaped. She returned the favor, and then soothed his abused lip with a soft swipe of her tongue. She continued to trace his lower lip lazily before he reclaimed control of the kiss.

Eventually, he drew back and without letting her go, he stared into her eyes. "That storm?"

"Yeah." It came out in a husky whisper.

Still reeling from his kiss, she sucked in air and pulled back. He reluctantly let her go, and they settled into their seats, neither one looking away. Red rode under his skin, and she was pretty sure the same color filled her face.

Quiet fell between them, neither one in a hurry to break it. When he finally spoke, there was a seriousness to his voice, an indicator he was done dancing around the question. "Why such a hard-on for Michael, Mercy?"

eleven

I t took everything Havoc had not to drag Mercy out of the tavern and explore the fierce storm of lust that boiled between them. Especially when he could see the same need reflected in the emerald shine of her eyes. But despite evidence to the contrary, he wasn't some horny ass teen whose dick reigned supreme. Nope, he was a horny ass man who could keep it in check until he got some answers. Then his dick could reign supreme.

Her heavy lashes dropped and severed the humming thread of awareness with a definitive snap. He resisted the urge to rub his chest at the strange sensation. Her kiss-swollen lips took on a sardonic curve. She deliberately lifted her bottle and took a drink. Only after she set it down did she met his gaze with cool calculation. "Why do you have such a hard-on for the Cartels?

It was probably twisted, but her repetitive evasive maneuvers amused him. Anyone else who played this cat and mouse game with him would find themselves on the wrong end of his knife. But with her, he found it...fun. The shock of that made him curt. "They stole something precious, something I can't replace."

She blinked, obviously not expecting such honesty. Instead of pushing for more, she returned the same unflinching truth. "He destroyed my world, and I intend to return the favor."

Instinct whispered if he continued to push, she would do the same. Since he was unprepared for that level of sharing, he simply replied, "Lofty goal."

Her veiled flash of disappointment made him pause, but before he could figure out why, she said, "I believe if you're going after someone or something, may as well go balls to the wall."

He chuckled at her wry statement. "Good motto to have, darlin'." He studied her profile, taking in the fine lines around her eyes and mouth as her attention went back to the action at the pool table. If not for the fact he could tell she was visually tracking their movements, he'd think she had fallen into a stupor of exhaustion.

Running your ass ragged would do that to you.

He'd been in her shoes a time or two, and since they were reduced to waiting for Istaqa and Vex to finish up their Q&A session, they might as well take advantage of the downtime. Lord knew, it wouldn't last. Keeping a grip on his bottle, he dropped his feet, and pushed up from the table.

She looked over and quirked her eyebrows. "We leaving?"

"Nope." He held out his hand. "Let's shoot some pool."

She unfolded from her seat, grabbed her drink, and took his hand. "Lead on."

He tangled their fingers together and led the way to the pool table in the corner where the previous players were notching their sticks in the rack. He and Mercy waited to the side and exchanged polite head nods as the group cleared out.

Havoc set his bottle on the small wall shelf, then did the

same for her's. After choosing their sticks, they used the Rock-Paper-Scissors method to determine who was up first. When his paper covered her rock, he grinned, then set the table and lined up his break.

A sharp crack and the balls scattered, the cue ball chasing the solid green to the left corner pocket. The green ball dropped, leaving the cue ball alone on the table. He adjusted his position, then bounced the cue ball off a side rail to send the red into the middle pocket before missing his chance to drop the orange ball.

Then it was Mercy's turn. She took her time studying the table. Stick in hand, he leaned his shoulder against the wall and studied her as she glided around the table's edges, picked her spot, and lined up. Seeing her intent, he shook his head. *Damn difficult shot.*

Her stick made contact and the cue ball kissed the rail and then pocketed her target.

"Nice shot," he murmured.

Her lips curved and she began stalking her next move. One game turned into two, then three. After the last ball dropped, they docked their sticks. A mellow mood replaced their earlier tension.

Next to him, Mercy laced her fingers, stretched her arms over her head, and arched her spine. The move pulled her t-shirt tight over her lush breasts. He jerked his gaze away from the mouth-watering temptation and looked around. He was surprised to see only a handful of patrons left. "You're a bad influence, woman."

She dropped her arms and shook out her hands. "Hey, I didn't hustle you, and I so could have, you know."

Yeah, he figured out she was a pool shark early in the second game. "Talking about the time, babe. It's late, we need to head back."

She sighed but followed him out of RedRock and into the

quiet night. Lights from the few open shops offered some illu-mination, but the desert night pooled deep in the places in between. They headed back to Istaqa's, both content to let the night fill the air between them.

When she cocked her head for the second time, he slowed and kept his voice low. "What?"

She shook her head, and when they passed through a spill of light from a window it revealed the rising tension that tight-ened her expression. "Maybe nothing."

Her sense of 'nothing' seeped into him and grew with each step they took until the skin on his neck threatened to crawl away. He wrapped an arm around her waist and drew her close, an instinctive move, one he knew damn good and well she wouldn't appreciate. Unfortunately, instincts never heeded logic.

She gave him a puzzled glance he ignored. His caught the shift of shadows underfoot as someone behind them crossed the lighted path and his gut clenched. "We're being followed."

Her initial stiffness faded, and she curved into his hold. "More than one, I think."

They continued with their unhurried pace. He rubbed his chin over the top of her head, using the motion to check their back trail. Sure enough, he caught a stutter in the shadow behind them. He buried his lips against her hair. "Got one."

Where there was one, there would be more. He knew Mercy could hold her own against a threat like this. She didn't need him to stand between her and the incoming threat, unlike the last woman who crawled under his skin. With a firm, logical foot crushing the neck of his protective instinct, he scanned ahead for options.

They were coming up on the deserted section of the marketplace. Stalls and haphazard shelters of canvas and other scavenged materials reigned, but the lack of light turned the benign area treacherous. It also made it their best shot at addressing the threat. First, they needed to confirm how many were on their ass, then they could get down to the why.

Mercy proved she was following the same lines of logic when she stepped away to dance a few steps in front of him. Without letting go of his hand, she spun around. The smile on her face was all kinds of fake, but her flirtatious laugh sounded all too real as her fingers tightened on his. Taking her hint, he tugged on their clasped hands and caught her as she threw herself into his arms in a mimicry of a woman enthralled with her man.

She buried her face in his neck, her breath warm against his skin, as his scruff snared the flyaway strands of her hair. "One at three, other at eleven."

His arms tightened around her waist as he dropped his head over hers, effectively blocking their exchange. "Got your blade?" He barely felt her tiny nod. "Let's lead them into the stalls." The last thing he wanted was to cause an obvious mess in Istaqa's front yard.

She unwound her arms and turned back to resume her previous position at his side. She used his bigger body to shield her movements as she freed her blade as they continued forward. When they reached the end of the street, Mercy, in her role of a woman intent on taking advantage of the man at her side, pulled him into the deeper shadows.

Once out of the line of sight, they didn't waste time. They slipped further into the maze of stalls and wound their way through to find a solid spot to make their stand. Havoc found it in an open patch of grass with limited access points and situated between two stalls that backed up to the canyon's wall.

He tugged Mercy close and put his lips near her ear. "We need to draw them in."

She scanned their surroundings, nodded, and then drew back. The metal blades in both of her fists winked in the night.

He pulled his blade free, met the undaunted anticipation in her gaze, gave her a fierce grin and mouthed, "Now!"

Her husky laughter filled the night. Even though he was looking right at her and knew it was bait, his dick didn't give a damn and went hard at the feminine sound. He ignored his ill-timed reaction and focused on the sounds of the approaching figures.

It was clear their pursuers weren't amateurs. If he hadn't been aware of them, he wouldn't have caught the slight sounds that gave them away—the shift of dirt under foot, the brush of cloth against corrugated metal, or the heavy breaths that merged with a soft breeze.

He and Mercy exchanged a look, then slipped into the pooling shadows near the stalls, him on one side, her on the other. He used silent hand signals to indicate he would circle around.

She dipped her chin in acknowledgement.

Then they waited.

It didn't take long before three figures inched into sight. They stayed close to the structures and took their time to ensure their approach. When they realized the clearing was empty, they stilled.

Dammit, they could be here all night.

Obviously having the same thought, Mercy sent a soft, needy moan into the quiet.

At the erotic sound, Havoc tightened his grip on his knife and made a silent vow if he ever got her alone, he would ensure a repeat of that sound.

The shadows inched closer, confident their targets were otherwise occupied. Not wanting any of them to escape, Havoc crept through the nearest stall and used the low counter to conceal his movements as he worked his way around. He needed to come in from behind and cut off their escape. And he had to do it before they got to Mercy. With a plan set, his mind settled into an icy calm.

He got into position, but when he straightened, his shoulder brushed against the nearest tent. The rippling the canvas alerted the figure bringing up the rear. He spun around and came face to face with Havoc. His vicious curse ripped through the night, warning the other two.

With the element of surprise gone, Havoc barely dodged the first lethal swipe. Tall with a longer reach, the attacker's leaner build gave him a speed advantage. Not a stranger to knife fights, Havoc kept his guard up, but couldn't avoid the sting, there and gone across his forearm, as he closed in, giving his opponent no time to retreat.

Havoc got inside the other man's guard and deflected the next strike, but he lost his chance to gain control of the incoming knife. He used his block to cover his move as he swiped out, his blade making contact, but not causing much damage.

The other man danced back, unwilling to chance a deeper connection.

They circled each other, steadily moving away from the stalls and further into the open area. There was a soft grunt from behind them. Neither looked, but the noise spurred a reaction from his opponent. He came in low, slashing at Havoc's stomach.

Havoc sucked in his abs and danced back, giving up inches to avoid being gutted. His retreat brought an evil ass grin to the other fighter's face. It didn't stay long. On the next lunge, Havoc captured his attacker's wrist and twisted with merciless strength. His opponent hissed in pain and twisted his body, trying to escape the wrist lock. Havoc moved in tandem, took a big step back and to the side, and drew the fighter's arm back at a relentless angle as he continued to wrench his wrist.

The fighter didn't give up. A solid blow landed on Havoc's

thigh, momentarily throwing him off balance as numbness sluiced down his leg. He shifted his weight and his opponent jerked free. The lean fighter stumbled back, regained his feet, and darted back in, head down as he charged Havoc with an enraged bellow.

Despite his unsteady stance, Havoc spun out of the way. A line of fire erupted along his back, a reminder to get the hell out of the blade's range. He balled up his fist and used his momentum to complete his spin and nailed the bastard with a left hook. The hit took the man to his knees, his knife tumbling from his grasp.

Havoc grinned and drew his foot back for a kick, when a heavy weight hit his back, and sent him stumbling forward.

Fuck!

Busy with the first asswipe, he totally forgot about the others. He dropped his knife to free both hands, then stopped the incoming blade from sinking into his side. With a brutal squeeze and twist, he broke the second idiot's wrist and sent the weapon tumbling away.

Havoc ignored the second attacker's pain-filled yelp, and dragged him around to use his body as a shield for the first attacker, who managed to find his knife and now charged in. He sank his blade deep into his compatriot's gut.

Havoc shoved the gutted man into his partner, who pushed him aside just as Havoc closed in. Things got nasty as a flurry of fists and hits ensued. Blood filled Havoc's mouth after a fist found his jaw. He returned the favor and split his knuckles on the other man's teeth. The bruising hits faded into the background as Havoc's world narrowed to specific targets—head, neck, gut, knees.

When a well-placed fist to the gut doubled his attacker over, Havoc used the opening to land an elbow to the base of his skull. His attacker dropped to the ground in a lifeless heap.

Havoc wiped away the blood that dripped into his eye,

and sucked in air, feeling the protest of aching ribs and various other spots. Nothing felt broken, just bruised.

He toed the man crumpled at his feet and got nothing—no groan, no muscle twitch, not a damn thing. He then shifted his attention to the man lying in the spreading pool of blood. Glassy eyes stared unseeingly into the darkness.

Satisfied neither one would be back for more, Havoc looked around and found Mercy, who appeared to have things well under control. In fact, if he wasn't wrong, the last attacker was about to get up close and personal with death. Since they needed one of the three breathing, he called out, "Babe, need him alive."

Mercy lifted her head but didn't release her grip on the hank of hair she was using to arch the man's spine. He was on his knees in front of her, with a blade stuck in one arm that hung uselessly at his side, the other flopping around like a fish out of water. His body hid hers, but there was no missing the glint of her blade that rested against his exposed neck.

As Havoc got closer, he realized the man's arm was flopping because it had been broken at the elbow.

Vicious little vixen.

Havoc stopped inches away and slowly dropped into a crouch, his face blank despite his body's protests. Mercy had the idiot well and truly caught, so no danger there. He rested his arms on his thighs as he studied the man. It seemed Felix wasn't the only Cartel roach to scuttle out of the cracks.

As recognition pierced the wild-eyed gaze, the kneeling man's dark eyes widened with horror and the swarthy skin paled to nearly translucent, making the distinctive ink that crawled up his neck even more visible. "*Madre de dios, el Verdugo.*"

Havoc didn't acknowledge the name that belonged to a man long gone, but obviously not forgotten.

Mercy peered around the man's head and her eyes

narrowed. Her mouth opened, but whatever she was going to say was cut short when she caught sight of his battered state. Temper darkened her eyes and iced her voice. "Might want to get to it, my hand is getting twitchy." As if to reinforce her words, her blade broke a thin line of skin, until blood beaded along the edge.

The man whimpered and Havoc's lips curled in distaste. "Start talking, amigo."

"Bounty, we were collecting the bounty for the bitch." It came out in short gasps as Mercy's hold made swallowing difficult, much less talking.

Flicking his gaze to her, he murmured, "Ease a bit, yeah?"

She shifted her hold to allow the man to talk, but her blade didn't budge.

Havoc sighed knowing that was all she would give him, and then he went back to his questions. "Who's paying?"

When the man didn't immediately answer, Mercy's blade offered some encouragement. "Suárez." The name escaped in a high-pitched squeal as the blade and Havoc's reputation overrode the Cartel-inspired fear.

Of fucking course.

He shared a look with Mercy. Grim acceptance filled her gaze, but she leaned in, menace turning her silky question into a ball shriveling demand. "How many others?"

"*No sé.*" The knife bit deeper at his claim of ignorance and he began babbling. "We paid a couple kids to keep an eye out and tell when they saw you. Don't know about any others. We just wanted the bounty."

There was a ring of desperate truth in his shaky voice. Havoc met the question in her gaze with a grim nod and pushed to his feet. Proving he wasn't a complete idiot, the man at her feet started to beg. His pleas abruptly stopped as Mercy's blade sliced his throat and reduced the current number of bounty hunters on her tail by one.

She shoved his body aside, wiped her blade clean, and straightened. "*El Verdugo*?"

"A long story for another time."

"Hmm." With that noncommittal noise, she dropped it.

Havoc didn't think her patience would last long though. He caught her wince as she stepped over the body. "How bad?"

"Got me good in the ribs, but nothing's broken." Her blade disappeared, and she ran a critical eye over him. "You?"

"I'll live." He motioned to the two heaps before them. "Let's stash these out of sight. Istaqa can send someone to clean up."

They worked together and piled all three bodies behind the last stall. They topped the pile off with a tarp Mercy liberated from another stall.

Havoc brushed his hands against his jeans. "You know, even if you strike a deal with Suárez, this shit won't stop." Because it still took time to spread the word that the bounty was pulled, and time was one thing she didn't have.

"Yeah, I know." She walked around the pile and fell into step beside him as they headed out of the marketplace. She waited until they were on the path to Istaqa's before speaking again. "But I'd rather look over my shoulder for a few weeks than whatever's left of my life."

The edge of realistic fatality in her answer rubbed him the wrong way, but he didn't have a clue why. It left his voice sharper than he intended. "Making a deal with Suárez could cost you more than a few weeks." He took a few more steps up the path's steady incline before he realized she'd stopped. He turned to find her standing there, hand braced against her side, her lips thin with either pain or annoyance, or maybe both.

"Not telling me anything I don't already know, Havoc." She sucked in a couple of shallow breaths before moving forward again. "Why the concern?"

Since he didn't have an answer, he dodged her question and kept pace with her. "Just want to be sure you know what kind of snake pit you're stepping into."

There was no amusement in her soft chuckle. "Don't worry, I'm highly aware no matter how I move, I'm going to get bit."

Yeah, that was what he was afraid of.

twelve

"How is it," Vex started, "That we leave you two alone for a few hours and you still manage to find trouble?"

Mercy pulled the bag of frozen corn from Istaqa's freezer and held it against her jaw, before turning to Vex. "More like trouble found us."

Vex ambled over, hooked a finger under Mercy's chin, and nudged her head back, exposing the darkening bruise. "Forget to duck?"

Mercy jerked her head away, and instantly regretted it when the drums in her skull woke with a vengeance. "Ow, dammit."

Vex's lips twitched but she dropped her hand, crossed behind Havoc, who stood over the sink cleaning the cuts along his forearms with a hand towel, and snatched up a half-filled cup from the counter. "Please tell me you left them bleeding out."

"Drained and gutted." He ran the stained cloth under the faucet. "And all wrapped up for disposal."

Vex rounded the island's far end and settled on the stool

next to Istaqa. Due to the kitchen's layout, the duo had a straight line of sight to Mercy and Havoc.

"I've got Daniel on it," Istaqa said.

Mercy put her back against the counter and held her impromptu ice pack against the heat of what, experience taught her, would be a spectacular bruise come morning. A numb haze was setting in as her earlier adrenaline slipped away and she caught herself watching the play of muscles in Havoc's back through the reflection in the night-darkened solar glass behind Vex and Istaqa. Even in this casual setting there was something compelling about him, an intensity she wanted to play with, regardless of the havoc it would create. She couldn't stop her small goofy smile at her unintentional pun.

Havoc's soft curse cut through her mental wanderings and yanked her back to reality. She turned her head carefully and saw he was trying to wring out the cloth with one hand. She blew out a soft, aggrieved sigh, set her ice pack aside, and took the towel from him. "Give me that."

He gave her a grumpy frown as she wrung it out, but he moved aside to give her room. She ignored the twinge in her ribs as she began cleaning his various cuts.

"You and Daniel get anything useful on your end?"

Havoc's rumbled question swept over her skin like the tantalizing brush of fur and caused her hand wrapped around Havoc's wrist to tremble. The unexpected sensation tripped over her nerve endings and trapped the air in her chest. Momentarily distracted, she snuck a glance under her lashes only to get caught peeking.

An utterly male spark of hunger lit the deep chocolate depths of his eyes, and an answering heat ran under her skin. She dropped her gaze, grateful her back was to Istaqa and Vex, as it made it easier to hide her reaction. Hell, she wish she could hide her reaction from the man himself, but standing so close, she was shit out of luck.

"Idiot believes he's working for Suárez." Istaqa's voice was rife with frustration.

"You don't sound like you feel the same," Havoc said, then flinched the tiniest bit as she cleaned one of the deeper cuts and she gentled her touch.

"I don't." There was no way to mistake the banked fury icing Istaqa's reply. "But he sure as hell believes it was Suárez giving the orders." A charged silence followed.

"I bet they're Felix's." Mercy's muttered observation slipped free without permission, exposing her frustration.

"Yeah, me too." Istaqa's admission carried heavy reluctance.

Determination stiffened her resolve and she pushed, "Going to let me call Suárez then?"

Vex hid her grin behind her cup and the combined weight of Havoc and Istaqa's attention fell on Mercy. In a bid for nonchalance, she turned to rinse out the cloth again and waited for Istaqa's answer.

He didn't make her wait long, but his voice was stiff. "After I discuss a few things with Suárez, yes."

A burst of relief hit and eased some of her tension. Not only would she get a chance to turn the tables on Felix, but depending on where the phone was located, she might be able to sneak back in and get word to her boss. She stifled her triumphant grin and wrung out the cloth. "Good." It was all she dared to say.

With wet cloth in hand, she turned to Havoc and changed the conversation. "Where else?"

When he didn't respond, she hid her antsy anticipation with a frown and met his singular study. His gaze was sharp with speculation and her closely held excitement took a downward turn. If he caught any inkling of what she planned, he'd stop her in a heartbeat. In effort to throw him off, she played up her impatience factor with a cocked hip and tapping foot.

Havoc whipped off his t-shirt exposing a wall of bronzed flesh. The air in her chest stalled and her thoughts scattered like a flock of startled birds in a myriad of directions. It took an unsettlingly long moment to recapture the flighty things before she motioned for him to turn around.

His lips curved up in a male dare as he held her gaze, and then he took his sweet time giving her his back. A thin, wicked slice ran just above the blood-soaked edge of his jeans.

She sucked a sharp breath through her teeth and got to work cleaning his wound.

At her first gentle dab, he stiffened, but other than that, offered no further signs of discomfort. In fact, his voice remained steady as he got back to the business at hand. "Give me a few more reasons, Istaqa."

"On what?" There was nothing in the man's question to indicate he resented Havoc's demand.

Havoc braced his hands on the island's top and blocked Mercy's view of Istaqa and Vex. "Why you're leaning towards Felix over Suárez."

Mercy wondered where Havoc was going with this since up until now, she was fairly certain Havoc believed her about Felix. *What did he think Istaqa knew, that she didn't?*

A chair creaked and Mercy peeked around Havoc's bulk.

Istaqa's elbows were braced on the island's counter, and he was rubbing his hands over his face. "It was the little things. Like comments that made no sense." He dropped his hands and met Havoc's gaze. "Not to mention the planning of this was sloppy. Laying multiple charges over extended periods of time, allows the possibility of discovery. Not only is Suárez far from sloppy, but he also isn't an idiot. We've managed to maintain a—" he paused, obviously searching for the right word, "—balance in our previous agreements. If I believe that Suárez is the one behind the plan to destroy the dam, then I also have to believe Suárez has lost his damn mind." He blew out a tired breath. "I want a chance to actually hear his voice before I make that judgment call."

"You think you're being played." Mercy continued to clean Havoc's back and didn't try to hide her compassion because Istaqa was in an unenviable, craptastic position.

"Not just me, but Suárez as well." He admitted grudgingly.

She didn't bother with the I-told-you-so's. Neither Istaqa nor Suárez could take Mercy's word for it, not with who and what each man was responsible for. Which meant her upcoming phone call would prove challenging on multiple levels.

She traced the edges of the bruise rising along Havoc's ribs and flattened her hand against his back. Warmth rose from his skin, hotter where the bruises formed. Tomorrow, he'd be sporting a plethora of colors.

"That's not the worst of it," Vex warned, signs of her earlier teasing gone.

Havoc's muscles locked under Mercy's palm and his voice rumbled through his frame. "Do I want to know?"

Vex answered, "You know that mole we worried was at Crane's?"

Mercy looked up. *The Vultures were worried about a mole? Not good.*

Havoc's nod was sharp.

Vex's jaw flexed and the lines around her eyes tightened. "It's a definite concern."

"Well, fuck." Havoc went to straighten, but Mercy's hand shifted with his movement, and pressed against his back in an attempt to keep him in place. He turned his head and growled at her.

She simply raised an eyebrow. "Two minutes, then you can do whatever the hell you want."

He twisted back around and silently waited with barely

leashed patience as Mercy finished cleaning the cut. Luckily his aimed his frustration at Vex. "Did you get details?"

"A few." She slumped in her seat, her expression dark. "But not sure they'll be much help."

"Anything's better than nothing." Havoc fell quiet for a moment, then, "We need to let Reaper know."

The other woman narrowed her eyes and angled her head. "Yeah, no. I'm not comfortable doing that in a phone call."

Mercy smeared a light coat of the honey and echinacea ointment over Havoc's cleaned wound and agreed with Vex. If you didn't know who you could trust, it was best to deliver such messages in person. It eliminated the chance of the information falling into the wrong ears.

Havoc took Vex's comment in stride. "You going to head back to Pebble Creek then?"

"Probably best."

He grunted.

Vex took it for the agreement it was and continued. "Since I want to see what happens with Suárez, I was thinking about taking off in the morning."

Mercy taped the last of the bandage over the deepest part of the cut and petted Havoc's back at just shy of the two-minute mark. "Okay, you're good."

He stood up, stepped away and went to pull his t-shirt back on, only to stop. His lips curled with distaste. Understandable, considering the t-shirt was trashed. He wadded it up and dumped it in the recycle container tucked by the counter on the far wall. "Let's see what happens with Suárez before we make any decision."

Mercy rinsed out the cloth, then spread it over the sink's edge to dry.

Havoc settled next to her, his hip propped on the counter's edge, his arms crossed over his chest, and his gaze on Istaqa. "When you planning on making the call?"

Curious herself, Mercy turned to watch Istaqa.

He looked between her and Havoc, then said, "Daniel's trying to set it up." He checked the wall clock ticking off the minutes and added, "I'm thinking we should have something confirmed within the hour."

"Good," Havoc grunted. "The sooner the better."

Mercy couldn't agree more and settled in to wait.

thirteen

Color her impressed. Less than an hour later, Mercy stood in what was clearly the communications room. The Free People had quite the collection. A half-moon desk took up one corner, its surface strewn with a mishmash of two-way radios, two old computer monitors—one of which had a permanent black line running through the top of a screen filled with some kind of code—a couple of old multi-lined phones, and a wall rack of black boxes with multicolored lights. She shifted her stance against the wall, tucked her hands behind her and tagged the two computer tower skeletons with Frankensteined parts nestled among the wire tangle under the desk.

Havoc propped a shoulder against the opposite wall and quirked an eyebrow her way.

She offered him a big old grin.

His lips quirked, softening the hard set of his mouth before he turned his attention away.

Her grin faded as she resumed her pose of casual disinterest. On the way in, she noted the room's location, a necessity since she had plans for a return visit. Now was the time to keep her mouth shut, her eyes sharp and her ears open.

In the room's center Vex was perched on the edge of a big blocky desk, one leg swinging as she listened. On the other side, Istaqa leaned over a speaker box connected to an old phone seeded with a multitude of wires. His face was dark, his palms pressed flat against the desk's surface, and his glare was aimed at the hapless phone as if he could fry Suárez on the spot.

"A threat, Istaqa? I thought we were better friends than this." Despite the scratchy speaker and questionable connection, it was easy to detect the wealth of anger simmering underneath Suárez's flippant response.

"Consider this a warning, not a threat, Suárez. One I'm not required to give." Hard as granite, Istaqa's response offered no apology. "The agreement we hold with the five Cartel families is clear. No one threatens the dams, or the water stops. Your man admitted he came here under your orders to set those charges. As the Cartels have clearly violated their agreement, I'm within my rights to deny access." He looked to Havoc as he continued, "Be grateful I called you first."

Mercy gave him credit for knowing how to deal with the old *jefe*. Head-on with no give. By calling Suárez prior to informing the families, Istaqa gave Suárez a chance to save his skin.

Like most of those trying to keep their grasp on the slippery reins of power, Suárez was all about survival and didn't suffer fools or blustering egos. As proof, instead of arguing about being tossed to the unforgiving judgement of the other families, Suárez confirmed Istaqa's assumption. "Whoever this *puta madre* is, he is not mine."

"Prove it, or my next call will end your entire family."

Mercy had to admit if she was on the other end of the line, she'd be shitting bricks right about now.

When a litany of Spanish profanity filled the air, there was no doubt that was exactly what Suárez was doing. "How do you think I should do this?"

Mercy took vicious pleasure in hearing the edge of desperation in his voice. She dropped her gaze to her boots just in case something in her expression gave her away. It might be sucky to take joy in another's pain, but the depraved old fart deserved every excruciating moment dealt by Istaqa.

"Not my problem." And Istaqa's clipped tones indicated he was about done.

Suárez spoke quickly, trying to ensure Istaqa wouldn't hang up. "I swear *en la Ave María Purísima*, he is not there on my orders."

Istaqa didn't back down. "Mary Magdalene doesn't have anything to do with this mess, Suárez. This is on you."

"No!" The denial was a harsh near shout.

The vehemence behind it jerked Istaqa upright. His brows rose as he eyed the phone, but he kept silent as deep breaths echoed down the line as Suárez fought for control.

When he found it, he spoke. "I will share with you what I've chosen not to share with any other. A gesture of my sincerity, yes?"

Istaqa shared a long look with Havoc and Vex, and let the silence stretch. "I'm listening."

A rush of air filled the line, then Suárez's voice came through, rage hardening it into diamond clarity. "Someone is after me. They killed my youngest son. I believe this is just another move in their game."

Istaqa's attention switched to her, and despite her inability to read a damn thing in his obsidian gaze, she held it. "Your son?" he asked.

Her pulse took up a dull beat. If Lady Luck decided she

was done with Mercy, this was where things would go
sideways.

"*Sí*, Tavi," Suárez confirmed. "The *puta* slit his throat
when he caught her going through my lieutenant's office."

She didn't think it possible, but Istaqa's gaze slipped to
below freezing. "A woman killed your son?"

"Yes." The snap of venom in Suárez's voice left a hiss on
the line.

Mercy bit the inside of her cheek hard to stifle the vicious
smirk that threaten to escape. It just chapped Suárez's ass to
believe a lowly female killed his precious son. Almost made her
wish she really had done the deed.

"A lone woman killed your son and is targeting the dam?"
Istaqa pressed with obvious skepticism.

"That is what I said." Suárez's impatience overrode his
caution.

"Why?"

"If I knew, we would not be having this conversation."

"No, I don't suppose we would," muttered Istaqa, he
tapped his fingers in an absent beat against the desk. "You have
proof that this woman is behind your son's death and the situation here?"

There was an obvious pause. "My lieutenant found her
crouched over Tavi's body, bloodied knife in hand. She ran.
That was enough proof for me to send my man to hunt her
down, and to offer a generous bounty, a guarantee she finds no
shelter."

The arrogance in Suárez's voice set her teeth on edge. The
vindictive bastard's bounty was going be a massive pain in her
ass. A fact her aching jaw and bruised ribs could attest to.

Istaqa's gaze shifted to Havoc and the two men appeared
to have some sort of telepathic moment, because they turned
to her in tandem.

Something in the way they stared at her that made her

stomach clench. A tingling started at the tips of her fingers and inched up her arms. A band of pressure tightened at the base of her neck, and her muscles locked, one by one. She braced.

Sure enough, Istaqa dumped her ass in the deep end. "Your lieutenant go by the name of Felix?"

Wary caution cut through Suárez's voice. "*Sí.*"

"Huh." Istaqa dangled his bait in the bloodied waters.

"Why do you ask?" Suárez's accent thickened as his temper frayed.

The silence stretched for a second, then two, and moved into three before Istaqa answered. "We heard a different story."

"From who?"

Taking the question as her cue, Mercy pushed off the wall and walked to the desk. With each step she buried her tempestuous emotions. She didn't allow anything to leak into her expression or her voice as she stood, Havoc at her back, Vex to her side, and faced Istaqa. "From me, Suárez."

There was a moment of quiet before Suárez exploded. While her Spanish was damn good, she missed a couple of the words, but based on context she got it. She was far from his favorite person and her parentage, or lack thereof, was reduced to impossible combinations. When Suárez went in some truly disgusting directions, Havoc's bulk slowly solidified. Finally, Suárez wound down, his heavy breaths filling the open line.

"You finished?" Boredom filled Istaqa's question.

"Is the bitch yours, Istaqa?" Menace replaced temper and left Suárez's voice a whip of contempt.

Mercy's '*no*' clashed with Istaqa's '*Hell, no*'.

Istaqa's raised his palm and Mercy clamped her mouth shut, letting him talk. "She's not mine, Suárez. She showed up in my territory and shared the information that led to stopping your man before he blew my dam. This she shared in effort to prove her first story regarding your son's death held merit. After finding your man and the explosives before the dam could be damaged, I have to wonder if her version doesn't hold more weight than yours."

"She must be good," Suárez snarled. "She has you fooled, just like she did my precious son."

Faint amusement broke through Istaqa's bland mask. "How so?"

"She must fuck like a damn goddess to blind you to the evil in her black heart."

Mercy frowned at the phone, trying to decide if she was pissed at Suárez's assessment or amused. Since his opinion of her mattered less than a speck of dust, she picked amused. And she wasn't the only one.

Istaqa threw back his head and laughed. "Suárez I wouldn't let her anywhere near my dick as I like it right where it is."

"So, what is the *puta's* story?" Suárez pushed. "She's the poor abused woman on the run from the evil Cartels?"

Istaqa's humor faded, and his voice and face reclaimed its previous hardness. "No, her story is your son was killed by the one who wants your position. She just happened to be in the wrong place, wrong time."

"She denies she's a killer?" Disbelief layered the question.

"No," Mercy broke in. "I'm a killer, Suárez, but I did not kill your son."

"You came into my home on a lie, *perra*, and then ran when my son ended up dead. Why should I believe you?"

"Because you give me time, I can give you, his killer."

"And who is this killer?"

"Felix."

Suárez's rough laugh could shred skin and when he was done, his voice came over the phone like a venomous snake. "You expect me to believe a man who has been loyal to me, to my sons, and considered part of *mi familia* slit my son's throat? For what?"

She leaned in, lowered her voice, not in sympathy, but so the old man would listen close, and laid it out. "In the last few months, your shipments have gone missing, you've been forced to step into territorial disputes because of baseless rumors, and each time something happens, you end up on the short end of the stick. This isn't by accident. Felix wants your position. To get it, he not only killed Tavi, but he's working with someone outside the Cartels, someone with enough power to back his play. Power enough to ensure he gets what he wants. And what he wants is your crown."

"You know this how?"

To gain trust, you had to offer truth, so she shared what she could. "I was sent into your home to verify you were working with this new partner and to bring back proof of who this partner is."

"Who sent you?"

Even though he couldn't see her, she shook her head. "Yeah, no, that's not going to be shared."

"Istaqa, tell me why you believe her." There was a lessening in the fury of Suárez's voice, an indicator that he was actually listening. "She could be taking a page from those damn Strix's and playing us both."

Istaqa grimaced. "Since the Strix were wiped out nearly a decade ago, I sincerely doubt that's the case. Besides, you're willing to believe that a woman who was in your house, with unlimited options to take out you and yours, but didn't, is willing to endanger every man, woman, and child in the Cartel territories to play you now? All she had to do was let the dam be blown and then stand aside and watch the fallout."

"Perhaps," Suárez grudgingly admitted. "But that does not answer my question."

Istaqa folded his arms and pinned Mercy in place with an

unrelenting stare. "I believe her because I don't think you're reckless enough to endanger not only your family, but the others as well. You remember how it was before the Border Wars, you know just what it means to be denied water. I think you value what you have. You would not risk any of it in some half-assed plan that has every chance of failure, and little chance of success."

A dry chuckle came over the line. "Ever the diplomat, eh?"

"If that's what you want to believe," Istaqa said. "Targeting the dam reeks of ego and desperation, two things you are not, but a man intent on taking what's yours is." He paused and then paid Mercy back in full. "So, yes, I believe she will get the proof you need on what part Felix played in your son's death, and in doing so, also prove to me who was targeting the dam."

She held Istaqa's unflinching gaze, placed a hand over her heart and bowed her head in silent agreement to his proposed deal.

His request wasn't unexpected, but now she had to figure out how to get Felix to squeal in such a way both the leader of the Cartels and the Free People would listen. Oh, yeah, she also needed to complete her initial objective for her boss and identify the damn silent partner.

God knows how much she loved challenges.

Suárez fell quiet, obviously pondering his options, and they waited him out. With each passing second Mercy's nerves tightened. Finally, he spoke. "A week to get Felix to admit to killing my son and planting the explosives."

She didn't wait for Istaqa. "Agreed. What proof do you require?"

"Don't worry about the type of proof, just get it."

That was not reassuring at all. In fact, being the paranoid woman she was, she figured it meant she'd have another one of Suárez's minions on her ass. *Fucking great.*

"Bounties?" The question came from Havoc.

"Remain in place," Suárez answered, no give in his voice. "Even if I were to call them off, it would take more than a week for word to spread. Besides, should she fail, I'll be more than satisfied with her head in exchange."

Yep, another damn Cartel member was out there somewhere.

Dammit. Dammit. Dammit.

Well, now she knew, which meant she might still make it to the other side breathing. Handling the bounties would be a nuisance, but doable. While getting them removed would've been icing on the cake, she'd take what she could get, for now.

A reprieve and a chance to do her damn job.

fourteen

"Guess this means you don't think I'll bolt in the middle of the night, uh?" Mercy sat cross legged on a bed in one of Istaqa's bedrooms. A bed Havoc gave serious consideration to sharing with her but seeing the exhaustion that lined her face and the bruise coming up on her jaw, common sense, the logical bastard, prevailed.

Between that and her earlier souvenirs from her run through the desert, she looked damn near done in. Strangely, it made him want to coddle her, a move that was sure to see his balls in agony. Therefore, he remained in the doorway with his shoulder braced against the doorjamb. "I'll be on the couch."

Her mock pout was cute. "Not the floor in front of the door?" Equal parts tease and serious intent rode her question.

Cheeky wench. Granted, after watching her mind spin so fast he swore smoke was coming out of her ears, his initial thought was to take that spot. The only thing that held him back was his battered body. He dodged confirmation of her assumption with, "You plan on making a run for it?"

"Nope." She popped the 'p'. "Going to crash so I can head

out first thing in the morning to hit Page and track Felix down."

"We," he corrected her, "will head out first thing." There was no way he was walking away from this mess, not when the Cartels couldn't be trusted to piss straight, much less honor their agreements.

Those green-gold eyes narrowed, and her pointy chin lifted, her mutinous expression filled with offended pride. "Don't trust me to do this on my own?"

"Don't trust you not to get jumped by bounty hunters and whatever the fuck else is out there looking for blood." As if he could leave her out there alone, like a juicy bone thrown to a pack of starving dogs. He hadn't missed when Suárez's dodged her question of proof, and prickly as she was, they both knew there would be more than just bounty hunters dogging her heels.

"Aww, I feel so loved."

He stifled his humor at her sarcastic rejoinder.

"Thank you." Her words were quiet.

"For?"

She studied him from under her thick lashes. "For bringing me here."

His body locked as something uncomfortable seeped into the cracks she created. "Didn't give me much choice."

His gruff response earned a small grin. "Still." Her grin faded, and she dropped her gaze to her feet, her finger twisting the loose material of her shirt.

"We're not done yet." He warned, wanting her to think twice about ditching his ass.

She blew out a heavy breath, a clear indication she was far from confident with whatever she was cooking up in that quicksilver mind and agreed. "No, we're not."

He squelched the rush of satisfaction at her unexpected submission and switched gears. "Got a plan for Felix?"

"Not yet." Her shoulders straightened and her chin took that determined lift once more. "But I'm working on it."

He had no doubt on that because nothing set a fire under your ass like a deadline with a death sentence. "Work faster, darlin', the clock's ticking."

Her nose wrinkled and he was surprised she didn't stick out her tongue. "Yeah, as if I wasn't aware." The starch in her shoulders started to fade.

He took the sign for what it was and decided to let the minx have her privacy. He straightened, then rapped his knuckles against the doorjamb. "Sleep well, Mercy."

"You too, Havoc." Her husky response curled around him like the sweetest touch and ignited a rapacious hunger.

Despite the merciless grip of his body's urges, he turned away, closed the door softly, and painfully made his way to the couch where a pillow and blanket waited. Low light came from the kitchen and joined the existing moonlight that left the room in shadow. He ignored Vex sprawled in one of the easy chairs, sat on the couch and forced his body back under control. He worked his boots off, and then stretched his aching frame along the couch with relieved sigh.

"What's the deal, big man?" Vex's voice was pitched low so it wouldn't carry beyond the two of them.

He folded his hands over his chest and closed his eyes. "Gonna tag along with her to Page, see if we can run down Felix."

"Think that's wise?"

The wariness in her question wasn't a surprise. Vex wasn't the most trusting sort. Hell, none of the Vultures were. Just another by-product of the life they led. "Think it's the only option we've got."

She let the quiet slip back in for a few, before finally muttering, "I'll follow you down and break off from Page."

He made a non-committal sound and hope she would trot

off to the last bedroom and leave him in peace. He didn't get his wish.

"What did he mean?"

Familiarity taught him that following her thought process was akin to herding cats, so he asked, "Who?"

"Suárez," she clarified. "He mentioned something called Strix?"

He wondered how she managed to curb her curiosity for so long and popped one eye open. Sure enough, she was curled in the chair, eyes on him. "More like who."

"Fine, who are they?" she demanded.

The girl loved her stories, and for the most part, he didn't mind telling them. The familiar exchange started shortly after he and Reaper picked up her and her twin from the streets of Portland. Vex had a hell of a time sleeping, so Havoc would sit up with her as the moon rose, and to rescue her from her nightmares, he would tell stories. Sometimes it worked, sometimes it didn't. Tonight, he knew, wasn't about nightmares, but because she was worried and trying to hide it.

Right then, guess it was time for a history lesson.

He closed his eye and dove into the tragic tale. "The Strix used to be the most lethal assassins out there. They rose out of the chaos of the Collapse and whispers of them grew to epic proportions as the years passed. After the dust settled, they remained nothing more than rumors and speculation."

"So, they weren't real?"

"No, they were very fucking real. They could get to anyone, anywhere, at any time. No one's certain just how many died at their hands because they were legendary at making that shit look natural. Never left any signs behind, just rumors. Drifted in like smoke, did their deeds, and disappeared just as quickly."

"Sound like those sneaky types—what were they?" She snapped her fingers. "Right, ninjas. One of the books my old man kept was about them. Maybe the Strix were just bad-ass ninjas."

He chuckled. "Maybe but doubt it."

She fell into their storytelling habit and followed his cue. "Why?"

"While that ninja shit makes for good stories, not so sure it's real."

"But the Strix were." Her voice held a healthy dose of skepticism.

"Yeah, they were." He dug through his memories and pulled up the more creative recitals he heard when he was younger. "There were a couple of stories of who they initially were. Back before the Collapse, the government used these spy types that were so dark no one knew they existed. Called them black ops. For all intents and purposes, they didn't exist except to do the dirty work of the government. Some say, the surviving black ops community, small as it was, managed to recruit new members and rebuild itself into the Strix. Others say the Strix are what remains of the old crime families, because when cities fell, so did their underground empires, and they turned their skills to new profit ventures."

Caught up in the tale, Vex frowned. "Crime families? Like the mobs?"

Although most people nowadays had no idea about mobsters, thanks to his dad's love of old movies, one he shared with Vex, she was quick to connect the dots.

His mind slipped to those quality times he spent with his did, bonding over a variety of hard to find recordings— The House on the Hill (not his favorite), Oceans 11, The Godfather (parts 1 through 3), Reservoir Dogs, Scarface, Inception (which initially made his brain hurt), Independence Day (which was laughable, as if aliens could be more vicious than humans), and his all-time favorite, Zombieland. Even now that movie left him wondering what the hell a

Twinkie tasted like to get that kind of devotion. All in all, he had to admit that the old world found the most twisted shit entertaining.

"Havoc?"

Vex's voice tugged him out of his memories and back to the present. "Hmm?"

"What happened to these legendary assassins?"

"Not sure, but one day they were there, the next gone. My guess, somebody wiped them out." Because that seemed to be the way things went. No matter how dangerous or deadly a group was, a bigger, badder predator always laid in wait. It was a fact that kept him and Reaper up at nights.

It was also Reaper's main reason for not wanting to align with Lilith, but after Havoc pointed out that there was strength in numbers, Reaper reluctantly conceded. Now the Vultures were part of a slowly growing alliance.

A move Havoc wasn't completely comfortable with yet. Reaper was pissed, and not just because of the alliance. There were other issues he had with Lilith. Issues that went deep and dark, beyond a point Havoc could help.

"That sucks," Vex murmured, hauling him back from the mental quagmire. Then she added, "Sounds like my kind of peeps."

He grinned because he could see that. "Yeah." His chuckle faded, the quiet crept back in, and he began to drift. An old memory rose, and he mumbled, "Met one once."

"A Strix?"

"Mm-hmm. It was back during the Border Wars. Ran across him in Lost Angels after being cornered by some Cartel foot soldiers."

Lost Angels once held the name Los Angeles, but after being ravaged by outbreaks, riots, rising coastlines and all the rest of the hell that belonged to the Collapse, there wasn't much left. Now, those who ventured there called it Lost

Angels because what remained was a creepy graveyard of what once existed.

As far as Havoc was concerned, losing it to the Cartels in the wars wasn't much of a loss. "He didn't look like much. Seeing him, you'd never guess what he was. But put a blade in his hand and he was stunning. Cold, ruthless, but lethal as hell. Taught me some useful moves while we were holed up. Afterwards, he was gone. Like smoke on the wind."

"Never ran across him again?"

"Nope." But after doing his time in the Border Wars, he hit the road with Reaper and did his best to forget the lasting scars of why he joined the fight in the first place. He shied away from those memories and focused on what the future held. "You be careful heading back to Pebble Creek, baby girl."

She snorted. "Worried about me?"

His lips twitched, but he knew better than to give her the truth. "Not you, whoever you run into."

Her laugh was soft and rare. "I promise not to leave carnage in my wake."

"Something I'm sure Reaper will appreciate." Then because it was too easy and he couldn't resist teasing her, he added, "Simon too."

A feminine sniff of disdain sounded. "As if Simon gives a fuck what I do."

Poor girl's heart was all tied up with Simon, not that she listened to it, or even admitted she had one. But almost losing him to the Raiders had messed with her head, which was probably why she wasn't sleeping.

He decided to give her something different to dream about. "Hate to break it to you, Vex, but that man doesn't give you shit, to give you shit."

"Right." Not an ounce of belief existed in her voice.

"A man doesn't care, he doesn't bother bitching." To reiterate his lesson on male logic, he added, "He cares, he'll bitch."

"Whatever," she muttered.

Can lead a horse to water, son, can't make it drink. Words from his dad crossed years to whisper in his ear. The sound of Vex getting out of her chair was followed by her move to his side. He kept his eyes closed.

Then came the soft brush of her lips on his forehead and her hair tickling his face in a poignant echo of years past. "Night, Havoc."

"Night, baby girl. See you in the morning."

He barely heard her move down the hall, and only caught the soft closing of the door when she made it to her room. Finally alone, he let sleep come. He wouldn't get much before Mercy made her inevitable move. And it was coming. She gave herself away with that moment of speculation in the comm room.

Although his gut told him she wasn't out to betray him, Mercy was shaping up to be a personal challenge. A challenge he was more than ready to take on, and not just because his dick was all about getting in there. But to get a handle on the game she was playing, he needed to be there when she did her thing. Besides, it might be his chance at ID'ing her boss.

fifteen

Mercy's trusted internal clock woke her up to the hushed silence of the dead of morning. The windowless room was pitch black which made it hard to pinpoint the time, but she figured she managed close to four hours of sleep. Which meant sunrise was on its way. She didn't want to leave the warm nest of the bed, but nefarious things were best done under the cover of darkness. With a sigh she threw off the covers.

Less than a minute later she stood by the door, toes curled against the smooth wood floors. Courtesy of her earlier visit to the hall bathroom there was a chunk of soap shoved into the door's strike plate. She inched open the door without the revealing snick of the latch.

That same earlier bathroom run garnered her a couple of safety pins abandoned in a drawer and confirmed Havoc was a light sleeper. Hence her four hours of shut eye to ensure the man was down for the count. When she had enough space, she slipped through and carefully pulled the door almost closed. No sense in making her departure too obvious.

Guided by years of experience in being in places she

shouldn't, she moved through the hall towards the main living space. Her pulse ticked along at a steady pace as the calmness needed for such endeavors held strong. She edged into the living room. Just beyond the window the night skies held the grey edges of early morning light confirming she needed to make this quick.

She inched her way by the couch, only to freeze in place when Havoc shifted. His breathing remained steady, while hers, on the other hand, stalled. Only when the ache hit her chest did she remember to breathe—carefully. *Move!* The harsh mental slap sent her skittering by and through the kitchen.

She left the main room behind and crept down the long hall leading toward the back warren of rooms. Low light spilled from scattered hall lamps, but it wasn't much help. She stopped at the corner just before the communication room and crouched.

She laid her hand flat against the floor and strained her ears. No vibrations met her palm, indicating the hall was most likely empty. Silence flooded the space, unbroken by the slight noises normally accompanying human presence. She took a chance and peeked around the corner, careful to make it quick.

Shadows stared back.

No guard? Seriously?

She pulled back and leaned against the wall. Okay, either this was a trap or a sign of arrogance. Maybe even both. Unfortunately, until she got closer, she wouldn't know, and this was likely her only opportunity to give her boss a much-needed heads-up.

Chances were high that Felix had already reached out to his silent partner and bitched about her screwing with his plans with whatever was in play back at the Suárez's homestead.

He wouldn't mention the dam, because admitting to that big of a fuck up was a guaranteed death sentence. Which meant, if she didn't stop Felix in Page, odds were high he would be headed north. Because he was the kind of low-life slug who was concerned with one thing and one thing only, saving his own ass.

Speaking of asses, time to move hers.

Trap or not, the longer she waited, the more likely she was to be facing Havoc. She headed to the communication room. At the door, she confirmed it was locked with a gentle, testing twist.

Instigate Plan B.

She pulled out the modified safety pins and starting a mental countdown, got to work. it took a handful of seconds of judicious effort with the makeshift rake and a tension wrench to pop the lock. She stashed her lock picks and slipped inside the room. Perhaps, later, she would consider counseling Istaqa on his over-confidence in his security measures.

Maybe.

She closed the door behind her, careful to keep it quiet, but the soft click of the latch still made her flinch. Then she chided herself on the stupid reaction since the hum of the old tech created enough noise to cover the small sound. Navajo City had power, not just wind, water and solar, but the electric kind. All because when the Free People took control of the dams, they also took control of the old power station just outside Page.

She used the weird glow created by the tiny electronic lights to navigate to the keyboard tucked under the non-cracked monitor. When they gathered in this room earlier, she had recognized the computer code for what it was—a gateway to what was left of the internet, an old technology that didn't reach anywhere near what it used to. Not that she needed it to. She just needed to get a message to the server in New Seattle.

Her fingers hit the space bar, and she gave a soft sigh of release when the monitor lit up. She typed in the commands memorized years ago for just such a situation and was thrilled when the screen flickered, and a prompt came up. Before it could disappear (because this kind of thing was spotty at best) she keyed in her coded message. If anyone other than its intended recipient saw it, it would make no sense. Message complete, she hit enter and waited just long enough to ensure it was truly out in the ether before she back out of the window and returned to the previously blank screen.

She moved to the door, gripped the knob, then waited for the monitor to black out before she opened the door just enough to check the hall. It was a limiting view, but she held on to her patience as that trusty sixth sense that never failed to alert her confirmed she was still alone.

She slipped out, taking time to pull it close. Unfortunately, she would have to leave it unlocked, but by the time someone discovered that fact, she should be long gone. If she was lucky, it would be shrugged off as someone forgetting to set it.

She all but ran back down the hall, the floor cool against her bare feet. She came to a stop at the corner, checked for incoming movement, and when the shadows remained still, started to head back. She was almost to the end of the hall when her luck broke, and her internal warning system flickered. She rocked to a halt as the shadows separated and anxious alarm hit.

Fuck brazening it out.

With a split second to choose, she pivoted on her heel to run, but didn't get far. A thick arm wrapped around her waist and trapped her arms. A heavy hand muffled her soft grunt and covered her mouth. Her feet left the ground as she was lifted, adjusted, and then a shoulder hit her stomach.

She didn't bother struggle because a familiar scent of male

heat and temper filled her nose. She hung over Havoc's shoulder and braced her hands against his bare waist, being careful to avoid his wound. The arm around her thighs tightened as she looked up to determine they were headed back toward the kitchen and front room.

Her fingers dug in at his waist and she pinched his side —hard.

His soft pained, hiss was followed by a sharp slap on her ass as he turned away from the couch and headed towards her room, obviously requiring privacy for his interrogation.

This sucked because if it was up to her, she would happily share information. After everything she learned during the last couple of days, it was getting harder and harder to keep her secrets, but they weren't hers to give. The only thing stopping her from following her gut was imagining her boss's temper tantrum if she opened her mouth.

Yeah, not a pleasant thought.

She was so caught in her head she barely registered that she was absently stroking his back just above the edge of his pants. They hit her room and Havoc didn't give her a chance to refocus before he closed the door, then tossed her on the bed. She hit the mattress and bounced. She pushed up on to an elbow, shoved her tangled hair from her face, and glared at Havoc. She opened her mouth but didn't get a chance to utter a word.

For a big man, he moved fast. He was on the bed, his arms braced on either side of her shoulders, and pinning her in place with his weight.

It wasn't right but the feel of him holding her down set her body alight. Given no choice she ended up flat on her back and watched him warily. Her hands went to his shoulders, but even she couldn't tell if it was to push him away or drag him closer.

He leaned in, his face thunderous. "Who'd you contact, Mercy?"

Her breath stalled as the vibration of his rumble raced through her. She blinked because angry or not, that was damn sexy.

He dipped closer, his unbound hair falling forward. Color rode under his angled cheekbones and fury left an unholy light in his eyes.

Oh shit.

The chaos in her body worsened and she squirmed.

He shifted his hips to still her movements, and suddenly he was pressed hard and thick against the ache blooming between her legs.

Double shit!

She swallowed an inappropriate whimper as nerves kicked in and tried to wrangle her lust back into its hidey hole. It didn't work. Her tongue darted out to wet her dry lips.

He caught the movement and his face tightened. "Who?"

Not keen to outright lie to him, she went with her best option—silence and shook her head.

He growled.

The sexy noise left her fighting her body's need to move this situation in a completely different direction. She curled her fingers into his solid shoulders and locked every muscle down in an effort not to trigger disaster. Any other time, she'd tempt fate, but right now was the wrong time, wrong place. It didn't help that she could feel his reaction, hot and hard, to their current position and a hungry fire smoldered under her skin.

His jaw flexed and something she couldn't read washed through his face. The muscles under her hands shifted and he dropped his head until all she could see was him. Feel him. "Talk."

"And say what?" Her question emerged unintentionally

husky. She couldn't help it. Hell, right now she was thrilled she could form coherent words.

"Who did you reach out to?" He gritted out, his breath hot against her face.

Fighting him on two levels proved to be too much for her. Something had to give. So, she offered a piece. "My boss."

His dark gaze searched hers and he demanded, "Name."

"No." She could taste her regret in the one word.

"Goddammit, Mercy." Frustration and disappointment edged his scowl as his eyes went hard.

That look stung so deep, that when she felt his body tense, she knew she was about to lose something she couldn't afford to lose. "I can't!"

It was pure reaction, not thought, that had her cupping his face in her hands to hold him as he reared back. His scruff was surprisingly soft against her palms and made her want to pet away his anger. But this was too important, and she needed him to hear her, to not give up on her. Not yet.

"Please." She held him in place and lifted her head, her neck tight as she got as close as she could. "I know you can't, but you have to trust me, Havoc."

He didn't move, but his nostrils flared and the lines on his face deepened. "Hard to do when you're sneaking around."

Okay, yeah, she understood that, so she gave another piece and prayed her ass would be in one piece when her boss found out. "My boss won't interfere with you and yours."

"You don't know that." Suspicion made his voice sharp.

"Yeah, I do." And she did.

But because trust was earned and in the short time they spent together, he had earned hers, but her for him? Well, the situation being what it was, made it downright difficult. Then, listening to her gut (or something a tad higher and rusty from lack of use), she went against years of experience and took the first scary-ass step to shifting her balance on that thin line of loyalty to this side of shaky.

It was a decision she couldn't, wouldn't, explain, not even to herself. "Those answers you—" then she corrected, "—no, the Vultures want, so does my boss. If it was up to me, I'd lock you two in the same room and make you both share."

His dark eyes narrowed, and she couldn't help but notice (since she was so damn close) how thick his lashes were. "So let me talk to him."

God, he was a stubborn SOB. Her hands tightened on his jaw. "That's what I'm trying to arrange."

He blinked at her unexpected answer. "Say again?"

Finally assured that he was willing to listen and wouldn't go anywhere, she dropped her head back to the bed, but she didn't let go of him, enjoying the tentative connection. "Can't pick up a phone like we did with Suárez, but I left a message. One I'm hoping he gets so we can meet. Preferably after dealing with Felix."

As she spoke, his body lost its earlier stiffness and sank into hers. The heat of him seeped through the thin material of her shirt. Her nipples peaked and something hotter curled much, much lower.

His gaze drifted down her chest and caught her obvious reaction. He licked his lips and when he lifted his gaze, it wasn't only temper that sparked in the velvety depths. "Where?"

Not wanting to push him over the edge that she managed to convince him to inch back from, she proceeded cautiously. "Not giving you specifics." In an effort to ease the sting of her refusal, she brushed her fingers along his jaw and offered a tentative smile. "You'll hit the road and leave my ass tied up in ditch somewhere."

"Might still do that." A hint of humor snuck around his grumbled response.

Her voice softened. "I'd dare you to try, but you'd probably take me up on it."

That got her a lip twitch. "No probably about it, babe." His attention dropped to her mouth and that fast he shifted their situation from one danger zone to another. "Consider it necessary seeing how you have a tendency to try my patience."

He shifted his weight to one arm, and she dropped her hand. He touched a finger to the base of her throat and drew a torturously slow line down the center of her chest, leaving an ache behind. "Could make you spill."

"You can try." And if he did, she was down with that.

Her pulse raced, her heart following in its path, and her lungs forgot how to function. The path his finger took sparked with heat and woke a hunger in its wake. It was a delicate touch that seared beyond skin and sank bone deep. Greedy need made her spine bow as she sought more contact.

His dark eyes smoldered as he watched her, hunger joining temper and tangling with male speculation. He continued to torture her with his slow, seductive touch. "Is that a challenge?"

Somehow, she managed to get out, "You up for it?" Part of her wondered if she lost her mind, tempting him this way. The other, hell, it was grinning like a deranged lunatic, loving every minute of pushing him.

"Oh yeah." His finger went away.

Before she could blink his big, warm hand slipped under her t-shirt, and retraced his earlier route over her sensitive skin. His palm inched over her stomach, and she sucked in a breath, holding it, waiting, wanting more.

He grinned and drifted a little higher. A feather light brush against the edge of her breast sent the air trapped in her lungs rushing out on a low, shaky moan.

He leaned in until their lips were a breath apart and she was trapped in his gaze. "You ready?"

Her 'yes' was less than a whisper, but he heard it. Even better, he heeded it and took her mouth with an intensity that curled her toes and snapped what little restraints remained on her lust. It swept through her and washed away the feeble reminders from her commonsense about why this wasn't smart.

Fuck being smart, she ached.

Her hands slipped from his face and tangled in his thick hair, holding him close. She expected hard and hot but got slow and smooth. His tongue stroked hers, teasing and tempting. She took his taste, all heat and spice, deep where it set off a series of shockwaves that rocked her body.

Trapped under his weight, she could only respond, and glided her tongue along his, taking what he gave. There was no calculation in her reaction, it was pure want, a desire to drown in what he offered. Then their kiss changed, became darker, more demanding, and dragged her deeper into the rising storm.

His palm cupped her breast, and his thumb brushed over her aching nipple, sending sensation tearing through her. Her hands left the smooth strands of his hair to drift to his neck where she found the heated skin of his muscled back. She stroked her palms over the luscious expanse and tried to absorb every inch.

He continued to tease her as he sank deeper into her. He left her breast and turned his attention to stroking along her ribs. The heat of his touch wiped away her body's myriad of aches and replaced it with something better, hungrier, but the ache between her legs gained strength.

She shifted restlessly and managed to get one leg out from under him. Once it was free, she hooked it over his hip and set her heel just below his ass. The move had the added advantage of pressing his long, hard shaft right where she needed it. The sensation rocketed through her, and she tore her mouth from his, her neck arching as she ground into him with a groan. "Oh God."

He upended her world with his clever hands and diabolical mouth, and desperate for an anchor, she set her hands on his chest where a light covering of hair arrowed down in a thin line. She continued to pet him as his mouth glided along her exposed neck. His tongue joined his lips and played along the sensitive tendons. Then she forgot all about touching him and just held on as a series of shivers broke over her body. It only got worse when he sucked at the soft skin where shoulder and neck met, hard enough she had no doubt she'd be wearing his mark.

She whimpered at the rasp of her t-shirt against her nipples as she writhed under him. "Havoc." It was all she could get out as her body went up in flames.

He ground the hard length of his cock against her with deliberate intent, proving she wasn't the only one caught in the need raging between them. He kept up the slow torture despite her repeated demands. If this was how he intended to get her to talk, she might be tempted to tell him anything he wanted.

Thankfully, he didn't say a word, instead he kept up his sensual assault and she gloried in the luxurious ride to the peak. Then he stopped, just before she reached the top. She blinked open eyes she didn't realize she had closed, to find him watching her. He nipped her chin and laid a trail of soft kisses along her jaw until his mouth was next to her ear. "Shirt off, babe. Want your tits."

She didn't have to be asked twice. Her shirt sailed to the side and left her bare chested, giving him exactly what he wanted.

Male hunger filled his face as he cupped one breast, dropped his head, and curled his tongue around her nipple. The lick of fire sent her eyes rolling to the back of her head as her hips lifted to ride the hard cock barely restrained by the barrier of their pants. His tongue disappeared, only to be replaced by his mouth and he drew her deep.

A soft, needy keen escaped as her spine bowed as he played with her breasts. She dragged her palms over his chest and mapped the rise and fall of his muscles. When she brushed one of his nipples, the mouth at her breast vibrated with his moan. So, she did it again and got a repeat reaction. Wanting to find out what else could get that reaction, she cupped his face and made her demand, "My turn."

He let her roll him to his back and his hands settled on her hips, the thin material of her sleep pants no barrier to the heat of his touch. With her knees braced on either side of his hips, she traced her fingers over his beautiful chest and through the light hair to brushed them over his nipples. When they tightened under her light touch, she braced her palms and leaned forward. The change in her position shifted his erection against her damp center, and despite the small explosions it triggered, she managed to press an open mouth kiss to the base of his throat.

Salt and heat met her tongue as she continued to kiss and lick her way down his chest, intent on following the trail genetics so thoughtfully left. His hand dove into her hair, tugging and pulling, to add a pleasurable bite and shoot her lust to the next level. She shifted back as she went lower, her palms skimming carefully as a small part minded the bruise on his ribs. She pressed another open mouth kiss to the soft spot just below his belly button when a sharp knock on the door ripped through her haze.

"Havoc, stop playing with her and get your ass up!"

Mercy stilled at Vex's wakeup call. Havoc's hands tightened in her hair, then loosened. "We're up!"

"Yeah, I bet you are." Her footsteps moved away from the door before he could respond.

Mercy pressed her face into his stomach to stifle her giggle. She nipped Havoc lightly, then settled her chin at the edge of his pants. She lifted her gaze to find him staring down at her with a mix of frustration, hunger, and unexpected humor.

He untangled one of his hands to brush a gentle stroke along the side of her face. He cupped her chin and swept his thumb over her lips. His gaze drifted over her face, his thoughts hidden. "Dangerous game you're playing, Mercy."

She kept her voice equally soft. "Not playing games, Havoc."

"Aren't you?"

She shook her head, but not enough to lose his touch. "Trying to help.'"

Some of his harshness softened. "You're treading a thin line, babe. You're not careful, you're going to fall."

His unusual perception proved he saw deeper than she expected, and it left her uncomfortable. "I've got good balance."

"For both our sakes, I hope you're right."

His response held a depth of sincerity that brought a lump to her throat, even as it sank past the shield protecting what was left of her heart.

Unable to answer, she turned and pressed a kiss against his palm hoped she was too.

sixteen

An hour after the sun rose Havoc led Mercy and Vex out of Navajo City and expected to hit Page by mid-morning. Mercy rode a bike Ed had scrounged up because while Havoc's bike could handle two riders, after this morning, he wasn't sure he could survive the temptation of having her pressed up against his back.

The plan was that once they hit Page, Vex would head towards Pebble Creek to get word to Reaper. Sending Vex off solo wasn't ideal, but no way in hell would Havoc let Mercy chase Felix down on her own. After all the discussions yesterday about what went down in Pebble Creek, what was happening here, and whatever Mercy had going on, Havoc's gut was in overdrive.

On the surface it might be a tangled mess of 'what-ifs' and 'maybes', but the more he turned it over, the clearer the picture became. The attack on Crane's supply routes, the kidnappings, the attempt on the dam, the set-up of the Cartels, all of it pointed to one undeniable fact—someone wanted to divide the various leaders and was willing to play them against each other while they consolidated the power and resources. There was only one person left on the table with enough mojo for that kind of shit, and that would be Michael.

The man currently held the territory that stretched along the west coast. It started up in what had been the Pacific Northwest and stretched down into Tahoe Forest situated just north of the Sacramento remains. It not only covered a huge ass amount of land but included numerous abandoned military installations and a couple of the remaining big cities— New Seattle, Portland, and Redding.

Michael had access to some seriously lethal resources at his disposal and there was no telling what kind of weapons and other nasty shit he had stockpiled. Stopping him would take the combined efforts of all those involved—Fate's Vultures, Lilith, and the Free People. And even then, Havoc worried it might not be enough.

Humanity wasn't what it once was, their numbers decimated during the Collapse and its aftermath. Population went from the millions to thousands, and in some places, dropped to single digits. Seventy-plus years may have passed, but humans were just getting back to living versus surviving, and an all-out war between territories could spell the end of what was left of civilization this side of the Mississippi.

Reaper, and by extension, the Vultures, recognized the inevitable end of this whole fucked up situation and so agreed to work with Lilith, and now Istaqa to ensure it never came to pass. As much as Havoc wasn't keen about taking on Michael, he was a hell of a lot less keen on playing the role of foot solider in someone else's war again. He had enough of that shit to last more than one lifetime during the Border Wars, even if those same wars taught him the necessary skills to save what little had been left of his soul.

He shook off of the dark memories and turned his mind to something a little less terrifying, although not by much—

Mercy. She was a bundle of contradictions, all secrets and boldness. She made no effort to hide she was down with exploring how dirty things could get between them. A trait he appreciated. Despite Vex's cock-blocking, his dick still ached, but with his dick out of the driver's seat, he had to admit it was probably for the best. As much as he wanted Mercy not everything you wanted was good for you, and he wasn't convinced she ever would be.

There were her knife and skulking skills, skills that were breathtaking to watch but weren't learned from being some garden-variety hired gun. Nope, skills like that were honed with precision for a specific reason. Reasons she wasn't at all willing to share.

He got that, really, he did. He carried a few dark paths of his own that he didn't want anyone trotting down.

His worry was hers would harm those he called his and that was a risk he wasn't sure he was willing to take. Her secrets went deep, so deep he wondered if once he stopped digging, he'd be able to find his way back to the surface. Yet he was the world's biggest dumbshit because even knowing that he still considered setting his shovel in her dirt to unearth those hints of buried treasure.

Last night she almost managed to sneak by him and he only caught her on her way back from the communication room. He couldn't even pinpoint what had given her away, al l he knew was one moment he was asleep, the next he was on his feet heading down the hall. He watched her slip out of the room and start back, recognizing her skill and knew this wasn't the first time she'd snuck around, nor would it be the last.

His anger as he hauled her to her room hadn't been with her because he knew she would try it, but with himself for failing to get ahead of her and losing his chance to find out who she worked for.

So, when he had her beneath him, he pushed and he pushed hard, setting that shovel deep. It was clear her loyalty was torn, and he admired how she handled the tough situation, by not lying, but giving what she did. It surprised him that she'd take such a risk and as much as Reaper would give him crap for it, Havoc believed Mercy truly wanted to share, but couldn't. He hoped to hell her balance was as good as she thought, because the loyalty lines she walked were gut clenchingly thin.

Even though her hatred of Michael, the depth of which couldn't be faked, added weight to her claim that he wasn't her boss, it still left one vitally important question unanswered.

Who the hell was she working for?

Adding an unknown into the volatile mix could throw things into a tailspin with a single act. As much as he wanted to sink into her body and take his time fucking her, he had to be damn sure she didn't fuck him in return. It was strange because when it came to women, he had no issue keeping it all about the sex, but with her, he couldn't. How she managed to get to him in a way no woman had since—he cut the thought off before it could fully form and refused to give it life. He couldn't go there. Not yet, or likely ever.

For now, he would concentrate on tracking Felix's ass down and making the roach to squeal on his partner, then he could worry about Mercy. If they were lucky, he might get proof of Michael's involvement at the same time. Things would be so much easier if he could just take the fucker out before things escaped containment and turned to shit.

Unfortunately, blessings like those didn't just drop from the sky, unless they were prepared to crush you beneath their weight. At that thought, he cocked a quick look to the expanse of blue stretched above him.

By the way, that wasn't an invite.

Thankfully, no one answered.

VEX'S DUST trail was long gone by the time Havoc led Mercy through Page's backstreets. They pulled into the small lot behind Lee's pub. The rumble of the two engines bounced off the narrow alley confines and turned deafening as they rolled to a stop. Havoc shut his bike down and dismounted as Mercy followed suit. The noise faded as he pulled down his bandana that protected his nose and mouth from turning into dusty wasteland, and then shook his head to stop the ringing in his ears.

Next to him, Mercy pulled off her beat-up baseball hat, bent at the waist and shook her hair out. A small dust cloud escaped and drifted away. She straightened, gathered her hair, and tucked it through the cap in a makeshift ponytail. Then she turned to him, her face shadowed by the brim and angled her chin. "Where to first?"

"Lee's Bar." It was the most logical starting place when looking for out of towners and despite the bandana he needed to wash the grit from his mouth.

"What about the bikes?"

"They'll be fine." Because no one messed with Lee's customers. It was one of the main reasons the Vultures crashed here when passing through. Throwing punches and raising hell was a great way to pass the time when you were bored, but not so great if you were aiming for a bit of shut eye. Therefore, the Vultures picked crash pads where such activities were highly limited. And Lee's was one such spot. "Come on."

He led the way through Lee's back door. They passed through what used to be some kind of screened in porch and hit the kitchen to find Lee manning the stove, a fairly clean apron wrapped around his thick frame.

He turned at their entrance, his face red from the heat with a spatula in hand. "Havoc." His gaze went to Mercy as Havoc's hand nudged her towards the sink on the wall. "Miss."

She flicked her fingers in a wave even and headed to the sink.

"Morning, Lee." Havoc followed Mercy, waiting while she splashed her face before he took his turn. He finished drying his face and asked, "We miss breakfast?"

Lee used his head to indicate the shelf of plates as he worked the stove. "Grab one, can fill you up before I shut it down for the morning."

Havoc tossed the towel on the edge of the sink and nabbed a couple of plates. "Grateful." He stood at Lee's side as eggs and bacon were shuffled on to the plates.

Lee slid the last piece of bacon in place. "Things okay up the canyon?"

"They will be."

Relief eased some of the lines on Lee's face at Havoc's answer. "Good, that's good." He turned off the stove, shifted the pan to a back burner, and took his spatula to the sink. "You sticking around?"

Havoc handed a plate to Mercy, who took it with a chin lift. He scrounged around until he found two forks, then handed her one. He settled against the counter's edge and forked up a bite of fluffy eggs. "For a bit, just need to track a man down."

Lee washed dishes and shot him a look over his shoulder. "Which man?"

"Hispanic," Mercy chimed in, motioning with a piece of bacon. "Kind of a dick, thinks he's hot shit, had two sidekicks stuck to his ass." She took a bite of her bacon and grinned.

Lee turned back to his dishes, his lips curved. "Yeah, they were here last night. Main one was pretty quiet, sitting back like he was lord of the manor, just liked to watch and drink. But one of his sidekicks tried starting something with one of the boys and got shot down real quick." He set a handful of silverware on a drying board. "Stayed a few hours, then headed out."

"Any idea to where?" Havoc asked then heeded his stomach's demand for more and took another bite, enjoying Lee's cooking.

"Margo's, I think." Lee slid him a look. "I'm sure she'll be happy to share with you."

At Lee's implication, Havoc frowned and looked to his plate, hoping to hide his wince. Margo made no bones about what she'd like from him, but it wasn't a shared thing. It also had nothing to do with her chosen profession, it was all Margo.

The woman ran a successful cathouse and presented the picture of independence, but the truth was, she was on the hunt for a man of her own. Last time Havoc had stopped in, she made no bones about wanting that man to be him, regardless of his wants. Therefore, he took pains to steer clear.

"Margo's?" Mercy asked.

Lee didn't answer but gave her a look and went back to washing.

Havoc cleared his throat and answered, "A brothel down the street. Most visitors end up there sooner or later."

"Cool. Guess it'll be our first stop then." Mercy didn't bat an eyelash but went back to her breakfast.

Havoc sighed and finished off his food. When they were done, they handed their dishes to Lee and headed out.

Havoc waited until they were on the street and heading to Margo's before he spoke. "You seriously cool about this?"

At his side, Mercy looked to him, confusion clear on her face. "Cool about what?"

"Going to a whorehouse." He wasn't even sure why he was asking. Hell, every time Vex visited one, she ended up making best friends. Something told him Mercy was made from the same cloth, but he found he still had to ask.

Her lips twitched and humor lit her eyes, adding a green shimmer. "Why? Think I haven't been in one before?"

He rubbed the back of his neck as he scanned the light morning bustle. Mainly so he wouldn't give in and take that mouth. "Most females find visiting such a place uncomfortable."

"I'm not most females, babe." To underscore the tease in her voice, she bumped her shoulder into his arm. "And to let you know, this ain't my first den of iniquity."

And male that he was, her statement brought to mind all sorts of wicked things and judging from her widening grin, she knew it. He wrapped an arm around her waist, tugged her close, and dropped his head to her ear. "You're a tease."

She threw back her head and laughed, never breaking eye contact.

It was stunning to watch and something deep in his chest where nothing reached, softened.

Her joy was plain to see, lighting her eyes, adding color to her cheeks, and taking her from pretty to beautiful. When she was down to soft chuckles, she didn't pull away, but kept pace with him, their hips bumping.

They made it another block before she spoke. "Let you in on a little secret."

He didn't miss the tentative offering. "What's that?"

He came to a stop when she did, and they both stepped back out of the flow of foot traffic. He had his back to a building when she turned into him, stepped between his legs, and braced her palms against his chest. He cupped her hips.

Her earlier humor was replaced by an intensity he didn't quite get. She held his gaze, worried her bottom lip, her body stiff, and then shared, "Spent my younger years with Momma as she worked the streets in Lost Angels."

He took the unexpected hit and didn't lose her gaze. "Must have sucked." He wanted to ask more questions but standing out on the street wasn't the place to do that.

"Yeah, it did." She searched his face, but when all she found was his ready acceptance, some of her tension disappeared. "But not like there's a lot of options for a woman when she loses her man. Especially when she's used to her man taking care of her and her baby."

Mercy shrugged. "Momma lost hers, and when she did, she did what she had to and made sure we had a roof and food." She paused and studied his face. He wasn't sure what she was looking for, but she must have found it because she continued. "So, no, visiting Margo's won't make me uncomfortable."

He squeezed her hips and gave her a grin. "Good to know." Then he decided to return her gift with one of his own. "Fair warning, I'm depending on you."

She arched a brow. "For?"

"Protection."

"From what? Overzealous girls?"

"Just one," he confirmed as he nudged her back so they could re-enter the street. He caught her hand in his, dipped his head close and explained, "Margo."

It earned him another laugh and a vow. "I promise to keep your virtue safe, babe."

seventeen

Mercy walked into Margo's and took a step back in time. Not a traumatic trip, but the memories gathered all the same. Her mother had initially worked the streets of Lost Angels solo, before Lacey, one of the better madams who made a killing supplying flesh for those with the credits to pay, took her under her wing.

So long as the credits were good, Lacey didn't discriminate on who she sent her girls (and boys) to, but she did have one standing rule—return her gifts in the same shape they arrived in. Not many pimps—male or female—took that level of care, especially not in the free for all that was Lost Angels. Caught between the territorial lines of the Cartels, Raiders, Michael, and Free People, Lost Angels was a volatile mix of personalities and survival was a solo gig.

Once Mercy's momma was settled in at Lacey's, Mercy was given free run of the house and the surrounding blocks, and she had made the most of it. Lacey's stable might be skilled in sex, but where they excelled was in dealing with the reality of the world around them.

Mercy had soaked their expertise up like a sponge. How to

interpret the language of faces and body to prep your mark, the best places to hide weapons in plain sight, how to distract, how to con, how to pick up useful tidbits, how to watch and listen without being seen—all of that and more encompassed Mercy's early education. An education that saved her ass once she lost her momma and the questionable safety of Lacey's protection.

As she walked inside at Havoc's side, it was like coming home.

A woman in a close-fitted top with more than a hint of cleavage was bent over a ledge on the high counter. She looked up, her artfully sloppy curls bouncing with the movement. Light from the pendant lamps above glinted off her cat-eyed glasses perched on a delicate slope of a nose as she gave Havoc a full-body scan. Her pen danced through her fingers and her red lips curved. "Heya, sugar." She caught sight of Mercy and her smile notched up a level. "Darlin'."

Mercy grinned, recognizing the tactic, and figured this sexy librarian couldn't be Margo, because if she was, she wouldn't have looked twice at Mercy. Instead, with the skill and speed of a master player, the woman was sizing up the possibilities of the incoming couple. A man coming in with a woman on his arm, meant the best way to make the most of your soon to be appointment was to ensure his female really enjoyed her experience.

So, no, not Margo.

Mercy and Havoc crossed the tastefully decorated and airy lobby. At some point Margo's had been a hotel and the two floors above curled around the main level. A decorative railing snaked around the second floor and guarded a line of closed doors. With the limited angle available, Mercy saw the third floor appeared to have the same layout. It was the perfect set up for its current reincarnation.

Interestingly, it didn't scream house of ill repute. There

were no red lights, no scantily clad bodies lounging on over-stuffed furniture, nor the smokey haze that indicated the use of substances you could snort, smoke or shoot. That alone kept it a step above most brothels.

Instead, the simple, but comfortable furniture was collected into various groupings that encouraged conversations, or, in the case of the three women and one man off to the side with various objects piled in the center, a long, lazy game of cards. Even the skin on display was tastefully arranged —shorts to showcase long legs, fitted tops with a peek or two of undeniable cleavage, understated make-up—the overall picture one of casual, but approachable beauty.

On the room's other side, a honey-skinned beauty painted her toenails, her bare foot propped on a coffee table. In the corner loveseat, a couple, one man with his legs propped on a low table played with the hair of the other man that rested his head on his thigh. Others were scattered around, and all watched to some degree as she and Havoc made their way to the counter. gave Margo credit, the whole vibe worked well. She returned the librarian's smile with one of her own and added a cheerful, "Hey, I'm Mercy."

Their greeter mirrored Mercy, propping an elbow on the counter, and setting her chin in her palm. "Hey, Mercy, I'm Sage."

"Heya, Sage." From Mercy's close-up position, she didn't miss the real humor the replaced the woman's earlier professional cheer. "Love your glasses."

"Thanks." Purplish-red nails managed to hold the pen as she nudged her glassed down a bit so hazel eyes could peer over the top of the frames. They drifted over Mercy's face then switched to the hard-to-miss man who angled so he could watch both the room and the counter and set his palm against the small of Mercy's back. "Love your accessory. Can I borrow?"

Her grin widened at the purred comment. "As much as I'd love to share, I'm looking for something a bit different."

Sage stiffened and her gaze snapped back to Mercy, her initial friendliness cooling.

Before it hit deep freeze, Mercy added softly, "I'm hoping you can help."

Sage studied her for a moment, then pushed her glasses back into place. "Shame, could've been fun." She arched a sardonic brow. "What kind of help are you talking about?"

"The information kind."

Thick lashes brushed the lenses as Sage narrowed her eyes and her lips thinned with obvious disapproval. "We don't kiss and tell, sugar."

"Not asking for details," Mercy clarified. "Just looking for a little direction."

Sage's feathers settled at Mercy's answer, but she didn't lose her frown. "Ask."

"Last night, you get a trio of men not from around here but acted like king dicks?"

Sage's frown deepened and new lines appeared around her eyes. It took a few seconds, but she gave a slow nod.

"Anyone catch where they're staying?"

Havoc adjusted his stance and Sage's gaze flickered to him, then came back to Mercy. "Think you have your hands full already there. Not smart to take on more trouble."

"Don't have much of a choice." Besides Mercy liked Havoc's brand of trouble.

Speaking of which, his hand on her spine disappeared, then he was crowding in behind her, his arm snaking around her waist. His fist appeared on the counter by her elbow, his fingers uncurled, and two thin squares of silver slid on to the counter and snared Sage's attention. "Be grateful if you shared, Sage."

Havoc's rumble hit Mercy's ear and she stifled her automatic shiver. *The man's voice was hell on her libido.* She delicately cleared her throat and found her voice. "Just need a starting point, Sage."

Sage studied Mercy for a long moment, and it wasn't hard to miss the mix of anger and fear that muddied her hazel eyes, but her thoughts stayed hidden behind her sultry mask. She slipped the credits across the counter and vanished off the counter's edge into her palm. "I can't give you one but know someone who can." She twisted to lean over the counter to Mercy's right and called, "Penny, come man the desk."

"Coming."

Mercy bent to look around Havoc and watched the honey-skinned nail painter set aside her polish and dropped her feet to the ground. She walked awkwardly on her heels with her toes lifted to preserve her art.

Sage moved to the far end of the counter. "You two." She got Mercy and Havoc's attention. "Follow me."

They followed her up the stairs to the second floor where Sage stopped in front of a purple door decorated with stylized birds and flowers. She knocked twice.

Mercy and Havoc stayed the side as someone moved around inside. Shadows danced along the gap at the base of the door, and then the lock sounded. The door opened just enough to frame a statuesque woman whose curves (top and bottom) did not quit. Tight black pants traced every feminine line and the matching corset worked wonders for the creamy skin. Raven black hair, so dark it carried blue highlights, curled over shoulders, and framed a face that stunned even Mercy.

Irate steel blue eyes rimmed by midnight lashes swept dismissively over Mercy before snapping to Havoc. The woman's initial temper disappeared like smoke on the water and filled with something equally hot as her aggressive stance shifted to sultry. "Havoc." Her voice was rife with invitation.

Mercy didn't need Havoc's unenthusiastic return grunt of

"Margo" or his arm that curled around her waist and shifted her into a shield position to recognize who answered Sage's summons.

At his not-so-subtle move, Mercy bit her lip, curled her hands over the tense arm at her waist, and dropped her head to hide her grin. *Guess he really didn't like Margo's attention.*

And Margo was definitely intent on having Havoc whether he wanted her or not. It was there, in the way she looked at him, as if it was simply a question of when, not if, she would sink her talons in deep.

Luckily for Havoc, Margo would have to claw her way through Mercy first, and that would be no easy feat.

"Sorry to interrupt, Margo," Sage murmured, drawing the other woman's attention. "They're here about the asshole from last night."

Mercy looked up just in time to catch the change in Margo's expression. Whatever fantasies she held of Havoc were swept away to leave behind harsh lines of fury. "Why?"

Havoc's muscles tightened under Mercy's hands and his tone was short. "Need to find him."

Margo, clearly unappeased by his succinct explanation, took her hand from the door's edge, propped one bare shoulder against the frame, and folded her arms over her chest. For a moment it seemed Margo's corset would split at the seams, but luckily, it held strong. "You going to fuck him up?" She didn't wait for his answer but gave one of her own. "You're going to fuck him up. When you're done, do it again for me."

"Happy to," Havoc said. "Want to share why?"

Margo unfolded her arms and used a hand to push the door wide, exposing the scene inside. "That's why." The two words came out in a near sibilant hiss, her fury unmistakable.

Mercy turned with Havoc to see a rumpled bed and on it, curled around a pillow, a spill of blonde hair that did not hide the bruised and battered face aimed toward the door. Havoc's arm dropped away, and Mercy didn't wait for an invite, but slipped by Margo, her attention focused on the girl who watched her approach with wary eyes.

Behind her she heard Havoc's low voice. "What the hell happened?"

"The bastard beat her." Margo's voice was equally low. "Skimped out on payment and hit the road before the security found her."

Mercy reached the bed and crouched until she was eye level with the girl. She curled her hands on the bed's edge because this close, there was no missing the damage inflicted. *Margo definitely needed new security measures.*

"Hey," She met the wary hazel gaze. "I'm Mercy." Under the bruises and swelling was an innate prettiness that broke Mercy's heart.

Those old eyes in a too young face studied her carefully before answering in a raspy voice, "Jenni."

Mercy's hands tightened on the bed as anger whipped through her. Jenni's voice carried the kind of rasp that came from being choked. It took sheer force of will to mask her fury and manage a small smile. "Jenni. Think you can answer a couple of questions for me?"

Jenni's gaze went to Margo in silent query.

Mercy didn't follow Jenni's gaze, because there was no point. If Margo didn't want her girl to answer, she wouldn't. Instead, she noted every bruise, every cut, the red lines still circling her wrists, and the ring of purpling finger marks that chained the delicate neck, all vicious reminders left by a twisted piece of shit. When she caught up to Felix, she would be sure to return the favor.

"Can try." Jenni's soft answer forced Mercy's thoughts of revenge to the side.

She focused on the girl. "I'll make this as easy as I can,

then. Don't speak if a nod works, okay?" After getting a nod in return, Mercy started. "The man who did this to you, he give you his name?"

Jenni nodded.

"Was it Felix?"

This time she shook her head, but added, "Santo."

Who the hell was Santo? Maybe he was someone new, because lord above knew there was more than one slimy ass bastard Cartel member scuttling about.

Jenni kept going before Mercy could ask. "Felix watched. Laughed." The girl's eyes darkened and shifted away.

Mercy caught the fear shining in the depths and nausea curled her stomach at what it meant. Her grip tightened on the bed until her knuckles turned white. *Motherfucker!* It almost hurt to keep her voice soft. "Both men came up with you?"

Another nod, this time with eyes averted.

Mercy couldn't turn back the clock, but she could make sure Jenni knew exactly who was to blame. "Jenni, sweetie, look at me." She waited until those eyes came back up. "Ever hear of Red Lacey?" After getting a chin dip, she added, "Grew up in her house, so no judgment here, yeah?"

Jenni searched her face, probably looking for lies, but Mercy waited her out knowing none would be found. Sure enough, it took a few, but Jenni offered, "Heard it got wild there."

Wild wouldn't be the word Mercy would use, but then again... "Yeah, it had its moments."

Jenni was seemingly reassured by Mercy's shared history and said, "Took Santo up, things were going along, then Felix walked in." She stopped, swallowed, and winced.

Based off the restraint marks on Jenni's wrist, Mercy read between the lines. "Santo let him in while you were tied?"

Another nod.

Right, which meant Santo belonged to Felix. "Then things went south?"

Jenni tried to curl up tighter and her nod was smaller.

"Okay," Mercy murmured, trying to ease the girl. "Just one more question and we'll let you rest."

"Okay," it was a whisper.

"Did either one of them tell you where they're staying?"

Jenni frowned. "Not staying."

The unexpected answer made Mercy re-evaluate her assumption on Felix's next move. Since he hadn't found her, she expected him to stick around, but if he wasn't planning to do that, what had lit the fire under his ass? "They say where they were going?"

Jenni's nod was uncertain. "Heard them when they thought I was out. Santo wanted to stay, but Felix was pissed. Said they were running out of time and needed to get to Salt Lake before shit hit the fan."

Shit like maybe the dam collapsing, or shit like Mercy had talked to the wrong people?

Anticipation streaked through Mercy and warred with a deeper worry. Could the fates finally be smiling on her? North would be perfect, considering her final destination lay in the same direction. But who, or what, lay up north? If she could catch up to Felix, she might get her answers.

Jenni shifted position and winced.

Mercy touched one of the few unmarred places on her arm. "Thank you."

Jenni looked at her, a hardness edging into her hazel eyes. "You'll find him? Make him pay—" she waved a hand down her body, "—for this?"

Mercy held the girl's gaze, shared a glimpse of her true self, and didn't hesitate to promise. "Yeah. He'll pay."

Jenni smiled. Not big because of her split lip, but it was enough. "Good."

Mercy straightened and turned to find Margo, Sage and Havoc watching. Havoc's face was blank, so blank, Mercy knew that what simmered underneath wouldn't be pretty. She walked towards Havoc.

Margo's gaze left Jenni, and shifted to Mercy, the soft edges in those spectacular eyes disappeared as speculation and questions formed. Questions, Mercy was betting, Margo intended to ask, just not in front of her girls. Sure enough, the moment Mercy reached Havoc Margo said, "Sage, honey, sit with Jen for me?"

Sage settled in with Jenni and Margo led Havoc and Mercy to the hall. She closed Jenni's door and said, "Minute of your time before you leave?"

"All we got to give," Havoc responded.

Margo raised a brow, pivoted on a booted heel, and led them to a set of stairs tucked at the end of the hall. They followed Margo's swinging hips up to the third floor, and when they stepped out of the stairwell, it was clear this was Margo's private domain. There were only two doors on this side of the floor. One was near the stairs, and the other was further down the hall.

Margo went to the nearest one, threw it open, and strode inside. Mercy was the last one through, so she closed the door and looked around at Margo's office.

At some point someone got creative and knocked down walls to make two rooms into one big, functional space. The windows (Mercy counted six) along the back wall were covered in sheers that let light flood the space. On the far side, overstuffed couches and chairs gathered around a stone fireplace. The other side was dominated by a massive desk, the kind rarely found anymore.

How did you find such a monstrosity around here? It wasn't as if Page was on the same level as, say, New Seattle, where such a piece of art would make sense. A desk like that—

polished stone top, equally polished dark wood that was wide enough to lay on and stretch your arms out—was proof that Margo's business was very, very lucrative.

Margo went straight to the mammoth desk, hitched her hip on its edge, and dove right in. "Who the hell are these two?"

Content to let Havoc deal with Margo, Mercy spied a chair off to the side close enough she could come to Havoc's rescue if needed and made a move to it.

Havoc's warm hand curled around her wrist and held her in place. She glanced back and found, other than his hand on her, his attention was centered on Margo. "Since Felix is Cartel, safe to say Santo is too."

Margo hadn't missed his proprietary hold on Mercy, but his answer shifted her glare to his face. Her eyes narrowed and disgust curled her lip. "Again? Don't they ever learn?"

Her gaze flicked dismissively over Mercy, only to return to Havoc and study him. Margo slipped off the desk, the avaricious light from earlier back, this time with a heavy ownership vibe. "Who started it this time?" She sauntered into Havoc's personal space as if Mercy wasn't even there, put a hand on his shoulder, leaned close and tilted her head. "You or them?"

The fingers on Mercy's wrists flexed and Havoc's voice was as hard as his unhappy expression. "Does it matter?"

"No, I guess it doesn't." Something Mercy didn't understand washed through Margo's face as her hand drifted from his shoulder and down his arm. "You ever going to finish feeding that demon?"

At Margo's question the air around Havoc went from cool to subzero. Mercy barely noticed as the depth of implied shared history scraped across her heart like a skein of nettles. The unexpected sting locked her spine and self-preservation finally kicked in. Determined to stay clear of whatever these two had going on, she tugged against Havoc's grip.

Unfortunately, he didn't let go. "Told you before, that demon doesn't exist. Even if it did, not yours to tame."

Mercy flinched. *Ouch!*

Margo took the hit as color rose under her skin, her mouth went tight, and her nails flexed against his bicep. "For something that doesn't exist, it sure as hell gets your ass into trouble more times than not, doesn't it?"

Havoc held her stare as the tension rose to a breaking point.

Margo finally let him go and stepped back, but not before saying softly, "Be careful it doesn't swallow you whole."

Havoc's grip on Mercy's wrist slowly loosened, but the heat of his touch lingered. She pulled her arm back and fought the urge to rub her tingling skin.

Margo walked around the desk and trailed her fingers along the top. "Cartel doesn't normally wander this far north, makes me wonder, why now?" When the desk was between her and Havoc, she stopped and braced her hands on the surface. "I don't need the complications they bring, so need to know if this is a singular situation or will there be others looking for you?"

Before Havoc let loose the temper that swirled around him, Mercy decided to refocus Margo's attention. "They won't be looking for him, just me."

It worked and Margo's head came around. "And you are?"

"According to the big guy here, trouble." Mercy held Margo's glare and gave her a big, old grin. Margo might have the arrogant bitch persona down pat but was wasted on her. "Not to worry, though. We'll be heading out so won't be trouble for you."

Margo looked to Havoc. "Trouble?"

Havoc made it clear he was done and turned to the door. "Appreciate you letting us talk to your girl, Margo, but we need to hit the road." He shot Mercy a look.

Reading it accurately, Mercy turned to leave but didn't get far.

Margo shifted the arrogant bitch from act to reality. "You've got a bounty on your head, girl."

Mercy stopped and felt Havoc do the same behind her. She pivoted on her heel, stepped around his big frame, and propped her hands on her hips. "Yep, I do."

Margo's lips tightened, a malicious light burned in her eyes. "You worth it?"

Mercy curled her lips even as she calculated all the different options available to ensuring Havoc never had to worry about his virtue again.

Proving she wasn't just a massive bitch, but an observant one, Margo paled.

Satisfied with the reaction, Mercy answered, "More than, actually."

Neither she nor Havoc waited for Margo's reply but walked out together and left Margo behind.

eighteen

As evening closed in, Havoc led Mercy along the road that ran along the foot of the Wasatch Front and into Salt Lake. In the valley between the Wasatch Mountains and the Great Salt Lake where what used to be a well-organized city sprawled a lakeside community. After years of flooding and crazy ass weather, the Great Salt Lake and the surrounding underground rivers reclaimed their ancient paths and submerged the western half of Salt Lake City. The locals had moved east and tugged their homes up the slopes of the Wasatch Mountains in an effort to keep their feet dry.

After their hours long ride Havoc was looking forward to a hot meal, but they needed a place to crash first. He turned his bike towards the main drag and the snarls of Mercy's bike followed in his wake. It took another twenty minutes of navigating the twisting warren of narrow streets in the cool evening air to find the place he wanted.

He pulled into a dirt lot where an eclectic collection of bikes (motorized and pedal) shared space with mules and horses tethered near various haphazardly parked wagons. He shut his bike down and felt the weight of curious stares. Not because travelers were unexpected, but because although Salt Lake was bigger than Page and smaller than say, Portland or New Seattle, rough looking visitors who rode into town on modified bikes earned wide berths from folks who called it home. Especially from nice little families like the one currently hooking up a swaybacked mare to a wagon.

He freed his bag from the back of his bike and met Mercy on the sidewalk that led back to the main street. A battered saddlebag was slung over one slim shoulder. The same bag that she nagged his ass to swing by to pick up despite before they headed north. That side trip had elevated his irritation level and left him surly.

It didn't help that when he left Margo's he was in a pisser of a mood, either. Not only did he not welcome her efforts to make something happen between them, but he really detested her attempt to resurrect history that was best left buried. All the way back to Lee's, Mercy kept giving him sidelong glances that asked all kinds of questions he wasn't ready to answer. Thankfully, instead of voicing those queries, she hounded him until they picked up her stuff. Once she had her bag, they hit the road.

Of course, that was miles of road and hours ago, so he had a felling her hiatus on questions was about to end.

"Where are we going?" She fell into step beside him, and they moved down the sidewalk and hit the street.

"Getting us a room, then a meal."

"Right," she muttered under her breath.

They moved with the light foot traffic, and the babble of voices mixed with the clatter of wheels, hooves, and motors as they wove their way between the shop-lined streets.

Havoc stopped near a four-story building, kept his attention on the street, and pressed a buzzer next to a battered, barred door under a yellow light. Above the door and attached to the weathered wall was a long narrow sign that spelled out ROYALE in faded red letters.

The buzzer echoed inside, and a squeaky voice came back. "Yeah?"

"Room for the night."

"Credit or trade?"

"Credit."

The buzzer sounded again.

Havoc pulled open the door and let Mercy take the lead. They stepped inside a narrow entryway where the frizzy haired night clerk roosted behind a pitted counter. The clerk didn't jerk them around, and in less time than expected, Havoc had a key as he followed Mercy's curvy ass up the dimly lit stairs. Lured by the graceful sway of her hips, his body reacted, and he briefly considered his chances at having a repeat of this morning, but with a more satisfying ending. He must have made a sound because when she shot him a dark look over her shoulder, he figured it was pretty close to nil.

He finally wrestled his attention away from temptation when they hit the top floor. The carpet underfoot was worn but clean, and the walls sported an unimaginative beige interrupted by framed sketches of generic desert landscapes. The air carried a hint of mildew almost masked by lemon.

The scent got stronger when Mercy stopped in front of the last room on the right next to a back stairwell. She used the key, and then pushed the door open with her shoulder.

He followed her in, only to pull up short when she stopped a few feet inside. Trapped between her and the open door, he put a hand to her hip and pushed gently. "Move it, babe."

She shifted to the side to let him pass. "That's going to make for a tight fit."

He walked to the double bed huddled under a thin patchwork blanket across from a narrow dresser holding a lamp and dumped his bag on the floor on the far side. "Maybe."

Just beyond the dresser was another door, presumably to the bathroom. Sun-faded drapes framed a window on the back wall. Everything was worn, but clean.

She shrugged her bag off her shoulder and moved forward the last few feet to set it on the floor. "No maybe about it, Havoc."

Amused by her disgruntled respond, he teased, "Scared, babe?"

Instead of answering, she glared.

He hid his grin by giving her his back. Then he stretched and worked the kinks out of his back and shoulders waiting to see if she had any further objections to their accommodations. When she stayed quiet, he couldn't help but think his odds might be shifting.

After one last spine-crackling stretch, he turned around and caught her checking him out. He let his grin fly.

Her gaze skittered to his and color rose under her cheeks, but she huffed and rolled her eyes before sweeping past him and into the bathroom. But not before he caught the lift of her lips as she closed the door.

Nope, she definitely wasn't objecting.

When the tap came on, he wandered to the window and used a finger to pull back the drapes to examine their limited exit option. The view wasn't much, just a narrow alley shared with the squat building behind them. He lifted the window and despite the fairly smooth glide up, the glass rattled in the solid frame.

He leaned out and tagged the metal fire escape that ended a few feet above street level. He wrapped a hand around the metal railing and shook it. The metal rattled against brick, but nothing tore free.

A tad iffy but would do in a pinch.

He ducked back inside and put the window to rights. "Hurry up, Mercy. I'm hungry."

She opened the bathroom door, her face now free of dust, and tossed a hand towel on to the counter. "Give me a minute."

She went and crouched by her bag. She dug through it and then tossed two thin blades on the bed. She dug around again, this time pulling out a brush. She used it, tossed it back in the bag, straightened and then gathered her hair and wove it back into its customary braid. When she was done, she snatched up the pair of blades, tucked them away and turned to him. "Let's eat."

He pushed off the wall he was leaning against, stalked close, and tried to pinpoint where the blades went. "You expecting trouble?"

Instead of retreating, she closed the last few inches between them, brushed his chest from shoulder to waist and then held on. She tilted her chin and looked up into his face, her green eyes streaked with molten gold. "Always."

Unable to resist her unspoken invitation, he wrapped one arm around her waist, pulling her up tight against the aching length of his dick and curled his other hand at the base of her skull. Then he dipped his head and took her lips as her hands rose to his cup his face. Between that possessive touch and her addicting taste, he careened toward a sensual oblivion.

Hard as it was, he kept their kiss short. When he lifted his head, her pupils were blown, and her chest rose and fell. He watched her tongue come out and sweep over her lips and knew his first assumption was spot on. She was all sorts of tempting trouble.

A stomach rumbled, his or hers, he wasn't sure, but her lips curved. "Food first."

His arm loosened at her soft reminder, and he reluctantly let her go. "Food first."

She stepped back, giving them both much needed space, and held his gaze with the mysterious depths of hers.

Before he could recapture her and convince her their stomachs could wait, she took his hand and led him away from temptation.

DETERMINED to kill two birds with one stone, Havoc decided to take Mercy to The Last Stand for both food and information. They left her bike behind as a placeholder for their spots and rode double on his, which he considered both a blessing and a curse.

Her hands looped around his waist, her tits pressed tight against his back, and her cheek rested against his shoulder. By the time he pulled up to the rowdy bar at the edge of town, a very specific part of his body ached, and it took an immense amount of restraint not to lay her on his bike and make it stop.

He rolled by the drunken pair throwing wild punches as they wrestled in the dirt by of one of the two bonfires outside Last Stand and shut the bike down. Mercy's weight against his back disappeared and her hands left his waist.

When he craned his neck, he saw she had scooted back on the seat and was now eyeing the idiots on the ground. When the dumbass on top nailed his opponent in the eye, she winced. "That's going to hurt in the morning." Then she turned to him and drawled, "You take me to the most interesting places, Havoc."

His lips twitched, but he patted her calf to get her to hop down. "Patrons are shit, but food's good."

"If you say so." She used his shoulders to balance as she swung her leg over and got off. Once her feet hit the ground she stepped back, giving him room.

Havoc swung off, wrapped an arm around Mercy's waist. Firelight from the bonfires danced off glass bottles and over hard faces with even harder gazes. Some of which were focused on them. He tagged those watchers with a warning glare to back the fuck off. Gazes skittered away as his message was received.

He one-armed his way through the door and they hit the bar's smoke-filled interior. Music, the kind with a heavy beat, played from somewhere. A three-sided bar held center court, booths lined the walls, and high-topped tables filled the rest of the space between. In the open space on the far left a game was underway at the pool table. Tucked to the right of that was a well-used dartboard currently sporting a mix of knives and darts.

Havoc scanned the scene, his gaze sliding through the crowd where a tatted waiter and two short-skirted waitresses, shuttled drinks, and food. He spotted his contact, but instead of heading over, he stepped in front of Mercy and forged a path to the bar, trusting her to stay at his back.

The stools were filled, so he stood behind them, got the bartender's attention, and flicked two fingers. He got a nod in return, then two bottles of home-brew skimmed the heads gathered at the rail. He handed one to Mercy who sent him an arched look.

He leaned in so she could hear him over the din. "What?"

She rose to her toes and kept her mouth close to his ear. "The food better be damn good."

"We'll eat, and if we're lucky, get some information." He touched his bottle to hers. "Let me do the talking."

She paused with the bottle halfway to her lips. "Got a choice?"

"Nope." He nipped her ear and didn't miss the shiver that swept through her. "Stay sharp." Then he straightened and took a drink from his bottle, his gaze roaming the floor. He herded Mercy to an empty booth, cutting off two bearded men with arms full of drunken females in the process.

"Hey, asshole, that's our booth."

Havoc gave the man a dark look. "Was your booth."

Despite their alcoholic haze, the men took Havoc's meaning to heart and stumbled away muttering under their breath.

He waited until Mercy slid in first, then he followed. She shoved the previous occupants' crap to the other side of the table, set her bottle down, and watched the scene. He let his gaze drift to a poker game at a table set off to the side.

Four men played, oblivious to the chaos that surrounded them. One wore a shit-eating grin and leaned forward to drop something onto the pot in the center. Light danced over the harsh angles of his face, illuminating the thin scar that ran from temple to chin and the sprinkle of white in his dark goatee.

The man to his left threw in his cards, then sat back and put his hands behind his short cut blond head, revealing dark ink scrolling along his skin.

The dark-haired man to his right, tapped a finger on the cards lying face down in front of him as he sucked on a cigarette, the haze of it adding to the sinister vibe of black hair, olive skin, and dark eyes.

The big man that sat across from the first wore a pissed off frown that was obvious even with the heavy brown beard he sported.

A waitress sidled up and set a bottle at the elbow of the grinning one. Before she could take the empty away, he snagged her around the waist, and pulled her into his lap. Somehow, she managed to hold on to her tray, even as she laughed and wrapped a free arm around his neck. He said something. She shook her head but lifted her face and took his kiss. When he was done, he set her back on her feet, slapped her ass, and watched her swing away.

When he turned back to the table, he said something. Whatever it was got chuckles all around, even from the angry one, who tossed his cards in before raising his bottle for an impromptu toast. The grinning lady-killer tipped his new bottle back and his gaze landed on Havoc. The humor in his face sharpened, and he tipped his bottle in acknowledgement, before taking his drink and returning to his game.

Connection made, Havoc sat back, laid his arm along the back of the booth, and stretched his legs out under the table.

Mercy shifted next to him, pressing close.

He dropped his arms to her shoulders and curled around. He looked down when her hand hit his chest and stayed there.

"Friends of yours?" Her voice wasn't loud, didn't need to be, because the high-backed booths buffered some of the surrounding din.

"Friendly, not friends," he clarified.

Her mouth opened, then shut as her attention shifted to the woman who stopped at their table and flashed an open, friendly grin. With hair out to there, a tank that barely contained her tits, and a skirt not much longer than the apron wrapped around her skinny hips, she gathered up the mess from the other side of the table. "Hey, get you two anything?"

Mercy braced a hand against his thigh and matched the woman's friendliness. "What's good?"

The waitress gave the table a quick wipe down, then straightened. "Burger and fries are your safest bet if you don't want to spend the night regretting it." Her gaze shifted to Havoc before returning to Mercy, feminine appreciation sparking her eyes. "And, sugar, I'm sure you have better ways to spend your night."

Mercy's grin widened. "Burger it is, then."

The waitress winked and looked to Havoc. "And you, handsome?"

"Same."

"Got it, be back soon." With that she spun around and took off.

Still leaning across him, Mercy turned to him, her eyes dancing with laughter. "Never would have thought it."

He quirked an eyebrow in question.

She shifted closer, until all he could see was her. "You need a chick repellent shield, my friend."

He blinked. "Excuse me?"

"Keeping females off of you is a full-time job," she explained. "First there was Nora, then Margo, now her?" Before he could say anything, she resettled in her seat and reached for her drink.

A strange warmth crawled through his chest and caught him off guard. He shook his head, lifted his bottle to his lips and muttered, "Trouble."

"And you love it," murmured Mercy as she mimicked him.

Yeah, he fucking did. He let her have the last word as his arm tightened around her.

For a few minutes they sat in companionable silence, then under the protection of the table, her hand on his thigh tightened in warning. "Incoming."

He clocked the man making his way towards them, bottle in hand. He slid into the seat across from them as they watched. He mimicked Havoc's position, his arm along the back, his legs sprawled to the side, and his heavily ringed fingers curled around the bottle's neck. "Havoc."

"Dog."

Dog's gaze went to Mercy. "Beautiful."

Havoc wasn't surprised when Mercy stayed quiet and simply dipped her chin in greeting.

In the streaked goatee, Dog's lips twitched, but turned his

attention to Havoc. "Strange seeing you here." He lifted his chin and did a deliberate scan before adding, "Especially on your own." His hooded gaze flickered to Mercy. "No offense."

She tilted her head in silent acceptance and took another drink.

"Reaper sent me on a run to Navajo City," Havoc shared.

That piece of information got nothing more than mild interest from Dog. "That right?"

The waitress reappeared and spared Havoc from answering. "Here ya go, two burgers." She slid the plates in front of him and Mercy, then swung her head towards Dog. "How about you, sugar? You need anything?"

The bottle poised halfway to Dog's mouth paused, and he grinned around it. "Nah, babe, I'm good."

"Right, then, holler if you need something." She sashayed away and Dog's eyes stayed glued to the swing of her hips.

Mercy shifted under Havoc's arm, and he lifted it, setting her free. She nabbed a fry and started in on her hamburger. The smell of grilled meat hit his nose. To keep his stomach from kicking up an unholy racket, he picked up his burger and took a bite.

When Dog turned back around, he took another swig, and set his bottle down on the table. He turned dark, steady eyes on Havoc as his early humor faded. "How's the grumpy bastard? Still pissed?"

Knowing damn good and well Dog was talking about Reaper, Havoc arched a brow as he finished his bite. "Considering you dumped the mess with perverted preacher on his ass, he ain't smiling."

Dog rolled his lower lip through his teeth and that ever-present amusement was edged out by banked anger. "Yeah, well, better he deal with that prick than me."

Since Reaper's tolerance for bullshit was below zero, Havoc was inclined to disagree. "You sure about that?"

"Preacher's still breathing, ain't he? In fact, the slimy weasel's back in town." Dog smirked, lifted his bottle by the neck, and tilted it Havoc's way. "Reaper's a big boy, he can handle it." Dog's attention wandered beyond the booth and his face was a study of darkness and shadows when it came back to Havoc. "Heard about Crane. Nasty deal there. Reaper needs us, holler, yeah?"

At the unexpected offer, Havoc set his food back on the plate and said, "Only taking you up if you don't leave our asses hanging, man."

Dog laughed, but there was nothing funny in the sound. "No worries there. World's twisting, me and the boys figure better to hold on to those who can ride the storm than those causing it."

Havoc wondered what kind of trouble Dog and his boys had found. Any other time, he would be all about discovering that answer, but right now, Mercy's brand of trouble was about all he could handle. So, he nabbed a fry and brought the conversation back around. "You want to help?"

Dog nodded.

"I'm chasing a scent, need a trail." He popped the fry in his mouth.

Dog shifted, dropped his arm, and stole a fry. He sat back as he chewed. When he was done, he asked, "What kind and how old?"

"The kind that stinks to high heaven, and fresh."

Dog stole another fry. "Considering we've got a few of those around here, care to elaborate?'

Havoc studied the other man and said, "Any of them carrying Cartel stench?"

nineteen

Mercy chewed her stunningly delicious hamburger and studied Havoc's buddy.

Tension shot Dog from laid-back flirt to hard-eyed focus. "Cartel?" he snapped. "Thought you were done with that shit, my man?"

Havoc didn't answer but took a bite of his burger without looking away the other man.

Dog held the stare and his mouth thinned with frustrated impatience, but the silent battle of wills continued. Finally, he sighed and leaned back, a disgruntled frown on his face.

Amused by the two hard asses acting like boys determined to one up each other, Mercy hid her amusement by dragging a fry through the ketchup on her plate and popping it in her mouth. As she ate, she felt minute the two men turned their attention to her. Determined to play it cool, she took her sweet time lifting her lashes to meet Dog's speculative gaze.

"That explains it," he muttered, then he turned back to Havoc. "You sticking around?"

The ever-eloquent Havoc rumbled, "At Royale."

"Good. I'll sniff around, share what I find." Dog snagged

his bottle, pushed out of the booth, and sauntered back to his boys and cards without looking back.

Easy silence settled between her and Havoc as they finished their meal. As unobtrusively as possible, she watched Dog reclaim his seat and resume his game. She had to admit hanging with Havoc was far from boring.

When Mercy's plate held only crumbs, she settled back against Havoc's solid strength as his arm slid around her shoulders. Their waitress did a run by to gather plates and set two fresh bottles of brew on the table. After she left, Mercy commented quietly, "Didn't know Fate's Vultures ran with the Dogs of War."

"Don't always, but sometimes they're good to have at your heels." He drained his bottle, set the empty back on the table, and then snagged the new one.

"Wasn't expecting company on this trip, Havoc." She wasn't trying to be a bitch, but she was used to working alone and having company she didn't invite made her neck twitch.

"Need usable information." His position didn't change but his gaze roamed over the room as a small grin played at his lips. He looked down, his gaze steady and sure. "He's good for it."

Since Havoc had yet to steer her wrong, she said, "Hope so."

"Know so," he reassured.

She grimaced and took a sip from her bottle.

"Dog's smart," he explained. "He hasn't failed before, won't be starting now. 'Sides, with the eyes he has on the ground, we'll find our roach a hell of a lot faster."

She heaved a sigh.

His lips twitched at her obvious doubt. "It comes down to professional honor, babe. He'll come through."

Professional honor she understood because like Fate's Vultures, the Dogs of War had a reputation to uphold, and when everything rested on your reputation, you didn't shit on it. Of the many gangs that straddle the line between profit and justice, it was a known fact that if you set the Dogs of War on a scent, they would run it to the ground. They were good at what they did because professional competition was a killer.

Literally.

Although organized enforcement existed in the bigger population centers, groups like Fate's Vultures, the Dogs of War, and others, existed in the outside communities because in the midst of chaos their presence offered some semblance of order, even if it came at a price. The Vultures tended to land, more often than not, on the side of justice. They choose not to lust after power over order, unlike the Raiders and Cartels, who tore through anyone dumb enough to stand in their way.

Some groups sat between justice and greed on the good/evil scale and were all about the profit, trafficking in whatever would line their pockets—weapons, protection, food—because everything had a price. And someone was always willing to pay.

Then there was her boss, who stayed in the shadows because he was all about revenge. She might not always agree on how he went about it, but she understood it.

That hadn't always been the case, though. Like acid, the memories retraced bone deep scars, but before they could corrode her fragile peace, she turned away from the abyss with the ease of long practice.

"How'd you know he'd be here?" Because this meet of Havoc's seemed freakishly convenient.

"Didn't."

When he didn't say anything else, she leveled a hard-to-miss glare at his profile.

He caught her look and kept talking. "Took a chance he'd be here. If not him, would've picked someone else." He tipped his bottled towards the rowdy crowd. "Dog's not the only option, just the best."

Her glare eased, but not her worry. "Forget the crap about professional reputation." She waited for Havoc to meet her gaze. "Do you trust him?"

He shrugged. "To tell me where Felix is holed up? Yeah. Dog's got more of a hard-on for the Cartels than I do."

Which reminded her...

She shifted in her seat to face him, pulled her leg up until her knee rested against the booth's back, and tucked her foot under his thigh. She set her elbow on the table and propped her head on her hand. "And why is that?"

The bottle he lifted paused as watched her settle in and he sent her a considering look. "Not my story to share." Then he tilted his head back and put the bottle to his lips.

"Not asking for Dog's story." She watched his throat work. "I'm asking for yours."

Havoc lowered his bottle to the table but didn't let it go. For a moment he didn't look at her and his face remained impassive.

Patient and determined, she waited him out as tension coiled around him and seeped into her. It left a heavy pit in her stomach, and she bit her lip to keep from pushing harder. She wished she could chalk up her need to hear his story to curiosity, but she couldn't—wouldn't—lie to herself. She needed to know what made Havoc tick. Her head began to swim and when he spoke, she realized she was holding her breath.

"Was married once."

The three words nailed her gut and the air trapped in her chest emerged on a hiss. In her lap, hidden under the table, her hand curled into a fist.

He stared into the bar without seeing it, giving her his profile. "Lived outside of Navajo City with Sienna. We grew up together. Always knew we'd be together. Made it official at eighteen. Lived with her parents because she was their only child. Didn't like leaving her alone since I worked on the dam. Living with them eased my mind, especially once she got pregnant."

This second hit carried a wealth of emotion and caused Mercy's heart to hurt, but she kept her mouth shut and listened, determined to give him a safe ear.

"She was a weaver. Made beautiful shit. Learned from her ma." Havoc stopped, his expression stark, and his jaw flexed.

Dread nipped at Mercy because it was clear this tale wouldn't end well. She laid her hand on his thigh. It wasn't much by way of comfort, but it was all she could offer.

Surprisingly, his hand covered hers and held on. "On the border things were heating up. We heard about it, just thought we were too far north to worry. Still, her dad kept a shotgun at hand, and Istaqa would send out riders to check. Not just on us, on all the outlying families."

A dark and brutal emotion swept over his face and left harsh angles in its wake. His hand gripped hers until her bones ached, but she didn't complain. "Cartel scouts hit our spread and three others. Left nothing but ashes and blood behind."

She didn't need anything beyond his sparse and blunt retelling to know it barely skimmed the surface of his scars. She'd seen enough horror in her life to fill in the blanks of the nightmares that tore through the protective heart of the man next to her. Unable to do anything but bear silent witness to his internal battle, she held back her unexpected tears knowing they wouldn't be appreciated.

His voice was as barren as the desert, the pressure on her hand relentless, and her fingers turned numb. "Came home, found them. Buried them. Then headed south. Spent the next few years earning a new name.

El Verdugo.

The name the idiots who jumped them used. It was

Spanish for 'The Butcher' and witnessing the ruthless aura that emanated from Havoc as he stalked through his memories, she knew it was a well-earned moniker. His profile turned dark, and she realized it was time to drag him back to now before he slipped too deep into the treacherous past.

She cleared her throat and eased empathy's stranglehold on her throat. "Works for me."

He shot her a look.

Reading it, she explained, "On why you're jonesing to help me with Felix."

"Glad you approve." The lingering chill in his voice indicated he didn't give a damn if she did or not. He eased grip on her hand.

Knowing they weren't out of the past's reach yet, she decided to guide him out by returning the honor he gave her. Some truths she couldn't share because they weren't just hers, but others...

"In the early years leading up to the Border Wars, Momma worked at Red Lacey's." She wove her fingers through his and took him along the streets of her history. "She caught the eye of an Artiza lieutenant. Became his favorite, actually."

The thigh muscles under hand turned rock hard and she knew she had his attention. She kept her attention on her bottle, turning it slowly against the table. "The Artiza's and the Suárez's were at each other's throats." Not an unusual situation since the two families might both belong to the Cartel, but they hated each other with a passion. "Who the hell knows what sparked the feud that time, but it was vicious and bloody. When they weren't focused on keeping others from taking Lost Angels, they sharpened their blades on each other."

She knew he was listening, could feel it in his stillness, but she couldn't look at him. This story hurt to tell and only one other had heard it, years ago. Havoc would be the second, and she wouldn't admit, not even in her secret heart, why she chose him. There was only so much a girl like her could take.

She swallowed. "Considering who he was and what he did, Alonzo wasn't so bad. He treated Momma well, giving her pretty things, making her feel special, never raised a hand to her. Even managed to tolerate me. He eventually moved us out to a small apartment, still in neutral territory but closer to the Artiza's hood. We'd been living there for close to a month and Momma was over the moon, thinking it meant more than it did." She shrugged. "Not like he did anything to dull her hope, just kept doing what he always did, making her happy."

And for the first time in her young life, she got to see her momma happy, really happy. It was a memory she cherished when life got dark because life always got dark.

"I came home one night and found the door had been kicked open. The neighbors were huddled behind their doors, because it wasn't smart to get involved in anyone else's drama." Memories filled with blood and destruction crowded close, rushing through well-worn grooves of her soul, and left her shaky. "Momma and Alonzo were in the front room where the Suárez dogs left them, their handiwork on display."

She gripped her bottle as the acidic wails of horror and grief rose to drown out the present and forced the nightmare back into its cage. "He died hard, she died harder, much harder." Strung up and gutted, Alonzo's unseeing eyes were aimed at her mom who laid below him. Her beautiful mother torn in places no human should ever be torn, then tossed aside like nothing more than trash.

Havoc's hand curled under her braid and wrapped around her neck, his hold gentle.

She sucked in a deep breath, regathered her composure, and shoved her childhood horrors back under the rug. She lifted her bottle and chased away the lingering pain with a long drink. When she set the bottle down, she finally met his gaze. "So yeah, I get you."

He studied her, his expression veiled, but compassion swimming in his eyes. "Yeah, I guess you do."

She forced a small smile to get them both beyond the past. "Guessing your stint in the Border Wars is where you hooked up with the other Vultures?"

Her detour worked.

He let her go, reclaimed his bottle for a long drink, and then set it down. "With Reaper, yeah." The edge in his voice smoothed out to his normal rumble. "Found Vex and Ruin a couple years later."

She hid her wince at her obvious mistake. Vex had to be close to her age, which meant she would've been just hitting the double-digit age range during that time.

"Story for later." Because now that she wasn't worried about leaving Havoc on his own, two and a half home-brews strained the limits of her bladder. "Right now, I need to hit the bathroom."

Havoc paused with his bottle halfway to his mouth and shook his head. "Light weight." He set it back on the table, slid out of the booth, and stayed close.

She used a palm against his chest for balance as she exited. Her head spun a bit with the change in position, but once on her feet, she patted his chest. "Don't go anywhere, don't fancy walking all the way back to town."

He caught her wrist before she could move away, leaned down, and brushed his lips against her ear. "You get back, it's my turn for questions."

She angled her head and pressed her lips to his heated skin, feeling the rasp of his stubble. "If you're lucky, I might answer."

His head shifted back just enough so he could stare into her eyes. Finally, he let her go.

She made her way through the bar and aimed for the short hall off the back. While she and Havoc ate, the patrons inside had multiplied, and she was careful to keep a low profiled as she slipped around tables and bodies.

The chances of the bounty hitting this far north were slim, but feasible. She kept her eyes sharp in case Felix decided to drop in, but since the lighting inside was crap, he wouldn't be easy to spot. Despite her caution, she took a few body bumps that thankfully didn't cause any trouble, as she hit the bathrooms.

She used her shoulder to push open the W branded door, only to hit resistance. A muffled curse sounded, and she backed off. The door was yanked open, and a pair of brunettes emerged. She stood to the side to let them pass but they still gave her the evil eye.

Once their asses flounced away, Mercy slipped inside, grateful to find the place empty. She didn't waste time making use of the facilities. Finished, she stood at the stained sink and washed her hands. When she couldn't find anything to dry them with, she wiped them on her pants. On the second brush she realized there was something in her pocket.

Frowning, she made sure her hands were as dry as she could get them before she reached in and encountered a crumpled piece of paper. Her pulse leapt, then steadied.

She pulled it out and kept it in her palm as she did another scan of the small bathroom to make sure it was empty. Then, she went to the door and leaned against it, not wanting anyone to walk in. She smoothed out the note.

To anyone else the chicken scratch would be indecipherable, but she scanned the familiar code and mentally translated.

Tomorrow. Noon. J and Tenth. Solo.

Math's timing as always was for shit, never mind his demand for a one-on-one meet. She balled the message, stepped to the nearest toilet, dropped it in, and flushed, watching it circle and disappear. Her boss, Mathis, or as he preferred to be called, Math, had made better time than she expected.

Frustration roiled. She gripped the edges of the sink and stared unseeingly in the chipped bowl. After the intense sharing session with Havoc and what brought her north, she wasn't ready for this meet, not yet. She needed to confirm Felix's whereabouts at the very least. Something she wasn't sure even Dog could do in a matter of hours. Then she had to figure out how to explain Havoc's involvement to Math. Plus, there was the teeny tiny problem of ditching Havoc.

Her mind ran through her limited options. Math would be livid when he found out about Havoc. Not just because she was working with someone, but that she was working with a Vulture. She had no idea what his problem was with Fate's Vultures, but he made it clear there was one.

She lifted her head and stared at the warped reflection in the cracked surface.

This wasn't good.

Her loyalty to Math was rock solid, but she knew, to the bottom of her soul, that the alliance being pieced together between the Vultures, Lilith, and the Free People, was exactly what she and Math needed to succeed with their own plans.

Convincing Math, who trusted no one, of the same, would be nigh to impossible. He had good reasons, but she wished he wasn't such a bullheaded idiot. You didn't have to let someone walk in your soul to trust them to fight at your side. If she could find a way to convince Math, then she could share information with Havoc, and by extension, the others.

She was very aware of what would happen when she and Havoc got back to the Royale. They would be alone and there was no way she could keep her hands off of him. Hell, she didn't want to, truth be known. It was reckless, it was stupid, but for once in her damn life she wanted something just for her. And that something was Havoc.

The road she traveled was more oft than not, cold, and dark, and choosing to be with Havoc, was playing with molten fire. Every time he stepped up, he colored her world with that same burning intensity, and she wasn't ready to go back to the shadows.

Maybe she was tired of being alone. Maybe it was knowing the future was shaky as shit. Maybe it was because the man managed to get in where most feared to tread, and she kind of liked having him there.

Honestly, it was all of that and more. The more being the feeling if she dug deep enough, she could unearth something in him she never had before, never really considered she needed, something perilously close to love.

It was the same thing she'd never, except in the loneliest hours of night, admit she envied when others found it. A partner, someone who'd treat her as an equal, maybe even cherish her at the same time?

She wasn't looking for a lifelong shield—those were fairytales. Her momma had a man she thought was her knight in shining armor. When he got his throat slit, she decided to find a new knight. But knights didn't exist anymore, and Momma never learned that, not until it was too damn late.

As for Mercy, she carried her own sword and kept the dragons at bay. It was hard work, but she never had to worry about finding her blade in her back or being left out for the dragons to eat. Still, there were times when it would be nice to have another blade at her side, to help drive a point home. Especially since, at the rate things were going, her life expectancy didn't stretch too far. Not that she ever thought it would, because the life she chose was brutal and short. So long as she managed to get her revenge before her last breath, she'd die at peace.

But before that final moment found her, she wanted a chance to walk beside Havoc. The hunger for that was strong enough to knot her stomach and she closed her eyes. Taking him to bed was basically asking for heartache to come on in and set up shop. He'd demand she share. He'd demand full disclosure.

Which meant if—*when*, she corrected—his need for the whole story came up against her need to keep to secrets, whatever they shared would fly apart at the seams in a catastrophic mess. He'd walk away (more like storm away) thinking the worst and leaving her heart sore. So, the question she had to answer—was it worth the eventual pain to play with his fire?

Math would be pissed.

She met her eyes in the cracked mirror and admitted, this once, she didn't care.

Havoc would be leagues beyond pissed.

She winced and rubbed the ache in her chest.

Probably, but it wasn't like his heart was involved, so he'd get over it. Eventually.

You wouldn't.

Nope she wouldn't, but it wasn't like her future was all that shiny anyway.

Her mind and heart clashed as she stood in a dingy bar bathroom, but in the end, her scarred, lonely heart won.

Life was too short to waste.

Time to test her balance on the loyalty line.

She made her way out of the bathroom and walked straight into the waiting fire.

twenty

Havoc decided they needed privacy for his questions and didn't give Mercy a chance to reclaim her seat when she got back from the bathroom. Instead, he caught her hand, and dragged her through the noisy bar.

Once outside, she didn't pull away, but waited until they were next to his bike to ask, "Thought you had questions?"

"I do." He pulled her around until she stood in front of him, put his hands on her hips, and tugged her close. She curved into him, and he bent his head, buried his face in her neck and took her scent deep as need warred with guilt.

He had a plan on how to get his answers and even though it was a dickish one, he was going to go through with it. He drew his tongue along her neck and ended his touch with a soft bite under her jaw. "Going to ask somewhere I can be sure I get answers."

Her hands curled in his shirt as she arched her neck, giving him more access. "You going to use underhanded techniques to get me to talk?"

He lifted his head and stared into her flushed face, taking

in the lust that added a slumberous cast to her eyes. "Yeah I am."

Based off the sexy, knowing glint that stared back, Mercy knew exactly what he was doing. But instead of pushing him away, her hands stroked over his chest.

Maybe his plan wasn't such a bad idea after all. "That work for you?"

Her answer was to bunch her hands in his shirt, rise on tiptoe and give him a hard, fast kiss followed by a wicked smile that left him off balance. She slowly untangled her hands from his shirt, stepped back, turned, and headed to his bike.

He followed, mounted up, and then waited until she was settled behind him before kicking it to life. When she pressed tight against his back, her hands dove low, and her fingers played teasingly close to the hardest part of him, he stifled a groan.

It was going to be a long ass ride back.

HAVOC PULLED his bike into the still-empty spot next to Mercy bike in the Royale's lot, waited for her to jump down to shut it off. They started the short trek to the Royale side by side, and he couldn't shake the uneasy feeling that crawled over his skin with each step. Salt Lake might be a quiet town, but predators still lurked in the shadows. At his side, Mercy's earlier ease was replaced by a rising tension. When she did a second surreptitious scan of their surroundings, he knew his neck wasn't the only one itching.

He pitched his voice low. "See anything?"

She did a slow head-shake that didn't do jack to soothe his whispering paranoia.

As they aimed for the door, he kept between her and the

shrouded street. He hit the buzzer, heard the click, and pulled the door open, letting her slip in first. He stepped into the doorway, did one more scan and got nothing.

They made it to their room without incident. He shut the door behind them and only then did the feeling of being watched disappear.

Mercy sat on the edge of the bed and began taking off her boots. "Someone's got eyes on us."

"No doubt."

Her hands stilled and she tilted her head to peer up at him. "You expected this?"

"You didn't?"

She went back to taking off her boot and muttered, "He moved fast."

He stared down at her bent head and his earlier paranoia circled closer. "Who?"

"Felix." She tossed one boot aside, slid him a look, then started on the second one. "Who else would it be?"

A crafty mind peeked around the sensually hungry woman, and he knew something was up. He waited until she dropped the second boot before moving in front of her and trapping her between him and the bed. "Don't know, but thinking you do."

She straightened at his unexpected move. Her hands pressed against his thighs as if to hold him back, and her head fell back as she frowned up at him. "What the hell, Havoc?"

A rush of lust hit as he stared into her flushed face positioned at a very interesting level. He breathed through it, and carefully pulled the tie from her braid. He began unraveling her hair, using the motion to soothe the ragged edges of hunger beating against him. When it was free, he ran his hands though the silky strands until no tangles remained. Instead of easing, the hunger turned and sank its edgy teeth in deep. He forced his touch to stay soft and his voice gentle as he put his interrogation plan into action. "Your turn for answers, babe."

She melted into his touch, her eyes closing, and dropped her forehead to his stomach with a soft groan. Her hands unconsciously kneaded his thigh muscles in a tacit agreement of his unorthodox inquisition. "Not fair."

"Isn't meant to be," he admitted gruffly.

He gathered her hair, tugged her head back, and bent down to catch her mouth with his. He took his time tasting her, his hands stroking over her hair to cup her jaw and angling her just so. Her mouth parted and he took what she offered with a lazy heat as he tangled his tongue with hers in a slow, seductive dance.

Her hands drifted to his hips, stroked up to his waist, and his cock tried to gain her attention by straining against the confines of his pants. To ease the pressure against his aching length, he set a knee to the bed and shifted his weight to the side, all without breaking their kiss.

She turned with him and inched higher on the bed so as not to lose his mouth. Her hands snuck under his shirt, drifted over his stomach, his ribs, and back down, leaving fire in their wake.

His groan was lost in their kiss as he rolled to his back, taking her with him. He slid one hand down her spine, the other to her hip, and down to her ass. He squeezed.

She nipped his lower lip in retaliation, then began trailing kisses over his jaw and along his neck. While her mouth stayed busy, so did her hands. They mapped his chest and brushed along his stomach to dip under the edge of his waistband. His eager dick jumped as the tips of her fingers teased the head. She undid the top button as her tongue drew intriguing patterns at the base of his throat.

He cupped the back of her head and brought her back to

his mouth. After a punishing kiss where her clever hands stopped trying to free him and curled into his waist, he used her hair to carefully pull her head back. His chest pumped as he sucked in air and tried to focus. It wasn't easy. Mercy's lips were red and swollen, her cheeks flushed, and her gaze was soft and dark. Instead of yielding to temptation and diving back in for more, he wrapped her in his arms and rolled her to her back.

Her hands flew to his shoulders and her legs shifted so his weight fell between them until his dick was cradled against her heated center. A half-gasp, half-moan escaped her as she writhed under him. The sexy sound scrambled his brain and pure needy reflex had him pressing deeper.

"Havoc." His name was a husky cry as her neck arched and her eyes fluttered close. Color washed from her neck to her face as the bend of her spine drove her tits against the thin protection of her shirt, the material stretching over distended tips.

It was too much and his grip on his libido slipped. He made quick work of her shirt and let her return the favor as he took in thin material of the no-frills bra that didn't do much for coverage. He cupped her tits, gently squeezing the curves that filled his hands, and brushed his thumbs over their distended tips.

Her lashes fluttered as another soft, needy sound escaped her lips.

God, he could get off watching her.

Just, not yet. He needed a few answers first. He forced his hands from the beauty of her chest and gripped her hips, holding her tight against him as a fast-rising tide of hunger rolled him under. He struggled to the surface and nipped her chin

Her lashes rose and he stared into a startling depth of need that stared back from gold shot emerald.

Shocked, his first question wasn't his intended. "Babe, how long?"

Her restless movements stilled as she tried to process and a frown wrinkling her brow. "How long, what?"

He didn't miss the strangely vulnerable confusion in her response and kept his voice gentle as he clarified. "How long has it been since you've been touched?"

Feminine pride shoved passion aside and the soft curves under him stiffened as her blunt nails bit into his shoulders. "Does it matter?" Her question carried a bite.

Instead of adding fuel to her temper by grinning at her pique, he settled deeper against her. "Does that feel like it matters?"

Her disgruntled gaze drifted over his face, her thoughts shuttered as her body slowly relaxed under him.

Undeterred, he repeated, "Does it?"

She bit her lower lip and shook her head.

"How long, babe?"

Her looked away and stared at her hands as they petted his shoulders and stroked down his chest. "For just me? Years."

At her hesitant answer, a claw dug furrows into his gut and sank deeper when her gaze hesitantly returned to his. He didn't want to ask what he asked next, but there was no avoiding it. "You sleep with Tavi?"

Her hands fisted against his chest and her chin lifted. "No, not Tavi."

"But others," he growled, even as he cursed himself for reacting. It wasn't like she was his to keep, nor did he have any rights over her who she chose to share her body with. The reminder did jack to ease the green-eyed beast inside him.

Her eyes narrowed, her lips thinned, and she caught his face, holding him in place as she lifted her head. "My job was to get in tight with the Cartels. Tavi was the weak link. He likes women, especially ones who can keep him guessing. I kept him guessing." She searched his face, and her voice softened. "But before that, other jobs required more."

He took the hit of her admission and let the burn move through him. He shifted and braced a hand up by her head and leaned in, the move forcing her hands from his face to his hair. "Your job sucks. Should think about a new one."

Her fingers curled and her nails rasped against his skull even as she turned her face away, but not before he caught the shadow of regret. "Like the one I've got, thanks."

Maybe she did, but it still bothered her. And seeing that eased a bit of his jealousy. "You sure about that?"

She didn't answer.

He took advantage of his position and laid a line of kisses against her jaw and down her neck. "You're working males you can't even mention without sneering." His mouth swept over her delicate curves and the combination of vanilla and spice hit his tongue. Hard as it was, he kept on track. "You've got a dick boss who won't let you talk, even if it saves your ass. Seems to me it's a shit job."

"He's not a dick." Her protest ended on a gasp because he set his teeth against her neck in gentle reprimand.

He lifted his head and angled her face to his. "He the reason you won't share?"

Her mouth tightened and a flash of temper sparked in her eyes as she tried to escape his hold.

"Think I can't see he's the reason you won't share, even though you want to?" When she remained stubbornly silent, he decided to play dirty. He stroked his hand up along her waist and ribs and took in every heated inch of softness he could on the way. He stopped just under the band holding her breasts, traced invisible lines around the material's edge, and then stroked his fingertips over her tempting curves, without really touching what he wanted. "What's he got over you?"

Her gaze locked on to his hand, need erasing temper and

her mouth softened as her lips parted to share a husky, "Nothing."

He palmed her breast, brought it to his mouth and trailed his tongue along the edge of cotton until a low whimper escaped her throat. Then he used his teeth to tug the material down over her flushed flesh so he could sweep his thumb over one turgid tip.

Her fingers tightened in his hair and her spine bowed in response.

He lifted his head. "A woman like you doesn't hold secrets for just any man."

Frustrated desire glittered in her gaze. "You don't know me."

"Hmm." He got rid of her bra and rubbed his chin over her breast, listening to her breath catch as his thick scruff rasped over her sensitized skin. "Only because you won't share, babe." Then he underscored his observation by curling his tongue around her pouting nipple.

"I can't." It was a near wail.

He pressed his lips to her tip in a barely there kiss and tried again. "Can't or won't?"

"Can't, Havoc, I can't." Wariness crept under her obvious longing, and she moved restlessly under him. "It's too dangerous."

The siren's call of her body's movements became his undoing, and he shifted his hips, riding his iron hard cock against her heated softness with a taunting, rotating grind. "For who?" he managed to grit out.

She shuddered with a low throttled groan as his aim proved true. She hooked one leg over his hip and dug her heel into his ass and planted the other against the bed as she rose to meet him.

Even with the barrier of their pants between them, it was fucking hot. His brain began to haze with a debilitating combination of hunger and need threatening his ability to remain focused on his agenda. It hurt to pull back, but he managed to get a bit of breathing room and repeated on a guttural growl, "Too dangerous for who, Mercy?"

She locked her hands on his shoulders and used her hold to lift her torso while she tried to wrap her other leg around his hip, in an effort to trap him in her silken embrace.

He put a halt to it, by wrapping his hand around her ankle, forcing her foot back to the bed, keeping those vital inches between them.

"Damn you!" Her curse was a hiss of sexual frustration that was echoed in the gold flash in her eyes and deep flush of her skin.

He stared down at the picture of decadent temptation caught under him and part of him wondered if he was crazy to continue to push. "Answer me, Mercy, or this stops."

Her body stilled and her eyes narrowed. "You wouldn't dare!"

To prove his point, he let go of her ankle, dropped his weight, and pinned her to the bed with his lower body. Then he shackled her wrists and locked them in place by her head. He held her gaze and leaned in without letting their skin touch as his hair fell around them. When he was a breath away from her, he whispered, "Wouldn't I?"

She struggled, not to get away, but to get closer. His hold meant she failed, and her wariness shifted to a quiet panic she tried to hide. "Dammit, Havoc, you're asking me to share something that isn't mine to give."

He might end up hating her depth of loyalty if it wasn't so admirable. It didn't help that he had the faint wish she'd give him the same.

A wash of emotions swept through her face, and he fought the urge to give in and make it easy on her, and him. "You have to give me something," he ground out. "Because I've watched you—with Istaqa, with me—and your balance is starting to waver."

Tangling between the sheets didn't require trust. But he wanted more than a quick fuck from the woman who managed to get under his skin and sunk deeper every day. Self-preservation was a bitch, but before she got to a level that would shred him, he needed to know where she stood when it came to him. "Fair warning, you need to make sure you land on the right side, or I'll make that decision for you."

Her brow furrowed and her "What?" was a confused whisper.

He laid it out, not hiding the edge of ice in his voice. "I need to know you aren't using me. To get to Istaqa. Or, even worse, Reaper. Too much unexplained shit is circling, and when it lands, things are going to be more fucked than they are right now. I get you're playing some long game, but I don't want to wake up tomorrow and find I'm pinned to the dirt with your knife in my back."

She jerked against his hold, hard enough to shake the bed and there was no missing the pain in her denial. "I wouldn't—"

"How do I know that?" Anger, jealousy, frustration, hunger, all gathered in a vicious storm, and he stared into her face as the erotic flush ebbed and her skin paled. He refused to let her injured expression touch him. "Even you admitted you're willing to do whatever it takes to get a job done. And, babe, in case you missed it, I am not a job."

She twisted her wrists and broke his hold.

He braced both palms beside her head on the bed.

She cupped his jaw, and her voice was soft, like she was talking down a rabid dog. "I know you're not a job, Havoc."

He blinked at her careful tone but was thrown by what he saw in her eyes. Yearning, vulnerability, a strange resolve, and something he couldn't afford to acknowledge. All of which he would've missed if he had been anywhere but where he was because she tucked it back behind her mask between one blink and the next.

She kept going. "I'm not out to screw you over. I'll give you everything I can, everything but my boss."

And with the grace of a cat, she found her balance on the razor thin line. It should've pissed him off, instead he was weirdly relieved. Still, he couldn't stop from asking, "Why would you do that?"

Her hands left his face, stroked their way over his chest, drifted down his stomach, and then dipped lower.

He didn't bother to check the instinctive thrust of his hips at her butterfly brush.

Her lips curved into a wicked smile as she did it again, then her abs contracted as she rolled up and pressed an open mouth kiss to the base of his throat. Her lips moved against his skin as she whispered, "Because."

He jerked when he felt her tongue come out to play. The she laid a path of destructive kisses in time with her teasing touches, the combination guaranteed to tip the erotic scales and shatter his control.

To ward off her seductive attack, he dipped to kiss one bare shoulder even as he stroked a hand from her waist up to capture her breast. "Because why?"

Her neck arched, her face flush with hunger and need. "Because I like the burn."

He was still processing her answer, when she shifted her hips, pressed her hands against his chest and used her weight to push him to his back. Not being a stupid man, he let her take him down. If she wanted to be on top, he was down with it, on one condition. His hands caught her hips before she could settle astride him. "I want these off."

She grinned, and got to her feet, standing above him on the bed. She started undoing her buttons and he matched her movements. They shoved their respective pants down in tandem.

He kicked his free and hers followed, but before he could enjoy the view, she dropped back to her knees and settled in. The feel of her, hot and wet, shot to his balls and his dick threatened to shatter. He held her in place as his hips rose to glide his cock through her silky heat. He did it once more before forcing his body to still.

Her head was tilted back, her hair spilling down her spine, and her tits rose and fell in a tempting wave above him.

He bent his knees up, curled his abs, and came up, forcing her to lean back against his thighs. Her lashes fluttered up and when he had her eyes, he went in for a carnal kiss. Lips, tongue, teeth, it stoked the flames into an inferno. When he lifted his head, he growled, "Time to burn, babe." He lifted her and ordered, "Position me."

She braced one hand against his shoulder and wrapped her other around his aching dick. Together they watched as she rubbed his tip along her wetness and then she held him steady so she could sink down and take him in a slow, destructive glide.

He gritted his teeth as hot silk swallowed him, holding him tight.

When she had all of him, she let go and gripped his shoulders. Then she made them both burn. Every undulation, every sigh, every groan, stoke the inferno into an incandescent wildfire.

Caught in Mercy's searing beauty, Havoc lost himself in the burn. They moved together and rode the tumultuous fury until it exploded, her cries mixing with his as it swept them both under in a breath-stealing wave. He gathered her close, rolled her to her back and took over, riding her slow and sweet as the reverberations ebbed.

WITH ONE ARM behind his head, the other curled over a boneless Mercy, Havoc laid on his back, his eyes open but aimed unseeing at the night-shrouded ceiling. Her head lay on his chest, one arm around his waist and her leg hitched over his thigh. He found he liked having her curled up against him. His hand stroked through her hair, enjoying the slide of silk through his fingers.

He managed to remember the condom for round two once their initial edge was blunted. Round three, they got creative, so protection wasn't needed. For now, the hunger that rode his ass like a demented demon was sated.

"Havoc?" His name was just above a whisper.

"Yeah?"

"Thanks." She pressed a soft kiss against his chest.

His arm tightened. "For?"

"Lighting me up." The raw emotion in her admission sank deep inside him and set off shockwaves, but she wasn't finished. "I really like your burn."

His emotional balance rocked by her confession, he managed, "Good, because I got a feeling it won't be the last time we go up in flames, babe."

She lifted her head just enough to tuck a hand under chin. Despite the gloom of the room, he could make out the softened lines of her face as she dropped the mask she wore and gave him a sweetly, vulnerable Mercy. "You sure you want that?"

Did he? Yes? Maybe?

Hell, he didn't really know. What he did know was he wanted a little more time to enjoy this woman who managed to get to him like no-one else. She swore he wasn't a job, and he wanted to believe her. He took his hand from his head so he could trace her cheek. "Yeah, Mercy, I'm sure." He got to her chin and hooked a finger under it, holding her in place, the gentleness in his voice replaced by a hard warning. "Don't fuck me over, babe, because it won't end pretty, for either of us."

She shifted up and kissed him. She did it long and sweet. When she broke away, she stared into his eyes. "I might fuck up, but I won't fuck you over, Havoc."

God, he hoped so, for both their sakes. He gave her a hard press of lips and tucked her back against his chest. "Sleep. Morning will be here soon."

She snuggled in and he closed his eyes against the cynical bastard in the darkest corner of his mind that shook his head in disgust and muttered, "Idiot."

twenty-one

Mercy woke up with Havoc's mouth on hers and his hands stroking the embers of last night's flames back to searing life. She relished the sensuous respite and let the incandescent burn cauterize her doubts. When the wildfire was finally banked, she lay in his arms, tracing random patterns on his chest as she listened to the steady beat of his heart.

Her peace was short-lived as self-preservation raised its ugly head and shredded it to pieces.

What the hell are you doing? He's going raze your world to ash.

Maybe he would, but since her current life expectancy was up for grabs, she figured better to go out in a blaze of glory than a sputtering spark. It wasn't like she ever expected someone like him to find his way to her well-guarded heart. Not that she planned on sharing that little tidbit any time soon because the minute she did, she'd find herself choking on Havoc's dust as he hauled ass.

And you don't think he'll figure it out?

She mentally rolled her eyes at her inner drama queen. She

wasn't an idiot. She understood her role in life, so long as she proved useful, people stuck around. Havoc wasn't racing to claim her, he just enjoyed fucking her. That's all this was, no matter what that tiny, stupid part of her wished.

The press of lips against the top of her head brought her out of her reality check. "You want a shower?"

She sighed and buried her face against his chest. *Time to get back to business.* "Sure." She snuck in a quick kiss, pushed off, and got out of bed. Buck ass naked she sauntered to the bathroom, adding an extra swing to her hips when she felt Havoc's attention zero in on her ass. She called over her shoulder. "Want to conserve water?"

"Works for me." His response was followed by the sounds of him getting up and his feet hitting the floor. Then he was crowding her into the bathroom.

She turned on the shower and asked a question she never thought she would as a solo operator. "What's on today's agenda?"

They bounced ideas around as both had occasions to visit Salt Lake in the past. Although they shared a couple of less savory contacts, Havoc's trips had been more recent than hers, so his information was more current. They took turns washing each other as they talked, an activity that led to much more pleasurable things. So, when Havoc proposed their first stop, she agreed, a decision that had nothing to do with the fact that he was buried balls deep in her and refusing to let her come until she gave in.

When they were ready to head out, they went downstairs and found Dog left a message with the clerk. He was busy sniffing out a possible lead on Felix and moved their meet to later in the day. With their morning now free, she and Havoc decided to do some tracking of their own, but first they hit the nearest cafe and fueled up on coffee and biscuits.

Havoc's first stop meant riding deep into the older

sections of the city and closer to the lake's edge. As they wound their way down narrow streets coiling between multistoried buildings lined with empty window frames, their glass eyes long gone, and draped in vegetation reclaiming what humans built, Mercy tried to shake off the disconcerting feeling that oozed from the bones of the past.

Not all the buildings were devoid of life. Smaller structures had been reclaimed, some as homes, some by vendors intent on trading goods and services. The upper floors of the taller buildings may be crumbling, but the lower ones had been salvaged to create a strangely warped cityscape. Humans were nothing if not resourceful and the newer version had woven itself together from the thread of the old.

Take the old mall that stretched along two blocks on the outskirts of the city proper. Although the majority of the structure survived the passing years, including the unusual bridge that connected the top levels, it had been repurposed into a two-story, open-air marketplace. Numerous businesses, both legit and not so legit, now called it home.

She followed Havoc past a wide entrance on their left with the skewed metal letters that spelled out Lark Planium. The uneven gaps between letters indicated some had been lost to history. He turned into a crumbling building that squatted across the street the roofline sporting nothing but spines of rebar. They didn't get far. An armed guard with a thick chested dog held in check by a chain, straightened from his position by a heavy rolling gate.

Havoc stopped his bike and set his feet on the ground but left his engine rumbling. "Need two, maybe three hours."

The guard gave them and their bikes a quick scan, clearly calculating the amount of trouble they brought. When he came to the obvious conclusion, he said, "Five gets you two, seven gets you three, ten gets you eyes."

Havoc dug in his pocket and flicked a credit into the air. "Eyes."

The guard snatched it out of the air with one meaty hand, pocketed it, and then waved them through.

Inside, the gutted space held a motley collection of transport. She followed Havoc past a couple of empty spots tucked between thick cement pillars and over to the back wall where the shadows hung heavy. He pulled into a narrow space next to the metal hulk of a bastardized truck that was now a hauling wagon.

She pulled up next to him, shut off her bike, and raised a brow.

"Our bikes stick out," he explained. "Less obvious back here. Plus, not sure ten will keep that jackass's vision twenty-twenty."

Silently, she agreed.

They left the garage behind and headed over to Lark's. When they stepped inside, the noise hit first, a low din of voices, with a few sharp calls mixed in. The smells followed, a cacophony of heated oil and salt with a twist of sweet. Food vendor stalls lined the rounded interior and offered those who wandered by a chance to stop and examine the offerings.

They made their way through the initial crowd that thinned as the wide walkways straightened out. Sunlight drifted down through the planks that covered gaps in the roof. Old storefronts lined either side of the passage. Some maintained the floor to ceiling glass windows that once displayed products, others had replaced those with boards and metal security bars. Those who couldn't afford permanent real estate, dotted the space between with makeshift and tinker wagons.

Although Lark's was a great starting point to finding anyone up to no good, with only a description of Felix to go on, their search was going to be a bitch. She and Havoc were going on pure assumption when it came to where Felix would go and who he would talk to, and that was never a good thing.

Mercy followed in Havoc's wake and kept her attention on their surroundings, taking note of those who paid attention to their passage.

The abundance of people meandering around didn't help. Unlike the atmosphere at the marketplace in Navajo City, where the everyday bustle was chaotic but calm, here it carried a tense undercurrent, a sense of get in, get what you need, and get out. Gazes slid away or stared openly with an avid light of calculation, and it left her gut tight.

She slid a blade into her hand, gaining comfort from its familiar weight and stayed at Havoc's back.

Ahead, a clamor of activity erupted. Havoc shouldered his way through the milling mass. Unable to see above the crowd, she stayed at his heels. The press of people eased, and she caught a glimpse of a wide area dominated by a low rising stage.

Havoc slowed and angled along the edge, his attention on something to his right. She pushed up to his side, so they walked shoulder to shoulder and clocked his dark frown. She left off with her crowd surveillance, followed the direction of his focus, and stiffened.

Fury boiled and her feet slowed. She didn't realize she had stopped until Havoc gripped her wrist and tugged. She turned and found him staring down at her, her anger reflected in the burning depths of his dark eyes.

"Keep it together," he warned in a low voice.

She sucked in a deep breath, locked her jaw, and fought for control.

On the stage a line of five young women and three men, all in their late teens, stood. Behind a podium set off to the side, stood a scarecrow masquerading as a man, and he was currently addressing the crowd. "These beautiful spirits come before you today to offer themselves to you out of love. They are here to serve you and by doing so, fulfill their divine duty to bring purity of blood to your families."

Nausea roiled in her gut as Mercy studied the children on the stage. Much like the dick at the podium, they were dressed in white, but with the sunlight pouring through the open ceiling above, their clothes turned virtually see-through. It wasn't that (okay not only that), but their expressions that bothered her. There was no fear, just sweet smiles and an innocence that would soon be lost.

She switched her attention to the asshole still spouting his delusional shit. It wasn't hard to spot the sick perversion that lay under the fanatical mask of false holiness. With his wide smile and bright eyes, he was the picture of sincerity. "Their hearts are open and willing to assist their fellow citizens, be it by helping with the land, or assisting with your house, or by serving as breeder. They understand their duty and have chosen to be here today. What will you offer for such blessings?"

Old, old demons rose, and she yanked against Havoc's hold only for him to lock her arm in place. She turned on him with a furious hiss. "What the fuck, Havoc?"

"Auction for Solamere breeders." His grip shifted and he jerked her into his side. Before she could move away, he wrapped an unyielding arm around her shoulder and forced her to turn away. He pulled her away from the crowd's edge, then shifted his arm to press his palm against the middle of her back and nudged her forward.

The sick in her gut rose to her throat as she shoved her way through the crowd. She breathed through her nose in a desperate effort to keep the contents of her stomach in place.

Solamere was home to a religious commune north of Salt Lake and considering Dog's comment yesterday, she was guessing the pervert was the twisted freak in charge,

Preacher. Somehow, he managed to convince his followers that he was the mouthpiece of God and their only path to salvation was his. Unfortunately, he was a damn good salesman because his members joined his brainwashed flock willingly.

Mercy didn't begrudge anyone their beliefs, but there was something just wrong with the inhabitants who called Solamere home. Not to mention, she had issues with a man who made a profit selling women and their potential offspring, like Preacher was with his breeders. Hiding greed behind the curtain of religion and misogyny was wrong on too many levels to count.

Unfortunately, after the rash of plagues during the Collapse, viruses remained a constant threat to humanity and those with natural immunities were highly prized. Throw in the demand from smaller communities who were always on the lookout for new blood and viola, a new market was created. Now, no one looked twice at the current practice of supplying breeders, something Preacher capitalized on, which meant auctions, like this one happened on a disgustingly regular basis.

Bids were shouted out as Preacher droned on and with each successive offer his voice got more and more smug. As they worked their way around the crowd Mercy kept her gaze averted, unable to watch as teens were sold and handed off. She wasn't the only one upset with the spectacle because tension radiated from Havoc as they finally made it to the other side and broke free.

Havoc's hand slid from between her shoulders to the base of her spine, then curled around her hip, and pulled her close.

She looked up at his strangely possessive action.

He jerked his head to the left.

She followed his silent prompt and saw a narrow green door set against dark wood, the word 'Enigma' arced above it in elegant script. Solar lanterns spilled soft light over the wood wall, revealing a beautiful raised, hand-carved scene.

Havoc took the lead, pulled the door open, and the bell tacked on the inside jangled. He held the door wide as she passed under his arm. She stopped a few feet inside and tried to figure out what they were doing in a bookstore.

Shelves covered the back and side walls and clustered along the free-standing cases scattered throughout the room. Worn cushioned seating and solid tables filled the rest of the space. In front of the back wall of shelves stretched a long wooden counter. There was enough room behind it for a couple of people to wander around. Currently, the only one back there was a man perched on a stool, who looked up from whatever he was reading to watch them approach.

Havoc stepped around her and headed to the desk.

The man behind the counter straightened and got off his stool. Taller than Havoc, but leaner, he wasn't the type Mercy would normally associate with a bookstore. His overly long hair held just enough curl to make a woman want to touch and was a mix of browns, blacks, and golds. He wore a faded t-shirt with a little boy and what looked like a cartoonish tiger on it. His expression morphed from welcoming to furious as they got closer. "Ah, hell no, Havoc. Get out!"

Havoc hit the desk and placed his hands on the top. "Calm, Dante."

Mercy stayed behind Havoc because Dante looked more like he wanted to rip Havoc's throat out than calm his ass down.

"Fuck calm." Dante mirrored Havoc and braced his hands on the desk. Light flashed off the thick silver decorating a couple of fingers and his arm muscles flexed against the leather bands wrapped at his wrists. "I just got shit back to normal after your last visit, man. No way in hell I want a repeat."

"Left Vex and Ruin behind." Havoc's voice was unperturbed. "It's just me."

The anger in Dante's expression eased so Mercy settled in next to Havoc and leaned a hip against the counter. Dante's gaze shifted to her then went back to Havoc. "Fine, since you left the twins from hell at home, what do you want?"

"Need to know if anyone's sharing stories about the Cartels."

Dante pushed off the counter and folded his arms over his chest as he frowned. "You know if I did, I'd share, man, but I haven't heard jack about those slimy bastards."

"What about any whispers about an attack on the Navajo City dam?"

Dante's face tightened, and his voice went frighteningly cold. "What kind of attack?"

"The kind that would wipe out Navajo City and compromise the water supply," Mercy supplied helpfully.

"That's whacked." Dante shook his head, rubbed his chin, and narrowed his eyes in thought. They waited and he finally said, "Don't know about an attack on the dam, but I've heard whispers that things are shaky in the putrid depths of the underworld."

Mercy fought not to roll her eyes because it was always shaky in the underworld.

"Problem is those whispers have whispers themselves," Dante continued before Havoc could ask. "Seems one of the power players isn't happy with the status quo, wants more, and is making deals with known devils to get it. No one's sure which player is making moves because the whispers can't decide."

Havoc's jaw flexed and his voice took a rough edge. "Which player's on top?"

The other man shrugged. "Varies with telling, but Lilith and Michael are head-to-head." The bell at the door rang out and Dante's attention shifted behind them, a professional smile slipping into place. "Be with you in a minute."

Mercy shifted to see a trio of teens enter. Two of the teens jerked their chins in acknowledgement, and the third didn't even bother to look up. All three started wandering the shelves, their voices low as they kept their discussion going.

Dante dropped his arms, set his palms on the counter, leaned in, and returned to their conversation. "There's another whisper, softer than the others," he added in a low voice. "About a new player, one with a vendetta but it's hard to make much out. Makes me wonder if it's not just wishful thinking on someone's part."

The air in Mercy's chest stalled and her heart gave a painful thud. *Son of a bitch!* There shouldn't be whispers, indistinct or otherwise. Not yet. It was too soon. She needed to share this with Math. Difficult though it was, she managed not hide the earthquake that rocked through her. Thankfully, neither Havoc nor Dante appeared to notice her minor freak out.

"Maybe it is," Havoc said. "Maybe it isn't, but whispers aren't going to get me what I need."

Dante rubbed the back of his neck and looked down, probably trying to hide his grimace. It didn't work. He dropped his hand and lifted his head, his face set in resigned lines. "What is it you need?"

Havoc's fingers drummed on the counter. "If I wanted to unearth a Cartel roach, which stone do I turn over first?"

"You want to make sure you catch that roach before it scurries away, so you have two options—University Hill or the Avenues. Either will probably send a bunch running for cover." With that, Dante marked the end of Havoc's Q&A by walking out from behind the counter and heading over to the teens. "Something I can help y'all find?"

twenty-two

Back at their bikes, Mercy went into a showdown with Havoc. The two locations were miles apart and she needed to convince him it was in their best interests to split up. Not only because it really was a better use of their time, but because her meet with Math was set in the Avenues. She wondered sometimes if Math had some kind of psychic ability because his tendency to be in the right place at the right time was downright uncanny. She wasn't sure how she managed, but she finally got Havoc's agreement to take University Hill and leave the warren of the Avenues to her.

She considered her next steps and straddled her bike. She was unprepared when Havoc wrapped a hand around her neck and pulled her close for a hard kiss.

When he lifted his head, he ordered, "Meet back here by three. You're late by even a minute, I'll tear apart the Avenues until I find you, got it?"

An unusual warmth bloomed in her chest and knocked her off balance. She curled a hand in his shirt and tugged, keeping his attention on her. "Same goes, babe. Watch your back."

That earned her a lip twitch as he turned away. They started up their bikes, roared out, and a couple miles east, she veered off. It was closing in on eleven when she started to weave her way through the narrow streets that made up the Avenues.

Interestingly, Salt Lake's roads had been built on a grid system, but the ravages of time and humanity had shifted parts of the grid which left her to navigate around sinkholes, rusted remains of cars, and collapsed homes. It wasn't fast, and it was far from easy.

Once upon a time, most of the neighborhood consisted of family homes and few small enclaves of livable homes still existed. Unfortunately, many residences were left to rot. There were a few bigger buildings that once were churches scattered throughout, but now their purposes were far from holy as they tended to be flophouses where addicts holed up.

It had been a while since she cruised through the Avenues, but she remembered two of those flophouses, one on the north end, and the other towards the east. Roaches tended to congregate in dark disgusting places, so those spots were up first on her list.

Deciding to start from the outside end, she used an old trailhead to bypass the interior streets. She tucked her bike in an abandoned shed that by some miracle was still standing and hoofed it to her intended target. By the time she cleared the flophouse and its tenants, it was closing in on noon.

Frustrated by the lack of coherent responses and leads, she pointed her bike to J Avenue and prayed she'd get better results after her meet with Math.

Since the streets were quiet and her obscenely loud engine drew unwanted attention, she stopped a couple blocks out and again stashed her bike in a run down, barely standing upright, vegetation encrusted shed.

She stood on the leaf-strewn sidewalk and took a moment,

unable to shake the feeling of being watched. She scanned her surroundings and tried to pinpoint the culprit but came up empty. Without the luxury of time for further investigation, she moved on and turned into one of the better maintained cluster of homes.

Trees decorated in purple, green, and yellow leaves lined the streets and stood witness to the carefully tended yards. She strolled along the cracked, but clean sidewalks, and just before J and Tenth, turned into a narrow alley between two homes. She hopped a fence into a large yard and hoped to lose whoever might be following. A couple more fences and a few gates later, she hit the overgrown and obviously abandoned basement apartment.

It didn't take her long to find the loose board on the side window and slip inside where she lost the daylight to hazy gloom. She palmed her blade and picked her way through the layer of Mother Nature's debris that carpeted the front room. She stopped at the pitted half wall that separated what, based upon the rusted tap and cracked sink, was left of the kitchen, and inched into the shadow filled hallway.

Peeling paint curled from the walls like dull earth-toned feathers and the warped wooden slats made for tricky footing. To her right an opening yawned, and a glance inside identified it as a bathroom. Just beyond it, standing opposite of each other, were two more openings. She ignored the one blocked by a crooked door speared by a tree branch and kept her attention on the murky opening to her left.

She took one cautious step, then a second, when a deeper shadow pulled away from the others and took shape. She jerked to a halt.

That shape was man sized and pissed. "What the fuck, Mercy?"

"Hello to you too, Math," she snapped, her hand tightening on her blade before she forced her grip to relax. Her temper, already riding a thin line thanks to last night's conversation with Havoc and the weight of this meeting, ignited, adding a sarcastic bite to her, "Fancy meeting you here."

"Don't be a smartass." He shifted out of the shadows but ended up creating more because at just over six foot with a set of shoulders Atlas would envy, he made the small hall downright miniscule. With long pitch-black hair, matched by an equally dark goatee and mustache, his steel blue eyes stood out against his gold touched skin. The entire picture screamed sinister bad ass.

She met his glare head on and shot back, "Don't be a dick." Greetings out of the way, she narrowed her gaze and addressed the fury tightening his face. "You need to check that anger you're wearing."

He folded his arms over his chest. "You want me to check it, then start explaining why your face is appearing on bounty notices."

That one was easy. "We can thank Felix, Suárez's lieutenant for that. Give me another day and it'll be over."

Unappeased, he growled, "Start explaining."

She kept it short and simple—how Felix killed Tavi, set her up for the fall, her run in with Havoc, the thwarted attack on the dam, the resulting meeting with Istaqa, including her take on the possible alliance, and ended with the deal she made with Suárez. She kept the personal details to herself as she drifted on her loyalty line and did her best to convince Math that teaming up with the others was a smart move.

Unfortunately, his temper went from red-hot to ice-cold as she spoke, and by the time she finished, the air between them was nearly vibrating with his rage. If she hadn't spent years dealing with his temper, she'd never dare to do what she did next. Her tone was belligerent when she snapped, "What?"

He closed in before she could blink. He was so close he forced her to crane her neck back so she could hold her glare. He leaned in and his hair drifted forward turning his expression sinister. "You hooked up with a goddamn Vulture."

It wasn't a question, but an accusation. The volatile mix of her emotions drowned out the logical voice that insisted she'd be better off taking a step back. Instead, she rose on tiptoe until they were nose to nose and drilled a finger into his hard chest. "That goddamn Vulture saved my ass, otherwise I'd be feeding the real ones somewhere between here and Page, so deal."

"Deal?" he sneered. "Are you kidding me? You partner up with the one group I told you to steer clear of after blowing a cover you spent months building and I'm supposed to deal?"

The disdain in his voice ripped along her temper and left behind a caustic edge. "Yeah, deal, Math, because the storm barreling towards us is bigger than we thought. Found out today someone's talking about our plans, not loudly, but enough to worry me. I don't know what your issue is with the Vultures. Hell, I don't want to know, because it's not my business." She held his burning gaze, her lips curled into a sneer, and her voice iced over. "What I do know is if you want to finish what we started, this is our chance to do it once and for all."

He pulled back, not much, but some. "How do you figure that?"

"We've been going at this alone, but they're teaming up. If you're smart, you'll do the same, because there is strength in numbers. Something you'd realize if you would just pull your head out of your ass. If you don't, what happened eight years ago will be a goddamn walk in the park to what he'll do to us next."

He jerked away from her and snarled, "Dammit, Mercy!" He stalked the scant few feet left in the hall and ran his hand through his hair. He hit the end of the hall, bowed his head, and locked his hands behind his neck, the dim light glinting off his silver rings.

She stood there, fists clenched, as worry and anger coursed through her, and tried to ignore the sting of frustration. She waited impatiently for him to find a path beyond his stubbornness. Not only was Math her boss, but he was also a rare friend. It would break something in her if she lost him.

Finally he turned, his face hard and unreadable. "You're walking a thin fucking line, Mercy."

She swallowed as he gave her the same warning Havoc issued. "My balance is good."

"Is it?"

"Yeah."

"It better be." He looked away and whatever worked in his head, did not penetrate his mask.

When he finally faced her, her heart seized. There was a distance, a distance she'd witnessed with others, but never with her.

He spoke and what he left unsaid landed with a brutal blow. "You share who I am, and I'll bury you."

It killed, that look and what it meant. She managed to squeeze out a harsh whisper. "Don't do this."

Unrelenting steel stared back, and his voice was empty. "You're not giving me a choice."

And there it was, his line in the sand. The blowback of his decision had the line under her feet swaying. She tried to steady it. "You always have a choice, Math."

"And you made yours." His cold, arrogant stare matched his voice and the two seared deep, freezing her from the soul out.

She closed her eyes to stem the hot pressure as the one solid relationship in her life fractured and her metaphorical foot finally slipped.

What did you expect, idiot?

She didn't bother to answer, instead, she took the wound he dealt her, and buried the damage under layer after layer of ice. Only then did she open her eyes. With no other choice, she continued forward, employee to employer. "Didn't get a name for the partner but got you a location. Warehouse District, New Seattle. Felix's initial meet was supposed to be four days from today, but chances are good he's moved it up. If I miss him here, it's your best chance to get a face."

Not expecting a response, she didn't wait but turned and left Math behind in the shadows, his unforgiving silence nipping at her heels.

twenty-three

Havoc walked out of the last building in Kingsbury Circle and dropped his sunglasses over his eyes to dull the sun's glare. It was closing in on two and he had one more location to check before he rendezvoused with Mercy at three. He spotted Dog leaning against the base of the cement wall running along the steps' side. Havoc started down the cracked steps and when he got Dog, he stopped and waited.

Dog didn't make him do it for long. "You and your woman sniffing around."

Deciding it wasn't worth it to argue the 'your woman' part, he stuck with, "That a question?"

"Nope." Dog pushed off the cement. "Walk with me?"

He fell in at Dog's side and they moved along the wide walkway.

A few steps in, Dog got to his point. "How well do you know her?"

Her being Mercy. Based on his previous experience with Dog, there was a reason to his question. Probably not one Havoc would like, but it was what it was. "Know she's working against the Cartels."

Dog's casual demeanor didn't change as he delivered his blow. "You sure about that?"

There was a note in his voice that woke the paranoid bastard in Havoc's head and knotted his gut. Both reactions pissed him off and left his voice flat. "Since I ran interference when Felix wanted her, yeah. No mistaking the bad blood between them."

They strolled past a group of tatted out teens sprawled under an old, leafy tree. A mix of Spanish and English made the rounds around as freely as the joint.

Dog wisely decided not to continue down that thorny path and switched directions. "Know you two hit Lark, then split ways."

Havoc held his tongue as he considered Dog's statement. The man was notorious for a variety of reasons and being damn good at his job was only one of them. Once out of the teens' earshot, Havoc came to a stop. "Not one for games, you know that."

Dog took a couple more steps before he stopped, pivoted on his heel, and shoved his sunglasses up into his hair. He stared at Havoc with his face carefully blank and folded his arms over his chest. "Not playing a game, my man."

"Then what's the deal? I asked you to track Felix, not her."

"Know what you asked," he shot back, "but I don't go into jobs where I don't know the players."

Havoc's temper started to rumble. "You know me."

"Yeah," Dog's jaw tightened but he didn't relent. "Know you. Don't know her."

"So you tracked us." Havoc made it clear that wasn't a question.

"Actually, was tracking Felix." Dog shook his head at whatever he read on Havoc's face and kept going. "Sent the boys out sniffing, decided to start where you did."

"Lark."

"Yeah, Lark's," Dog bit out, obviously starting to lose patience. "Which led to canvasing the Avenues—upper and lower. Was making my way north when I heard a bike, then spotted it out on the trailhead. Considering who you have me tailing, I got curious. Hung back a bit until I recognized it was headed to the flophouse at the north end. Once I got a closer look, realized it was your woman. Not keen on letting a female walk into one of those places all alone."

Just in case Dog didn't get it from looking at her, Havoc pointed out, "Mercy's a female who could handle it and then some."

"Don't matter, she's still female, brother." Never one to stand still for long, Dog shifted his weight and started rocking on his heels. "When she finished, I tailed her down, watched her stash her bike and stroll through one of them nice neighborhoods." He rolled to his toes and held the position. "Was about to let her be, when she did a disappearing act."

Christ, if Dog didn't spit it out soon, he'd be jumping like a kid with an overfilled bladder. "So, you followed." Havoc started walking, and Dog fell in with him.

"Curious behavior makes me itch," Dog shared as they walked. "She hit an abandoned apartment, disappeared inside, stayed a bit, and came back out looking like her world just got blown apart. Was about to go in and nose around when this big motherfucker came out. He's better than her, she moves quiet, but he moves like a ghost. They're both hard to follow." He muttered the last little bit, obviously bent out of shape by that fact.

Havoc rocked to a stop. The big motherfucker had to be Mercy's boss. Bitter anger surged and he wasn't sure which was worse, that she met with the ass, or that she lied to him to meet the ass. He throttled his desire to hit the road to track her down, and forced out, "Where'd he go?"

Dog's disgruntlement disappeared replaced by calculation.

"Now that's the interesting part of this. He took off and headed down into the city."

Havoc guessed. "You lost him."

Dog's mouth tightened like he just sucked a lemon. "Yeah, I lost the bastard."

Havoc eyed the other man as his thoughts twisted. Doubt raked cruel claws over the fragile skin of his trust and sent his emotions into a dark downward spiral. He tried to stay above the storm, holding tight to Mercy's voice from last night telling him he wasn't a job. But his grip slipped and the swirling doubts edging the storm sucked him in. "Know she's answering to someone."

Dog studied him with something close to concern. "Get that, brother, but I'm worried about who it is she's answering to."

So was he, but probably not for the same reasons as Dog. "Why?"

Dog wrapped a hand around his neck, turned away, and squeezed. "I've seen his face before, just can't place it." His hand dropped and he turned back to Havoc, his voice hard. "Not yet anyways. My gut's telling me he's trouble, with a big, fat capital T."

Havoc didn't doubt Dog's gut, not when his had the same issues. In fact, his was so loud it drowned out the echo of Mercy's whispered promise, *"I might fuck up, but I won't fuck you over, Havoc."* Maybe she wouldn't, but life taught him not to count on such oaths given after getting off. His voice was harsh when he demanded, "You find out, you share."

Dog flicked two fingers from his forehead in acknowledgement, turned on his heel, and headed out.

Havoc watched him go, his chest aching and his head filled with insidious whispers that couldn't eradicate the faint, lingering hope that Mercy wasn't lying to him.

Havoc brought his bike to a stop across from the entrance of Lark's and checked his watch. He was fifteen minutes early and there was no sign of Mercy. He shut his bike down, walked it back under the spreading shade of a massive tree, and settled in to wait. He used his time on the ride over to come to a decision, and that decision put the ball firmly back in Mercy's court.

It went against every instinct he had, but he couldn't get what she shared last night out of his head. Everything she said, every breathy promise, tightened the death grip hope lit in his brain. No doubt he was the world's biggest idiot, but it had been a long time since he felt that meagre light, and he wasn't quite ready to lose it.

There was no doubt Mercy knew about her mysterious meet before they split (otherwise why the push to take the Avenues?), but before he jumped down her throat, he wanted to give her a chance to come clean. Whether she'd take it was a question he couldn't answer.

He heard her before he saw her. With five minutes to spare, she rounded the corner and rolled up to him. He waited as she shut the bike down and came straight to him.

As she got close, he caught the storm that raged in her eyes. She curled on hand around his neck and twisted in his shirt with the other. His wrapped his arm around her waist and brought her in close. She used her hold to tug him down as she rose on tiptoe to kiss him.

Her taste hit his tongue and the hunger in it seared away his concerns under a wash of heat. She dropped to her heels and her tits slid against his chest, as her warmth settled against his dick.

He liked her greeting, liked it a hell of a lot. His arm tightened and forced a small gasp from her. A gasp he caught as he took over the kiss, shifting the initial burn into a darker flame. He tangled one hand in her hair and held her still so he could take what he wanted. His mental state seeped around the locked edges of his control and added an edge of punishment to his touch. Mercy sank deeper into him and didn't pull back.

A sharp dog whistle cut through his rising lust, and he tore his mouth free, barely registering the bawdy laughter that drifted by. He stared into her flushed face, the earlier turbulence in her eyes replaced by a need that shot straight to his dick. Since he couldn't bend that delectable ass over his bike and ease that ache, he locked his hunger down and concentrated on the here and now. It took every ounce of control he had to win that fight, so instead of revealing how shaky his hold was by opening his mouth, he arched a brow.

"Shit day," she muttered, reading him correctly.

Between Dog's recital of her movements and the lines around her mouth and eyes, he didn't doubt it. He just wasn't sure it was shit for the same reasons he thought. Slowly, he let her go, and she inched back, putting some much-needed space between them. He asked, "Find anything?"

Because he was watching so closely, he caught the telling shadow that flitted across her face before she dropped her gaze and shook her head.

He gritted his teeth. *She was going to fail before she hit the first hurdle.*

Unaware of his thoughts, she barreled forward. "Cleared the flophouses in the Avenues. No sign of Felix or his buddies. A few junkies shared some rumors." She grimaced. "Waste of time but chased them down. Got nothing but dead-ends." She moved back as she spoke, and he let her go. Free of his arms, she angled so they were side by side. "How about you?"

It was hard, but he tamped his rising anger down. "Heard things." He bit the words out and folded his arms so not to give into the urge to shake the truth from her. Unfortunately, his anger escaped his hold and iced his voice.

She cocked her head and narrowed her eyes, clearly catching his change in tone. "What things?"

Damn her! She was going to play this out to the bitter end. And didn't that hurt like a bitch? Done with her games, he snarled, "Why don't you tell me?"

Her head jerked, her brow furrowed, and eyes sparked, but there was a wariness slipping under her temper and confusion. "Tell you what, Havoc?"

The tentative anchors on his control broke with a nearly audible snap, and temper swept patience under like a riptide. He ripped his sunglasses off, stepped into her space, and leaned in uncomfortably close. "Who the fuck did you meet, Mercy?"

Her eyes widened, giving him a glimpse of panic, and strangely pain, before both disappeared under offended attitude. "You followed me."

He didn't relent, his voice brutally hard. "Who did you meet?"

"Don't do this." Her warning came through loud and clear despite the soft tone.

He curled his lips into a derisive sneer and raked her from head to toe with mocking disdain. "Not my choices taking us there, babe. That's all on you."

Her jaw tightened, and red replaced the pale in her face as her hands curled into tight fists at her sides.

"Who did you meet, Mercy?"

Instead of reacting like any intelligent being would in the face of his anger, she got in his face and hissed, "Who do you think?"

He exploded. "What's his name?" he roared.

The skin around her eyes flinched but her mouth went mutinous, and she took a deliberate step back.

"Right," he clipped. "Can't share your boss man's name." Her continued defiance sent the curious pain in his chest spiraling deep and spurred his anger and resentment higher. The noxious mix created a vicious demon. "Let's see if you can answer this one then. Were you planning on telling me about the meet?"

She jerked as if his question carried a physical impact and her eyes slipped to the side before she could stop it.

"Right." This time, it came out on a disgusted mutter as the tiny spark of hope he harbored sputtered out. He straightened, and ran a rough hand through his hair, shifting his gaze beyond her. Silence stepped between them and gained weight as he locked his emotions down, one by one. When he turned back to her, his voice as empty as he felt. "Everything you said last night, it was all just bullshit, then?"

Her throat worked and her eyes brightened, but she didn't answer

He choked out a bitter laugh. "That's what I thought." He shoved his glasses back in place and started to turn away.

Mercy clutched his arm, holding him in place. "I'm not fucking you over, Havoc."

He dropped his gaze to her hand, unable to look at her. "Bullshit."

Her fingers tightened and she stepped to his front, forcing him to see her since she stood in his face. "I'm not." She stared up at him, as if she could see through his glasses. "I'm just..."

When she trailed off, he snapped, "You're just what, Mercy?"

She grimaced and it was her turn to run a hand through her hair. "Trying to keep my balance—with you, with him, with all of this shit."

He hardened his heart. "Warned you about that."

Her eyes narrowed and her voice was snippy with frustration. "Yeah, you did, still I'm doing everything I can not to fall."

"Wise up, woman." He shrugged off her hold. "Your balance is for shit and you're already tumbling head over ass."

His barb found its mark and she flinched, took a step back, and wrapped her arms over her waist.

He ignored her reaction and stabbed a finger at her. "Word of advice—you better figure out how to land on your feet because right now, because no one's there to catch you."

She stilled and her face went carefully blank. "Think I don't know that?"

He blew past the sting at the brittle bite of her question and didn't temper his answer. "Honestly, I don't know what you think and I'm not sure I care anymore." He gave her his back and prowled to his bike.

Her quiet, "Fuck you, Havoc" had him turning to look back. Something painful flashed through her face before she hid it.

He refused to acknowledge it, or the pain carving through his chest. "You already did, babe, and I've got the burn marks to prove it."

"So do I." Her expression was set in a cold mask, but what raged in her eyes singed his already lacerated temper.

"Yeah? And?" he shot back, his voice rough. "What did you expect, Mercy? We fuck and suddenly I should believe you have my back?" He shook his head and got on his bike. He caught her gaze, unable to curb the ache in his gut or shake the cold grip on his chest. "Shit like that doesn't happen. And it sure as hell doesn't happen when you're too busy trying to play both ends against the middle." He ignored the pitch of his stomach as her already pale face went ghost white. "If you manage to find your balance, you know where to find me."

With that, he kicked his bike to life and rode away.

THE SUN WAS LONG GONE, and the moon had taken her position on center stage, when Havoc shoved up from the chair, he occupied for the last few hours as he stared at a door that never opened.

She crumpled at one fucking argument.

No way in hell would he continue to wait around like a whipped dog. He ignored the twisting pain hollowing his chest, grabbed his jacket, and shrugged it on. His earlier anger was now encased in ice, leaving him frozen from the inside out. Mercy hadn't returned, and his bitter disappointment crushed his earlier fragile hope.

His gaze swept through the room and snagged on Mercy's bag at the side of the bed. He waged a mental battle between hauling it downstairs to the clerk or leaving it. Unable to bring himself to touch it, he muttered, "Fuck me," before slamming out of the room.

twenty-four

Mercy reeled under the double blow of Havoc and Math's reactions. Havoc's especially left a hollow ache in her heart, almost as if it was breaking apart, but that was dumb because she wasn't stupid enough to have given the silly organ to him.

Right?

She ignored the telling silence that answered.

Havoc had been right on one thing, she was falling, and no one was there to catch her. But that was what she expected, so why did it hurt so much?

The rumble of Havoc's pipes slowly faded, unlike the pain of his verbal blows. His hits rippled like a pebble thrown into a still pond, each one gaining strength until she couldn't catch her breath. She didn't dare move as she fought her way through each wave. Finally, the merciless grip on her chest eased and the pressure that threatened to send her to her knees relented.

The world came back into focus. The afternoon sunlight drifting through the leaves of the huge shade tree. The occasional conversation or laugh as the passing people came and went from Lark's. The ache in her fingers.

To fix the last she forced her hands to uncurl. The sting in her palms indicated she would carry the marks of her nails for a bit. Not that it mattered. But unlike the ones on her heart, eventually those marks would fade.

She moved towards her bike despite the protest of her stiff muscles. She got on, kicked it to life, and turned it away from Lark and Havoc. With no set destination in mind, she rode, struggling to find her legendary balance, knowing it was all she had left.

She concentrated on the simplest of the multitude of messes facing her.

First, find Felix. Since sniffing around had done jack shit so it was time to play bait. There were areas, ones she knew if she showed her face in, word would make its way to Felix. Once he crawled out from under whatever rock he was under, she could flip the script and take his ass down. Unlike the situation in Page, she wasn't trying to stay a step ahead. She just needed to nail his ass and get a name before turning him over to Suárez, preferably alive.

If the name turned out to be who she thought it was, she could share it with both Math and Havoc and then finish what she started. While the two arrogant assholes slugged it out and argued over who had the bigger dick, she would what she should've done eight years ago and finish the job once and for fucking all.

She was done with Math. Done with Havoc. Done with the whole, "hey let's work together" bullshit, because it was a great big fucking lie. A lie she heard eight years ago, and again today. *When would she learn?*

She was obviously a glutton for punishment. Take her crazy ass belief that Math would always have her back, or that Havoc was somehow different from all the rest, that he could accept who she was—all of it—the good and the really shitty parts. Or, here was the whopper, that either one wouldn't leave her ass hanging in the proverbial wind.

Boy did she get that wrong.

Still, she meant what she said to Math, there was strength in numbers, which was why, despite his threat, she would see this through and give him and Havoc the information they needed. Even if Math never teamed up with the Vultures and company, it wouldn't hurt to have three different hunters locked on the same target. If she managed to sink her blade in first, all the better. Then she could disappear, become someone else and never have to worry about this kind of shit ever again.

It was a good dream to have, even if her chances of ending this as food for desert scavengers were high.

Decision made, she spent her afternoon trolling through the filth that lay under the thin veneer of civilization. The longer she spent on her quest, the more her surroundings matched her mood. Dark, twisted, and odious.

Even as she hunted for Felix, she kept her eyes and ears open to catch bits and pieces, each tidbit adding to the weight in her gut. Whispers of plots and bargains that made no sense, unless she matched it with what she already knew. Power was shifting, resources were being manipulated, and none of it was good. It made her suspect that what happened with the Cartels and with Istaqa's people, and even the Vultures, was only the leading edge of the disaster yet to come.

It wasn't easy, but she stayed focused on drawing Felix out because she was highly aware there was only so much she could do. She moved through each pit where flesh, the younger the better, was nothing more than a commodity, and the pursuit for the ultimate high recognized no boundaries. By the time she surfaced, she stared blindly into the setting sun and vaguely wondered if the layer of grime that stained her skin would ever disappear.

It wasn't that she didn't know this ugly underworld existed. Hell, Salt Lake's hell was levels above New Seattle's or Lost Angels', but it didn't do a thing to ease her queasy stomach or the relentless ache at her temples.

Knowing she couldn't do a damn thing to save them hurt worse. She tried for years to save others, starting with her momma, which didn't end well. Hell, she spent years after her momma died trying to pull people free from the flood of shit life kept pouring out.

Some of those jobs didn't even involve a paycheck.

Her failures were like stones tied to her ankles. Her inability to save the hollowed eyed children sold so their families could eat. Not being able to stop the lost soul who sought escape at the end of a needle. Being too late to save those she called family. Each one dragged her deeper into fetid waters.

She thought by working with Math to take down the biggest monster of them all, she would find her way to the surface. But now, after crawling through the festering nastiness, she wondered if it would be worth it in the end, because each time she slayed one monster, another rose, stronger and more vicious than the last. It was a never-ending cycle that held no apparent escape.

A far away rumble of a bike jerked her head around and hope sparked under her dismal thoughts. The rumbles faded and with it her short-lived expectation. The events from earlier rushed back in and battered at her already damaged soul.

"Your balance is for shit."

Havoc's brutal assessment echoed, and with her anger scoured to a dull ache, it was easy to admit he nailed it.

"You share who I am, and I'll bury you."

The vicious claws of Math's threat flexed deep in her heart, the sting ripped open a wave of frustration and pain. That he would walk away, after everything they survived, shattered the bonds of loyalty with a force that sent her shaky balance into a free fall.

"You better figure out how to land on your feet right now, because no one is there to catch you."

Wasn't that the truth? Yet for a moment she though one person would, say the protective brute who refused to leave her side. Then, he walked away, and an endless pit opened under feet. Now she hung there by the thinnest thread of her tarnished honor.

Honor or pride, idiot? Her inner voice did not cut her any slack. *Did you miss the part where he gave you a choice? Either find your balance and take a chance he'll catch you or be stubborn and let go. Which will it be?*

Grim determination seared through guilt and hardened her resolve. It was time for her to woman up, go after what she wanted, and damn the consequences. She knew exactly what side of the line she was on so Math could go fuck himself. As for Havoc, if he really was giving her a choice, she would pick him because it was time for her to find a little faith in the heart of the man she'd chosen.

Decision made, she moved to her bike and kicked it to life, determined to check out one last spot before she hauled her tired ass back to the Royale and hopefully, Havoc.

MERCY PULLED into a narrow alley between a tattoo parlor and a bar and left her bike under a rusted metal roof of a lean-to filled with dilapidated boxes and cobwebs. Hopefully anyone looking would assume it belonged to someone inside and leave it alone.

She seriously considered hitting the bar next door because

a drink would wash away the bitter taste in her mouth. Instead, she turned away and headed down the street, her intended destination a transportation office that served as a front for one of the larger gangs in the city.

The day's emotional roller coaster took its toll and left her distracted. Not a good thing considering where she was headed. It didn't help that the feeling of being watched returned with a vengeance as she moved down the street. As carefully as she could, she tried to locate her watcher but couldn't get a lock on them. In fact, caught up in trying to find them, someone else found her. A couple of someone's actually.

She passed another one of the narrow spaces between buildings when they hit her from behind. They dragged her backwards with a cruel grip in her hair and a meaty hand covering her mouth.

She fumbled for her blade with one hand and mentally cursed the face she hadn't kept it at the ready. She used her nails on the hand at her mouth and felt the flesh tear as a heavily accented, vicious curse erupted. She lost her footing when the hand in her hair gave another brutal jerk.

She twisted and used her fall's momentum to escape her assailant. She stumbled back and barely managed to stay on her feet. Before she could do more than suck in a breath, an agonizing blow landed low near her kidney. The sucker punch sent pain ricocheting through her nerve endings.

Responses honed by pitiless training kicked in and she locked the physical pain away. She dodged an incoming fist, barely yanking her face out of the way as it skimmed a hot, stinging line across her cheek. Gripping her blade, she twisted away and came back around to sink it deep into the gut of the one who sucker punched her. As he bent forward, he caught her wrist, but she used her other hand to grab his greasy hair.

Then, with a grunt, she pulled him forward, and shoved his bulk between her and the second attacker.

The move bought her a second, maybe two.

Fire gnawed along her side as he tried to pull out of her grip. She brought her knee up and reintroduced his balls to his throat. His hands fell away from her wrist. She yanked her blade out of his gut, twisting her wrist as she did so, ripped her hand out of his hair, and nailed a brutal kick to his fatal wound.

His guttural scream blended with more curses as he slammed back into the other man and shoved her back against the brick wall. He dropped to his knees, one hand at his groin, the other at his stomach, his furious gaze locked on her. "*Pinche puta.*"

Since he was no longer a threat, she kept her attention on his partner who stepped around him. She shifted the hold on her blade and the brush of a boot against the pavement came her left. She dared a glance and stilled.

Guess her plan worked.

"And here I thought you were looking for a meet, *chica.*" On a swagger, Felix moved deeper into the alley. His gaze went to the two men, his lips curling under his trimmed mustache as he gave the evil eye to the one on his knees. "Get up, *pendejo.*"

He didn't wait to see if his orders were followed but turned back to Mercy. He stopped just out of reach.

Since dying wasn't on her to-do list, she didn't take him up on his silent, but taunting offer. The minute she made a move, he'd gut her, which would mess with her plan.

He stood, legs braced apart, arms folded over his barrel chest, as he ran his smarmy gaze over her. "Wasn't expecting you to make this so easy."

With her temper on ice and the bruising ache of the

kidney punch shoved in a corner, she managed a cold, little smile in return. "I live to disappoint."

He matched her smile with one of his own, except his was more malicious. He spread his arms wide. "Really? Then do your worst, *avecita*."

Shock raced through her at his term for little bird. *Did he...?*

"That's right." He dropped his arms, bared his teeth and a vicious light fired in his eyes. "I know your little secret. I know exactly who you are."

She prayed he was bluffing. *Please God, let him be bluffing.*

Apparently, no one was listening upstairs because he kept talking and lightning didn't strike. "In fact, as soon as I found out, you went from being a pain in my ass and easy scapegoat to the best bargaining chip a man could ask for."

With every word he spoke her priorities changed, shifting her role from pretend bait to real bait. It sucked big time, but she really had no choice. Unfortunately, it also meant being a no show for Havoc.

A wrenching regret joined the bitter bite of anxiety, but she buried both, and kept her voice flat and unimpressed. "I wasn't thrilled with being your scapegoat, not sure I'm feeling any different about being a bargaining chip."

He shrugged his thick shoulders. "You don't matter. But the *cabron* I work with, does."

At the sneered reference to his possible partner, ruthless practicality snapped to life. Her mind spun through available options, none of them ideal, most of them piss poor, before locking onto the only one left. To get a shot at her intended target, she'd have to play along. For now.

But Felix wasn't done stroking his ego. "You know the nice thing with bargaining chips? They don't have to be in the best shape to work." He kept his beady little eyes on her. "Your choice on how this goes down."

With no back up imminent she knew that getting through the next handful of hours would test the limits of her abilities. But that realization didn't dull her desire to see this through to the bitter, probably lethal end. It also meant she couldn't appear to give in too easily.

She flashed a taunting smile and braced. "*Vete a la verga culero.*"

His amusement was swept away and replaced by vindictive satisfaction, proving her Spanish was spot on. "It's not me who's fucked, *puta.*" He barked a sharp order to his last standing sidekick, and together they closed in.

She put up a respectable fight. Even threw away her blade. But in the end, she hit the ground bruised and bleeding. She lay there, listening to Felix spit out his orders and watched the fragile dream of possible happiness hit the road without looking back. The dark promise of her future closed in with chilling familiarity.

No surprise really, but maybe she'd get a chance to fulfill one wish before she died.

She stifled her groan when she was yanked from the pavement and hefted with no care over someone's shoulder. As she hung there, ribs screaming, trying to relearn how to breathe, she managed to curl her split lip in a sly smile as Felix took her straight to her target.

twenty-five

Havoc lifted a half empty bottle of brew from the growing collection that lined his table near the bar. He returned to The Last Stand, not because he was looking for Mercy, but because he was looking to find trouble. Specifically, trouble he could get into with his fists. So far, no one was obliging. Even Dog and his boys were a no show.

Go fucking figure.

He scanned the floor and caught the speculative gaze of a long-legged brunette playing a round of pool. When she knew she had him, she gave him a slow wink and with seductive ease, leaned over the pool table to line up her shot. The short band of material that doubled as a skirt rode dangerously high, then higher when she hitched her weight to one leg and sent her stick forward into the gathered balls. The cue hit and she turned to blow him a kiss.

As tempting as it was to work his anger out in a different kind of activity, it wasn't happening tonight. He didn't want hot and soft, he wanted the hard bite of mind-numbing pain. His view was blocked when someone crossed the floor and headed his way. He shifted his alcohol smeared gaze and blinked.

What the fuck was Reaper doing here?

Dressed to menace, longish black hair pulled back from sinister features lined with an equally dark beard, the man moved through the crowd. It was only as he passed under one of the overhead lights, that his resemblance to Reaper faded. Despite his height, he didn't carry Reaper's bulk and he wore way too much silver.

What was up with that?

As the stranger got closer, Havoc's brain kicked into sluggish gear and matched Dog's earlier description of the man Mercy met to the thunderous face headed his way. Ugly suspicion crept in and Havoc's hold on his frayed temper slipped. He carefully set aside his bottle, pushed back his chair, the legs scraping across the floor with a sharp shriek, and got to his feet, his hands fisting at his side.

The stranger came to a stop in front of him, on a wave of pissed off fury that boiled the air around him. "Where the fuck is she?"

Havoc didn't pretend to misunderstand. "Figured she was with you." He raked the other man with a contemptuous sneer. "Since you like keeping her on a short fucking leash."

Havoc found the trouble he wanted when the fury surrounding Mercy's boss went ice-cold and he shot a silver lined fist at Havoc's jaw.

Havoc yanked his head back, but not fast enough to avoid the ring-lined knuckles opening a line of fire along his jaw. The sting of pain was lost under savage satisfaction as he sank his fist into the stranger's gut and then nailed a hit to his ribs. The brutal impacts earned him a grunt but did shit to slow the other man down.

Havoc caught a ringing blow to the side of his head before they crashed back into the table. The combined force of their weight cracked the wood and sent the table skittering back into the bar.

With an outlet for his rage, Havoc ignored the sound of breaking wood and sharp screams as patrons scattered and let fly. The next few minutes passed in a blur of fists, marked by the occasional dull thuds of impacted flesh and pained grunts. Havoc landed a series of solid blows, took a few in return, and then pulled up short at the deafening bark of a shotgun blast.

"Goddammit enough!"

The command echoed through the room and heavy breathing filled the resulting silence. When neither Havoc nor the other man broke their staring contest, the barkeep cocked his shotgun.

At that telling noise they turned and found the barkeeper giving them the evil eye as he shifted his shotgun to his shoulder. "You two want to kill each other, fucking take it outside." When they stood there, he barked, "Now."

Havoc straightened slowly. Mercy's boss did the same. Their chests pumped and their gazes locked. Havoc investigated the sting on his cut lip with a tongue and tasted the familiar copper of blood. He spit to the side, then growled, "Outside."

Mercy's boss gave a sharp nod, ran a set of scraped knuckles through his hair, then turned on his heel and headed for the door.

Havoc followed.

The crowd parted and did their best to get out of their way.

Mercy's boss slammed the flat of his palm against the door and shove it back on squealing hinges.

Havoc used his forearm to avoid getting his face smashed as the door rebounded. The stranger stomped down the steps and into the dirt lot. Unwilling to lose a chance at getting some answers, Havoc followed but kept a sharp eye on their audience in case someone stupid decided to join their discussion. No one dared to meet his gaze so he figured it wouldn't be a worry.

The dark-haired bastard stalked past the far edge of the building where the firelight didn't reach and stopped. He did a slow pivot, folded his arms, and waited for Havoc to join him.

When only a few feet separated them, Havoc stopped.

It didn't take long for the arrogant ass to open his mouth. "Where the hell is she, Vulture?"

In the face of the other man's obvious fury, Havoc's rioting emotions settled into an icy detachment. "My answer hasn't changed since the last time you asked."

"Fuck," the other man muttered as he spun away to stare into the night. "Thought she'd be with you."

Even though he didn't want to, Havoc couldn't ignore the niggle of concern at the man's reaction and snapped, "Why?" When he failed to answer, Havoc grabbed his shoulder and yanked him around. "Not asking again."

The man wrenched violently free of his hold, and then raked Havoc from head to toe with a scornful glare. "You're an ass."

Havoc resisted the urge to rearrange the idiot's teeth and gave him a toothy smile, his voice hard and vicious. "I'm an ass? I'm not the one that threw her to the Cartels."

The man's head snapped back, his eyes narrowed, his jaw went tight, and his face turned dark, but he didn't back down. "I didn't have to throw her, she knew the score."

Oh, Havoc had no doubt she did, but there was something more going on here, because the loyalty Mercy showed this dick was rooted deep. Like the type of deep that started at the heart level. "Did she? Because from where I'm standing, you got that woman wrapped so tight around your finger she'll die for you."

A malicious glint burned in the dark blue eyes. "Jealous?"

At the question, Havoc gritted his teeth, because if he was honest with himself, the answer to that was—probably. But he'd be damned if he would share that with this smug jackass. "Nope, more like furious."

"Right." The one word carried a heavy load of disbelief.

Havoc decided he was done. "Right," he snarled. "Furious, because some asshole is so intent on stroking his own dick and playing whatever long game he's twisted in, that he doesn't give a flying fuck about the pawns he's using."

The accusation hit its mark and those eyes narrowed into glacial slits. "She's not a pawn."

His denial fell on deaf ears and Havoc kept at him. "Could've fooled me, with the way you jerk her ass around and throw her to the wolves. If that doesn't scream pawn, I don't know what does."

With only inches between them, it wasn't hard to miss the scorn on the man's face. "You don't have a clue what you're talking about."

"Don't I?" Havoc wiped out those few inches until they stood chest to chest. "Then shine the fucking light on it for me."

The other man held his gaze and Havoc watched him battle back his temper, hoping to Christ the ass would lose. He was destined for disappointment.

"Why should I?" Mercy's boss regained control and stepped back. "It's not like you know her."

Havoc didn't hesitate to pick up the challenge. "Know she grew up hating the Cartels after watching what went down with her momma. Know she has your back, even when it's not deserved. Know she's playing a dangerous game to cover your ass, not just with the Free People, but with Suárez."

With each statement, the other man's face tightened but he continued to stare back towards the bar, giving Havoc his profile.

"And if she fails," Havoc finished, "it's not you bleeding out. It's her."

He turned just his head and met Havoc's gaze. "You think I don't know that?"

Havoc shot back, "Don't know you and don't know what the fuck you know. I only know what I see—you hiding in the shadows and her taking center stage."

A muscled jumped in the other man's jaw and he gritted out, "You trying to ride to her rescue?"

Havoc didn't bother to check his harsh bark of laughter. "The last thing she needs is rescuing."

"At least you can see that," the man muttered.

But Havoc wasn't done twisting his point deep. "Doesn't mean someone shouldn't be watching her back."

That earned a less than humorous laugh from the other man. "Right, because that goes over well with her."

After only knowing Mercy a few days, Havoc couldn't argue that. "That shouldn't stop you." *Or you,* his internal bastard sneered.

The other man's eyes flashed. "It doesn't."

Havoc ignored his self-imposed guilt. "You sure about that?" He didn't wait for a response but switched directions. "She wants me to work with you. That's not going to happen unless I know who the hell I'm working with."

The man shifted until he faced Havoc and studied him, his expression hard and unreadable. "I give it to you, you taking it back to the others?"

Curious to what this man actually understood about the overall situation, Havoc went fishing. "Going to have to be more specific than that if you want an answer."

The cynical smile was so quick it could be mistaken for a grimace. "The other Vultures, Istaqa, and Lilith."

It seemed Mercy hadn't jacked him around when she said

she planned on laying it out for her boss. "Depends on if your plan is going to mess with ours."

"If what Mercy's suspects is true, chances are damn high we're all facing the same person."

Hearing that did not ease Havoc's worry. "Start talking."

Mercy's boss obliged. "Eight years ago, Michael decided he wanted a clear playing field."

A vicious wrench hit Havoc's gut and his body locked in place.

The other man slid him a dark look. "To get that, he had to knock out the only group that could check his ass should his lust for power override his common sense. Initially, he depended on this particular group to help cement his hold on his power. They were specialists who understood that for others to live and breathe free, someone would have to get their hands dirty and keep shit buried. They took the jobs no one wanted, because they knew in the end, the results would keep the rest of the world safe. They thought his goals aligned with theirs, despite repeatedly voiced concerns to the contrary, and the decision was made by majority vote to give him their trust. Although the agreement was honored, they watched."

A fissure of foreboding crept through Havoc at a tone in the man's voice, but he held his tongue and kept listening.

"When they realized they were being played, they did what they've always done." There was a grim darkness invading the story. "They worked in the shadows, destabilizing his partnerships and dealings, all in a futile effort to rock his balance of power, but they didn't know how deep his rot had spread."

That fissure in Havoc's chest widened as the inevitable end of the tale started to come clear.

The other man kept talking, his voice empty. "When push came to shove, their group splintered, and they weren't prepared. Those deep in the bastard's pockets turned and took out the others. It was a fucking bloodbath, but a few escaped. They buried themselves so deep as to be ghosts."

When he said nothing more, Havoc gave those ghosts a name. "The Strix."

The man nodded.

Havoc stared into the night as images of Mercy blew through his brain. The way she fought in Navajo City, her exceptional knife skills, her ability to sneak by him, and how she tended to blend into any crowd. It all came together, but he still asked without really asking, "Mercy."

He got another nod, this one slower. "That long game you accused me of," the other man turned back to face him, his eyes burning with retribution, "I've been playing it for eight fucking years. So has she, not as deep, but she's been there every step of the way. The last thing I want is to watch it get screwed. So, this afternoon I cut her ass loose."

The news hit Havoc hard and left a mark. As much as he didn't want to get where this asshole was coming from, he did. If he gave into Mercy's demand to step forward it would throw a massive wrench in his game plan. And since Michael was much a rabid dog with a bone, if you wanted to steal that bone, you had to be crazy patient and fucking smart to get away without losing a hand.

Havoc wrapped a hand around the back of his neck and paced away, trying to pick his next move. Right now, the Vultures were working the crazy patient part, with an eye towards the fucking smart goal, hence the alliances. It wasn't their first choice in this mess, but it was their best.

He knew Reaper was far from happy to be working with Lilith. There was a history there, one Reaper never fully shared, but Havoc hadn't stood by his side through hell and not noticed its existence. Still, whatever Reaper's beef was with Lilith didn't outweigh the hatred he carried for Michael. In fact, while Havoc and Vex were sent to bring back Istaqa's boy and get the leader of the Free People on board, Ruin and his woman were in New Seattle trying to get evidence of Michael's involvement in Crane's murder.

However, if what Mercy's boss said was true, he'd make a strong strategic ally. Unfortunately, Havoc couldn't speak for Reaper, but he could make sure Reaper was aware of the potentially available resources.

Havoc stopped and made an offer he hoped wouldn't come back to bite him in the ass. "Can't make guarantees considering who we're up against, can only confirm we have the same goal in mind. If that's enough for you, I'll reach out to Reaper."

The other man studied him, something working behind his eyes. He finally worked his way through whatever it was and said, "Give him the name Math." A bitter humor crept under the hard expression. "If he doesn't lose his shit, have Mercy contact me."

Havoc frowned at Math's assumption that Mercy would return to Pebble Creek with him. "Not sure she'll be showing up anytime soon."

Math gave an unconcerned shrug. "She'll turn up."

"Hate to break it to you," Havoc reluctantly admitted. "But I'm pretty sure she's in the wind."

Math gave him an unreadable look. "And I have no doubt that wind will toss her ass back on your doorstep." At Havoc's disbelieving snort, Math gave him a sharper look. "You don't think so?"

Havoc raised a brow. "You do?"

At that, Math gave him a bitter smile. "Yeah, because she made it crystal fucking clear where she stood this afternoon." He turned to walk away. "And it wasn't with me."

The roar of approaching bikes ripped through the night before Havoc could respond to that unexpected revelation. Havoc and Math turned to watch five riders roll in and settle off to the side. The lead rider dismounted and scanned the crowd.

When he cut to where Havoc and Math stood, he locked on to their position and stalked towards them. As he moved, he jerked off the bandana that covered the lower half of his face and firelight played over Dog's grim features. When he got closer and took in Math, grim turned dark.

The uneasy sensation Havoc carried and buried since he left the Royale, broke free as Dog approached. When he stopped in front of them, he asked, "You two lose something?" He held his hand, palm down just under his chin. "Stands about yeh high? Wields a wicked blade, smart mouth and a tight little body?"

Havoc's mouth opened, but Math got there first. "Where is she?"

Dog eyed him dispassionately. "Gone."

Havoc blocked Math's lunge with a straight arm. "Where?"

"My man lost them in the Warren."

Havoc clenched his teeth at the news. The Warren covered the flooded remains of the old airport and its surrounding neighborhoods. It was dangerous, unstable, and a nightmare to track through. Math stilled and stopped shoving against Havoc's arm.

Havoc lowered his arm and concentrated on the more important part of Dog's answer. "Them?"

Dog gave a sharp nod. "He caught sight of two men, one hauling her, the other helping the walking dead, but was too far away to be able to stay close. He lost them near the Park. He tried to pick up their trail and got nowhere, headed back in."

Thank Christ they had a starting point. It might not be much, but it was better than nothing.

Dog held Havoc's gaze and kept talking. "Found her bike stashed by a tattoo shop near the Square. Few blocks away found signs of a struggle in an alley. From what my man saw and what I picked up from that alley, I'm thinking your woman managed to introduce one of them to her blade before they took her down."

"Bullshit." Math's growl earned Dog's attention. "To take her down, had to be more than three. She could handle three men blindfolded."

Dog rocked back on his heels and his arms went over his chest. "You calling me a liar?"

Math shrugged. "Saying it doesn't add up."

Dog's eyes narrowed. "Then you're calling me a liar."

All the air left Havoc's lungs and his body locked. If Mercy's attackers had been straight up bounty hunters or low-life street rats, she'd have no issues wiping the floor with them. For her to get caught, it had to be planned abduction, which meant a trap. And the one person who had a serious hard on for Mercy was Felix.

Before things degenerated into a brawl and he was forced to play referee, Havoc tried to reclaim the conversation. "We don't have time for this."

It didn't work.

"Fine. I am." Math got right in Dog's face and proved his logic wasn't far behind Havoc's. "Because there's no way three lazy ass Cartel fuckers took her out."

Dog grabbed the front of Math's shirt, yanked him forward, and whipped out a familiar knife. He set the edge against Math's throat. "No one calls me a liar, asswipe."

Havoc grabbed Dog's wrist, twisted, and wrenched the knife free. Then he stepped between the two, forcing Dog back a step and blocking Math's access. "Where did you get this?" He held the distinctive blade under Dog's nose.

Dog snapped, "Kicked off to the side in the ally."

Havoc twisted at the waist and showed the knife to Math. "Tell me I'm not seeing things."

Math took it, ran a thumb over the hilt and then along the notched blade. "It's hers."

A silent rant of curses ran through Havoc's head as he shoved Dog back, then stalked away on knees gone weak. He tried to get a handle on the debilitating mix of fear and fury that curdled his gut. Age old nightmares crowded close, determined to remind him of what could happen to a woman who found herself unlucky enough to be at the Cartel's non-existent mercy.

Behind him Math and Dog kept at it. He ignored them until Math's voice pulled him up short. "Havoc, this isn't the only one she carries."

He turned.

Math, his forehead furrowed, played the knife through his fingers in a mindless pattern Mercy used. He asked Dog, "Was this the only one you found?"

Dog looked between Havoc and Math before nodding.

"You're sure?" Math pressed.

"Yeah," he bit out. "I'm sure."

Math's frown deepened, and he muttered, "That doesn't make sense."

Havoc stalked back. "What?"

Dog snorted. "Not sure what good a knife will be in getting your woman back from the Cartel."

"This is one of many she carries." The knife in Math's hand stilled as he balanced it between his thumb and forefinger. He glared at Dog. "Mercy has never, and I mean, never, carried less than three blades on her." He turned to Havoc. "If they managed to get rid of one, where are the other two?"

It was slim, so heart-stoppingly slim, but Havoc held tight to the sliver of hope Math offered. "She has them."

The other man tilted his head in agreement.

"Then why in the hell wouldn't she use them?" Dog asked.

Math growled, "Because—"

"She's playing bait," Havoc cut Math off. Saying it out loud left an icy dread curling through his veins, and worse was the fear that crowded in behind it. His hands curled into fists and his vision went red. "What the fuck is she thinking?"

Even as he asked, he knew. *He fucking knew,* and the knowledge seared his soul and made him flinch. As far as Mercy was concerned not only had Math cut her loose, but for all intents and purposes, so had Havoc, both men leaving her out there without a safety net. And Mercy being Mercy, was going finish what she started—alone.

Truth blazed through his anger and worry, seizing his hear in an unforgiving grip. He had left the woman he loved swinging in the wind.

twenty-six

Mercy reconsidered the wisdom of playing bait for a psychopathic lunatic with masochistic tendencies when another savage jolt ripped through her, locking her jaw, and sending fire scouring through her bones. Especially when he had access to a damn car battery. The whip of agonizing lightning stopped, but the wave of pain continued to tear along her nerve endings.

She hung limp in a straight, ladder-back chair and breathed through the muscle twitches. The only thing that kept her upright was the thick rope coiled around her chest and anchoring her to the back of the chair. Her wrists were strapped to the armrests and, even worse, the cuffs at her ankles that kept her bare feet in a puddle of water left no room for movement.

Her head was yanked back by her hair and when she slit her eyes open, she found Felix's shit-eating grin staring back.

"How much more do you think you can take, hmm?"

A flat metallic taste coated her mouth, probably from biting her tongue. Like every time before, she didn't bother to answer, not that it was an option with her neck at that painful angle.

At her continued silence, his grin shifted to a tight-lipped sneer. "Stubborn bitch." He touched the metal contact point to her ribs and laughed as she danced under the electrical current.

Dimly she registered another voice call, "*Jefe.*"

Felix shoved her head forward and dropped the cable connected to the old battery sitting on the floor somewhere behind her. The force of his shove made the chair wobble.

A spate of Spanish broke out, but between her jittering brain and ringing ears she couldn't make it out what was being said. She worked up enough moisture in her mouth to get her sore tongue to move, then she checked her aching teeth. Between the hits and the shocks, she was surprised they were all still intact.

When her synapsis stopped misfiring, she blinked away the lingering white dots that streaked her vision and took a couple of slow blinks to get things to focus. From the ache and heat that surrounded her right eye, she figured she was now the proud owner of a stellar shiner. Thankfully, it wasn't swollen shut, so while Felix and his buddy continued their conversation, she checked out her surroundings.

The nippy air and lack of ambient light meant night had set. Light from the two standing solar lamps illuminated the water pooled at her feet. Unlike the water Felix supplied, this was a brackish, standing water clouded by minerals and grit. Which meant she had to be on the edges of the city somewhere near the Great Salt Lake.

Salt water and electricity, what a shocking combination.

She blocked out the nutty ass voice in her head and concentrated on wiggling her toes. Abused nerves attacked her feet with pins and needles, but when she managed to finally flex them without locking her arches in agony, she let out a shaky breath of relief. At least she wouldn't have to crawl when time came for her to leave.

Light and shadows danced over the water and revealed wavering lines of cracked tiles set in broken cement. *Not natural flooring then, man-made.*

Unwilling to add more aches to her already throbbing head, she was careful as she cocked her head for a better angle. The cement of the floor curved up into the walls. There was something on the walls, but she was too far away to make it out. A shadow cut through the light, then cruel fingers dug into her jaw and yanked her chin up, forcing her to meet Felix's gaze.

Her stomach lurched when instead of the expected contempt and arrogance, there was a calculated consideration. It didn't help when he said, "Seems I may have overestimated your value."

She might not be able to bitch about her current circumstances, since she only had herself to blame, but it didn't mean she couldn't act the role. "Oh goody."

His fingers tightened at her flippant remark. "Advice, *puta.*" He leaned in close, but not close enough, which proved that there was a brain in that thick skull. "Watch your mouth. I don't need it working to get what I want."

She ignored the sliver of dread ignited by his very real threat and tried to jerk her chin free. "What the hell do you want?"

With a cold smile, he made her fight for it, before he let her go. "First, payback."

Well, that didn't sound promising.

He moved behind her, grabbed the edge of the chair, tipped it back, and started dragging her out of the water.

With her weight forced against the chair's back, she let her head fall back and kept her attention on Felix. "For what?"

He didn't answer but continued to drag her until he had

her between the two lights. Then he shoved the chair forward so hard that the two front legs hit with a sharp crack.

The impact rang through her battered skull, and she grit her teeth.

He came around and crouched in front of her. "Knew when you showed up shaking your tits in Tavi's face you were going to be a pain in my ass."

While pissing him off wasn't the brightest move, she couldn't afford to back down now or it would give away her game. "Hate to break it to you, but that wasn't my goal, just a happy coincidence."

"That may be—" his eyes glittered, and he rested his hands on his knees, "—but I'm thinking your coincidence just shifted shit decidedly in my favor."

There was something in his voice that worried her, but since there was no safe response, she kept her mouth shut.

"Probably not what you expected, eh?" He chuckled. "See, at first I tried to figure out your game. Why target Tavi?" Felix didn't wait for an answer. "I'm guessing it's because he was the weak link. Now Xavier is the better target, being the oldest and all. But he would've seen through your shit, fucked you, then tossed your ass back on the street. No way would he allow you to get in as deep as you did. But Tavi—" he shook a finger in her face, "—he likes pretty, and that boy was weak. You come in, fuck him, and he's done." He made an inarticulate sound that held a wealth of meaning, none of which sounded good. "Now, he's really done."

Irritated by his smug tone, she snapped, "That's on you."

His voice hardened. "No, that's on you. You used him, stuck your nose where it didn't belong, and he got in the way."

"Is that how you plan on explaining it to Suárez?" She forced her split lips to curve. "I'm thinking he won't take kindly to you telling him you killed his son because he was in the way."

"As if that's a conversation that will ever happen." He cocked his head and his dark gaze reminded her of a crow's beady, glassy eyes. "He knows who his son's real killer is —you."

Now it was her turn to be smug. "You really think he's going to believe that?"

Felix barely batted an eyelash. "Why wouldn't he? He sent me after you, and once I have everything in place, I'll send him back your corpse and that will be that."

She pulled against her bindings to lean forward as far as she could and bared her teeth. *Time to shake Felix's delusional world.* "Hate to burst your crazy ass bubble, but you might want to reconsider reaching out to your boss. Unless you like wearing your tongue as a necktie." Needing him off balance, she laid it out. "See, I had a little chat with Suárez. He knows exactly who killed his son, since I told him, and he doesn't give a shit about me, but he sure as hell has a hard-on for you, *amigo.*"

"*Mentirosa.*" It came out on a hiss. "As if he'd believe you."

"Since we struck a deal, I'm thinking he does."

"*Lo que sea!*" Since normally the imminent threat of Suárez's displeasure would be enough to make any Cartel member flinch, his dismissive 'whatever', proved Felix was a blind idiot.

He rose to his feet, clamped his thick hands on her wrists and squeezed, keeping the pressure on as he got in her face. "You think that scares me?"

Since her answer was, *yeah, it should*, she kept her mouth shut. She did however flinch at the unrelenting pressure on her wrists. If he broke those she was screwed.

Malicious pleasure flared deep in his eyes and his lips curled with satisfaction. He doubled down on his punishing grip, but before her bones could give, she let out a soft whimper. She hated to do it, but she had to play this just right.

Pleased by her sign of weakness, he slowly released her. "Besides," he sneered. "Suárez isn't going to be around long enough to do anything to me."

She rushed the opening he gave her. "I don't get it."

When she said nothing more, he picked up the verbal bait. "What?"

She targeted his ego and started to poke her holes. "Even if you take out Suárez, what's going to guarantee the other families don't strike out in retaliation? Seems to me, between killing Tavi, trying to frame the Cartels by blowing up the dam, and now some hare-brained plot to take out Suárez, you're asking for them to gut you. No way the families will stand for this type of shit."

Temper darkened his face telling her one of her hits was a bull's-eye. "*Las otras familias*," he ground out. "Respect those who can use their power to get what they want. And I'm well on my way to getting exactly what I want."

She managed a dry chuckle despite her aching ribs and bruised stomach. "Yeah, that's where you lost me. See, I don't get how turning me over to some asshole is going to get you a shot at taking over the Suárez family."

"Well, then, let me put your curiosity out of its misery. Try to pay attention." He gave her abused cheek two deliberate sharp slaps.

She jerked her head away.

He chuckled. "See, I'm not turning you over. Told you, your role has changed." He caught her chin and forced her to hold his gaze. "Since you pissed all over my plans for the dam, plans that my partner and I spent months putting together, it's only fair that you help me trade up. Consider it penance for being a nosy ass bitch."

Her head might hurt like hell, but it still worked. She just didn't like the picture it was creating. To be certain she wasn't giving Felix too much credit where it wasn't due, she asked, "Penance?"

"Penance," he repeated in a silky voice. "You're going to bag me the bastard pulling your strings, *avecita*. The same bastard that's been a thorn in my partner's side."

She fought to keep her face blank as nausea bloomed. She swallowed hard, forcing it back. *How the hell had Felix found out about Math?* It might be a useless endeavor, but there was no other option but to play this game all the way through. "There's no one pulling my strings."

"Don't lie to me." He nailed her cheek again, this time hard enough to jerk her head to the side and force her teeth against the inside of her cheek, causing it to split. slam the inside of her cheek against her teeth, causing it to split. "You think I didn't recognize that *pinche pendejo* in Page?"

Page? Her mind scrambled before she realized he was talking about Havoc. That distinction didn't make it better, in fact, it made it much, much worse. She spit a mouthful of blood on the ground.

Felix got right in her face. "You would have never got a meet with that Indian if it hadn't been for that fucking Vulture. Since both of you screwed me, I'm going to enjoy returning the favor. I hang your ass out there, he comes swooping in. I bag two birds with one stone and my friend will owe me."

She dug deep, found a mocking laugh, and forced it to her lips. "Your plan is flawed. He doesn't give a damn about me, so your leverage. Gone."

Felix straightened to tower over her. "I don't believe you."

"Do or don't, I really don't care. Just don't be surprised when you end up looking like a dumbass in front of your partner."

"You better hope he shows, *puta*." His smile evil enough

to chill her blood. "Because pissing off Michael never ends well."

The name of the monster who wiped out her world in one brutal betrayal echoed through blood and bone. She tucked Felix's unexpected gift close as a curious mix of elation and fear washed through her. Once the initial wave broke, it left behind a numbing clarity. She didn't need Felix's low laugh to know she was doing a piss poor job of hiding her reaction. She didn't care. Fear wasn't a weakness, it was strength honed by relentless determination.

Felix was right about one thing, when Michael realized who he had in his grasp, hell didn't even scratch the surface of what she would endure. As Felix stalked away, a sobering certainty settled over her. Her time was marked, but there was one small flicker of hope in this whole shitty situation. Havoc wouldn't come. Not after what happened this afternoon.

She didn't think she'd ever be grateful for him turning away, but, right now, knowing what her future held, her gratitude went soul deep. If she was lucky (and God, she could really use some luck right now) he would be long gone, just like Math. Which meant she needed to get her shit together and prepare, because she would have one shot, and only one shot, to put an end to this.

One way or another.

twenty-seven

Havoc spent the night crawling through the flooded ruins of the Warren, too wired to feel the bite of the late spring chill. He and Math worked their way out from one side of the Park, while Dog's posse took the other side.

The Warren earned its name because way back when whoever the idiot was who designed the neighborhoods chose to pack in a shit ton of homes on top of each other with some larger buildings scattered throughout with no rhyme or reason. Now after the ravages of time and Mother Nature, Felix had a mixed bag of options to hole up in.

Although moving through the water-logged structures in the dark was the height of stupidity, neither he nor Math gave it a second thought. There had been a brief argument on where to start when they first arrived. Then Havoc snapped that Felix wouldn't waste his time torturing Mercy in a fucking bungalow. At which point Math agreed to clear the largest structures first.

Armed with solar powered torches and working in tandem, it still took time. Time Havoc wasn't sure Mercy had, and with each passing hour, his worry started to outpace his frustration as his mind conjured images that messed with his head.

Dawn was cracking the sky when Havoc met Math back on the mangled mess of what once was a street next to a faded green metal sign wearing a heavy veil of evergreen. "Anything?"

Math shook his head, grimaced, and wiped a hand against a shallow cut on his forehead. "How sure are you about Dog's intel?"

Since it was the fourth time Math had asked, Havoc didn't bother to answer. Dog had no reason to fuck him over. Besides, it wasn't like they had an alternative option at hand. What they had was a sighting by Dog's man in this godfor-saken pit of crumbling structures. A pit he would crawl through until he found where that bastard had buried Mercy.

So instead of ramming his fist into Math's face, he turned towards their next target, a two-story building surrounded by partially hidden, rundown homes under a heavy cover of trees. "We clear that, we move to the next neighborhood."

He ignored Math's bitten off curse and beat feet to the building. They skirted the decaying cement walls and found the gaping holes that once held glass. Once inside, he and Math split up.

Havoc worked his way through the bottom floor and left the questionable second level to Math. The first positive signs of Mercy's presence appeared when his light danced over a pair of familiar boots. Unfortunately, they were empty and lying at the edge of what used to be a huge ass pool.

He aimed his torch into the cement-lined pit and the narrow beam hit the dull shine of standing water and the upended legs of a rickety ass chair. But it was the corroded car battery and two solar lamps that left him cursing.

He put the light between his teeth, crouched down, and gripped the broken cement edge, ignoring the sting in his palms. He dropped inside and his feet hit with a soft splash. He went straight to the fallen chair and carefully skirted the metal tipped cables snaking through puddles. He swept his light around and the picture he put together left his gut cramped and his jaw locked tight.

"Got a body upstairs." Math's voice echoed through the cavernous space and came closer. "Looks like Mercy's work. Probably been there a few h—What the fuck?" The question came when Math's light hit the scene where Havoc stood.

There was a scramble of movement, the dull thud of boots hitting the ground, then Math was at his side. His light went over the scene and he muttered, "Goddammit."

Havoc unlocked his jaw through sheer force of will. "Dog said three men, one walking dead."

"The dead ain't walking." Math used the toe of his boot to nudge one cable into a heavy puddle. Sparks lit and a flurry of curses erupted from Math.

When he was finished, Havoc continued. "So, two men, and Mercy's not taking advantage of the new odds."

"She's either hurting—'"

"Or waiting," Havoc cut him off, unable to endure the additional weight of Math's conclusion on his worse fears.

Math turned, paced away, and came back, his voice as empty as Havoc's. "She's still alive."

Havoc's gaze lingered on Mercy's discarded boots, and he wanted to agree, but the question remained, for how much longer?

Unaware of the direction of Havoc's thoughts, Math kept speculating. "Mercy said Felix was heading to New Seattle for a meet. I'm thinking that plan has changed since he picked her up." He paused. "If he takes her to the meet, and it's who we think it will be, she's going to make a play."

That's what Havoc was afraid of. His heart squeezed. "Going to be tricky." He caught Math's look and explained.

"She needs Felix sporting a pulse to get Suárez to call off his bounty. Limits her options for taking his ass out so she can focus on his partner." Because if it was Michael and he showed his face, Mercy would do whatever it took to take him out.

Dog's signal, a sharp whistle, pierced the air and jerked their heads up. Havoc took one last sweep and prayed there was something more here for them to use. When nothing appeared, he followed Math as they jogged up the incline that would take them back up to street level.

To keep his shit tight, Havoc did his best not to think about what the scene at the pool meant, but it proved to be a fruitless endeavor. Fury rode hot and thick under his thin control, and it would only be a matter of time before it shattered.

They exited the building and found Dog straddling his bike, his face lined with exhaustion, but there was a predatory gleam in his eyes that made Havoc still. "You found her?"

Dog jerked his chin. "Caught movement heading towards the old Railway building. Hauled ass to you."

Could be Mercy and Felix, could be whatever bastard Felix was meeting. Either way, it was time to join the party. With a solid lead to follow, the heavy fist clamped around his chest loosened. "Go, we'll catch up."

Dog didn't need much more encouragement. He yanked his bandana into place and gunned his bike as Havoc and Math ran to where they stashed their bikes and got ready to ride.

twenty-eight

Mercy stumbled on bare feet behind Felix as he dragged her into another abandoned building, the sharp edges underfoot barely registering. Sheer stubbornness was the only thing that kept her moving. The soles of her feet were long past pain's reach and sliding into an alarming wooden numbness. The bastard tugged viciously on the rope leashed to her bound hands and she barely stayed upright.

She ignored the snicker from the pissant behind her and reconsidered her decision on keeping Felix alive. In fact, she was certain Suárez would find Felix's confession etched into his dead body a perfectly acceptable form of proof.

A hard shove between her shoulder blades jolted her out of her savage daydreams and sent her to her hands and knees. The impact ripped the skin of her palms and bit through her torn jeans. She didn't get a chance to regain her feet before a kick sent her sprawling on her back.

She laid there, sucking in much needed air around cracked ribs, and heard Felix's short, "Watch her."

She listened to him walk away and when the soft rasp of a match being struck was followed by the scent of tobacco, she closed her eyes, and catalogued the aching reminders of her conversation with Felix's fists and the electrifying dialog with the battery. It was a daunting list and a little part of her was seriously concerned about her odds of eventual success. However, the driving need to see Michael bleeding out at her feet was a good motivator. But if she didn't get off her ass, she'd miss out.

She opened her eyes and rolled over with a groan as her body protested any movement. Pride went by the wayside when necessity kicked in. It wasn't pretty, but she managed to crawl to a nearby pillar, dragging the rope leash behind her. A few gasps and a couple of pained grunts escaped as she folded her legs Indian style to give the soles of her feet a break, and then, to ease the tightness along her ribs, she leaned back against the pillar.

Over by the gaping hole where a front door used to exist, her half-ass guard was busy smoking a cigarette. If her feet weren't so mangled and she didn't have to stick around, she'd teach his lazy ass a lesson and make a run for it.

She studied her surroundings and realized they were in some kind of office lobby. Early morning light sifted through the varied openings, and a chill breeze carried a whiff of decay, stronger here than before, so wherever they were, they had to be closer to the lake. Closer meant the Warren.

She wondered who picked the spot for the meet—Michael or Felix. Considering this was the perfect spot for, say, an ambush, or a dumpsite for getting rid of body, she was betting on Michael. Besides, the big man would never risk meeting Felix somewhere he could be recognized. Plausible deniability and all that nonsense.

She studied the two halls that branched off to either side from the lobby and decided they probably hid stairwells. Which, if good old Mike was looking to take Felix unaware, would be where he would stash his men. It was also the most likely place that Felix, despite being an arrogant asshat, was searching right now.

There was a wall that blocked her sightline to the back, so she shifted to the side of the pillar. The wall was thick, and she wondered if it contained an elevator shaft. She looked up and winced as the move pulled at her ribs. She sucked in a shallow breath, braced, and did it again, this time angling so she could see through one of the many holes in the ceiling. She counted two, maybe three stories, so it was highly probable.

She sat back, blew out the breath she held in a whispered whimper, and did another guard check. He was puffing away near the front door and paying her no mind. *Good.* Since Felix had disappeared about five minutes ago, she wouldn't have much time before he returned so it was time to even her odds.

She slowly shifted her legs, first stretching them out, then wiggling her toes. Hot, sharp needles whipped up her legs and woke an answering ache in her abused feet. She clenched her teeth, shoved the pain aside, bent her knees, and gingerly set her feet on the ground.

Thankfully, the dipshits had bound her hands in front. She looped her arms over her knees, bent to rest her less sore check on her knees, and kept an eye on Smokey, as she forced stiff fingers to work out the thin blade hidden in the seam of her pants near her calf.

The worst thing about this particular hiding place was that thanks to her dance with electricity, she now had burns along the outside of her calf. Which was fine, except every time her pants moved, the material rasped against her raw skin. She got the blade free just as Smokey turned to look at her.

She hid the blade between her palms and held his stare with half-closed eyes, trying to figure out what was going through his tiny brain. He brought his half-smoked cigarette to his lips, stalked to the corner, and muttered to himself.

She heard the distinct sound of a zipper going down and

didn't know whether to laugh or curse. Instead, she took advantage of his inattention as he took a piss, angled the blade, and with tiny movements worked the blade's edge against the rope binding her wrists.

The razor-sharp edge made quick work of the rope, and the last strand gave way as Smokey turned around. She tensed her arms against her shins to keep the cut rope in place and through lowered lashes watched him close in. She evened her breaths and pulse, shut away the aches and pains, and shifted her grip on the blade, waiting for her moment.

Smokey crouched beside her, pulled his cigarette from his lips, and exhaled in her face. The smoke hit her, and she coughed. He grabbed her hair and yanked her head back, forcing her to meet his muddy gaze. She winced as he wrenched her neck. He leaned in and brought the glowing tip of his cigarette to hover just below her eye, so close she could feel the heat. Primitive instinct left her lashes fluttering.

His lips curved into a cruel, satisfied smile. "Not such a tough bitch now, are you?"

Well, actually...

She whipped her arm up and sank her blade into his neck. She twisted her wrist, then yanked it out.

Too late he jerked back and took a handful of her hair with him. His cigarette tumbled to the floor as his hands scrambled to cover the spurting wound. His hoarse shout echoed in her ears.

She adjusted her aim and drove the slim blade into his eye socket. His scream rang through the lobby as he fell back, ripping free of knife. Teeth bared in a silent snarl, she followed him down, switched her grip on her weapon and sliced his throat. Smokey's body did a jerky death dance as she rolled away. She got painfully to her feet, bloody blade clenched in her fist, and watched the life fade from his eyes.

"Now that was beautiful to watch."

Mercy spun around and froze when a woman stepped out of the shadows of the hall with a furious Felix at her side.

Dressed head to toe in black, including her shoulder holster, the woman wore intimidation well. The ink black of her mohawk matched the intricate designs decorating the bare sides of her skull, and her ears were lined with metal. Kohl darkened eyes of startling blue sat above angled cheeks that narrowed to a pointed chin. All in all, it was a dangerously compelling beauty that just dared you to touch.

The air of power she wore like a familiar coat, triggered a faint sense of recognition to Mercy's wary brain before it slid out of reach. "Glad to entertain. I'd be happy to provide an encore, but I'd need to borrow Felix."

"Yes, I'm sure you would." The woman moved further into the room with a fighter's grace. "Unfortunately, I'm going to have to deny you that pleasure."

Dark forms emerged from the surrounding shadows behind her, all armed with the distinctive shapes of handguns. They spread out with a telling methodical choreography. Some disappeared down the halls, while four stayed behind and took up guard positions.

Great, instead of Michael, she got the wicked witch and her flying evil monkeys.

"Too bad," Mercy murmured as she tried and failed to keep everyone's position in sight. Faced with four armed men, a pissed off Felix, and the armed mystery woman, she was outnumbered and out gunned. Instead of being scared shit-less, a strange, detached calmness descended.

"Oh, no need to apologize." The woman's smile didn't reach the chilling depth of her eyes. "I'm sure you'll prove more than useful soon."

Bitter disappointment swept through Mercy as she realized Michael wasn't coming. Two armed guards glided closer as she held her position and tightened her grip on her blade. "I hate to be the bearer of bad news, but I think you may be bound for disappointment."

The woman's gaze didn't waver, neither did her smile. "No, I don't think I will be." Her hand flicked. "Felix promised me that you'll bring me quite the unexpected gift."

With unsettling speed, two guards moved in tandem and disarmed Mercy with a merciless twist that left her fingers numb. They forced her to her aching knees and twisted her arms high behind her. That fast Mercy lost her chance to fight her way free.

She caught Felix's smirk and forced her rising panic and grinding disappointment to the back of her mind. Even though Felix's partner wasn't who she expected, she stuck with her plan to divide and conquer. To ensure she was believed, she had to start with obvious and work her way to the big reveal.

Despite her unfortunate position, she shook her head and heaved a big sigh. "Oh, honey, I don't know if you've figured it out yet, but Felix is real good at making promises he can't keep." She cut a hard look to the now red-faced Felix. "Like the promise he made to take out the dam."

Felix lunged forward, only to draw up short when one of the guards blocked him. His face washed from red to white and back. "Shut up, *puta*!"

Mercy turned her insolence from Felix to the woman. "How did that work out for you?"

Other than a slight tightening around the woman's mouth, she barely blinked. "My understanding was we have you to thank for that."

Despite the guards' hold, Mercy managed to shrug. "Maybe, maybe not, but it was only because he didn't leave me much of a choice."

Felix growled and curled his hands into fists as he glared at her. "You s—"

The woman held up an imperious hand and shut Felix down all without taking her disconcerting attention from Mercy. "Do share."

Mercy was more than happy to because it was becoming clear that the idiot was trying to do an end run around his partner. It was a hell of a risk and could easily backfire, but if Lady Luck was paying any attention at all, it might buy her time to widen the tiny fissure between Felix and his partner. "If Felix hadn't killed Suárez's son, then this—" she rolled her eyes to indicate the three of them, "—wouldn't be necessary."

Any lingering trace of pleasantness disappeared from the woman's face as it turned stone hard. She turned to Felix with chilling precision and her ice-cold question made even Mercy brace. "*You* killed Suárez's son?"

Felix fell back a step, his swarthy skin turning pasty, and his eyes widening and ran straight into the guard behind him. Felix jerked away, straightened his shoulders, and did his best to deflect, a move Mercy could've told him was pointless at this point. "She set Tavi on my ass. He started snooping around, and when he found the plans for the dam, he threatened to expose me. He left me no choice."

Bookended by her two guards, Mercy didn't have time to enjoy hearing Felix's confession. The air around the woman dropped from cold to bone-chilling. Even the lone guard by the elevator reacted and drifted further into the room.

Instincts screaming, Mercy stilled.

Felix braced.

"You fucking idiot." The woman swung her fist out, and the impact sent Felix stumbling back into one of the guards, who helpfully shoved him back towards her.

Felix lifted his head and tried to stem the blood pouring from his now crooked nose.

The furious female got in his face and spat, "What the fuck were you thinking?"

Felix flinched. When he caught his revealing movement, his cheeks flamed and his eyes went hard and bright, fury wiping out any semblance of intelligence as he unwisely defied his furious partner. "If I hadn't, he would have squealed to his father. I go down, you go down."

"So, you decide to kill his son, which guarantees Suárez's attention?"

Felix swiped his grimy hand under his nose and wiped it on his pants, then sneered, "I didn't know she'd run straight to *los putre Buitres* or warn the Free People."

Obviously done with Felix's excuses, the woman reached to her shoulder holster, pulled out a gun, and then dug into a pocket. When she brought out a silencer and calmly started screwing it in place, Felix lost his composure in a flurry of panicked Spanish.

Unfazed, she aimed and pulled the trigger.

twenty-nine

The biggest drawback to using bikes, in Havoc's opinion, was there was no quiet way to make an approach, especially early in the morning when the only things awake were birds. He trailed Dog around the lake's edge and into the flat expanse of an old parking lot. They drove right through wide openings no longer guarded by doors and stashed their bikes. As they got ready to head out on foot, Dog explained ordered his boys to hang back. Since there was no telling who or what they faced, Havoc didn't blame Dog him.

Despite the need to hurry that pushed at him, Havoc was forced to go slow as they picked their way over the unstable ground. Between the lake and underground rivers, it was a crapshoot if the seemingly solid piece of earth in front of you would hold firm or swallow you whole. The fact the area wasn't currently sitting underwater did work in their favor, so long as the weather held. If one good storm blew in, it would be a completely different story.

They crossed the remains of the Beltway and stayed north of their target as they picked their way to the old Railway building. None of them were surprised by Felix's choice of a meeting place. The squat, three-story brick structure sat in the middle of nowhere, in a lot surrounded by the pitted remains of large satellite dishes. It was a prime location if you didn't want to be seen and wanted to ensure no one could sneak up on you.

On their approach from the north, they hit a couple of ramshackle outbuildings and a dilapidated fence. Havoc wouldn't normally favor such a bold approach, but since Felix had his hands full with Mercy, and was down to one guy, their chances of arriving undetected were high. Well, so long as he was still alone.

He, Math, and Dog ducked inside a small shed just out of sight of the building to discuss their infiltration options.

Dog started. "How do you want to play this?"

What wanted to do—kick his way in, gut Felix, and drag Mercy's ass out of there—wasn't feasible, so he turned to Math. "Depends. What's important to you?"

Math's face went hard. "Fuck you, Havoc."

He ignored Math's fury. "It's a legit question. What's your end goal?"

Math's brows lifted in disbelief. "If I say Mercy, you going to let me have that?"

Fuck no. The knee jerk response settled something shaky deep inside him. "She's mine, but what I need to know is how you want this to go down so we can determine our approach. You want the mystery guest alive, we get in position, and wait. You don't care if he's breathing..." he shrugged.

Math's eyes narrowed. "You sound sure there will be a meet."

"Because I am." Before Math could press for more, Havoc gave it. "The Cartels aren't the most intelligent beings, especially when their dicks get involved. Felix and his man messed up a woman in Page, and let it slip they had to hit the road or risk missing a meet. You decide to pass on your chance at the mystery guest, that's on you. But I'm getting Mercy out."

Math's face was impassive as he studied Havoc. "And Mercy's deal with Suárez?"

Havoc shrugged. "He can make do with a corpse."

"Not sure that will pull the bounty off Mercy."

"I'll deal with that shit later."

Dog, who watched their exchange in silence, made a snort of disbelief. They both ignored him.

Math cocked his head. "You know, either way it plays out, it's a trap. She's breathing, she's bait."

"Yeah, figured that when Felix kept her alive." And right now he was grateful that Felix was a greedy asshole. "Thing is we're not sure which one of us he wants. I'm thinking better me than you. So, I'm asking—where's your head at?"

Seconds ticked by as Math considered him with an unblinking intensity. Finally, he answered, "We go in and wait."

Decision made, Havoc turned to Dog. "Need you keeping eyes out, make sure we don't get blindsided."

Dog gave him a fierce grin. "Gotcha covered, my man." Dog headed to the door.

Havoc went to follow and stopped when Math's hand clamped on his arm. Dog disappeared outside and Havoc looked at Math. "What?"

The other man faced him, something at work in his eyes, but Havoc didn't know him well enough to understand it. "Michael shows, he's mine. You just worry about getting Mercy out."

Not in the business of making promises he couldn't keep, Havoc clarified. "If she gets a shot, I'll help her take it. You go down, and there's no way I'm going to be able to hold her back." Nor would she forgive him if he tried.

Math's mouth tightened, obviously not a fan of Havoc's answer. "Fine."

Done pissing around, Havoc shook off Math's hold and headed out. "Right, let's move."

HAVOC AND MATH used a pile of rusted out machinery and rubble as a makeshift ladder and climbed in through an opening on the backside of the building. They dropped into a large room as the rising wind nipped at their heels. It slipped through the building and added a hollow echoing wail that rose and fell in a haunting wave.

Havoc grimaced. *Listening for others was going to be a bitch.*

He studied the room and noted what walls remained were covered in grey, peeling paint. A few surviving crumbling support posts held up a strange collection of shattered light fixtures and one or two ancient ceiling tiles inside a metal grid. He prayed that the pitted supports wouldn't decide to give up the ghost while they were inside. He carefully made his way towards the door that led deeper inside the structure.

He inched past metal racks and the rusted-out shelves decorated with faded graffiti that lined one side. The floor was a tricky maze as entire sections were missing. When he looked closer, he realized the missing sections didn't open to the floor below. Instead, it was as if the floor had been built a couple feet above another floor, which created a hollowed layer.

Weird.

He shook off the architectural mystery as he and Math made it to the door. Havoc cautiously peered around the edge, made sure they were alone, and then moved out into the hall. The sunlight had a tougher time penetrating this far into the interior, so it was shrouded in dim shadows. Unwilling to reveal their presence to anyone lurking nearby, Havoc used hand signals to direct Math to clear one side of the floor, while he worked the other.

Math slipped away and faded into the gloom.

On his own, Havoc ghosted through the offices lining the hall. He made quick work of clearing the top floor even though he was sure Felix wouldn't be there. Most offices didn't have functioning doors, and the ones that did, proved not to be hiding anything more dangerous than rats.

He found a set of stairs, blocked by a mound of what once was part of the ceiling above it. Since he hadn't planned on using them, he kept going until he found what he wanted, the elevators because elevators meant elevator shafts. Luckily the shaft was guarded by only one of the old doors, the other long since gone. He braced a hand against the wall because he didn't trust the strength of the remaining door and stuck his head inside to check out what he was working with.

The nose curling stench of stagnant saltwater hit and made his eyes water. No surprise there since like most buildings around here, this one had a basement, and it was flooded. Thanks to the hole in the roof, sunlight danced across the dark surface and illuminated the murky pool that lapped at the crumpled remains of the rusted-out cage of the elevator car. But what lay just above that made Havoc smile.

The shadowed opening to the first floor.

Finally, a piece of good news. He found his access to the main floor. Curious, he leaned a little further in. He ignored the wind that pulled strands of his hair free and whipped them about his face and stared down. There didn't appear to be any doors blocking the entrance, so it should be a fairly simple shot. If he could get to it.

He eyed the rickety pipes that lined the shaft and crossed them off. No way in hell could they hold his weight. The shaft was too wide to consider using his legs and arms to inch down. He crouched and guesstimated the distance between the floors.

Twelve, maybe fourteen feet?

That was a hell of a drop without knowing who or what he faced once he cleared the shaft. If anyone was there, armed or not, they'd have a clear shot at him. Hell, one good shove and he'd have a straight shot into the pit. His best bet was to stay to the side and drop below the opening so he could go in low.

He did another visual sweep of the shaft, and this time noted the shallow hollows that lined the deteriorating walls. His balls shriveled as the thought of depending on crumbling cement for finger and toe holds, but it couldn't outweigh his worry at leaving Mercy in Felix's not so tender care.

He got a solid grip on the wall's edge, sucked in a breath, and leaned out until he could reach the closest one. He slid his fingers into the narrow crevice and jerked down to test if the pressure would send a shower of cement into the watery pit below.

When the cement held, he shoved his head and shoulders inside and mapped out his climb, marking where each hand and foot would have to go as he made his way down. There were a few tricky spots, but he was confident he could make it.

He got his boots off, then his socks. There was no way the thick toe of his boots would fit in those cracks and the socks might catch at the wrong time. The howling wind from above should cover most of the noise from his descent, and if it didn't, he could only hope that no one came to investigate. He used his socks to loop his boots to his belt because he had no intentions of being barefoot when he made it to the bottom floor.

As ready as he could be, he leaned in, reached up and found his first two holds. With a deep breath he slowly swung into the shaft. He was about halfway down when the wind dropped to a soft moan, and he caught the sound of muffled voices coming from the main floor. He held his position as the seconds ticked by, but he didn't dare move without the wind's cover. As he clung to the wall, the burn in his muscles morphed into an agonizing ache.

To block the rising burn of his body's protests, he tried to concentrate on the voices, but couldn't make out the words. From the pitches, he was guessing two, maybe three, voices, but couldn't be sure.

The cement under his right toes started to drift away in a shower of dust. If he didn't move soon, his ass would splash-down into the murky pit below. With as much care as possible, he shifted his weight, and his foot slipped, the rough surface scraping away skin. Sweat rode his spine in a clammy line as he bit back his curse. His muscles screamed at the additional torque, but he managed to reposition his foot just below the crumbling niche.

He rested his clammy forehead against the rough wall as his muscles shook. He waged an internal debate on the risk of moving, and just when he was about to say the hell with it, the wind finally decided to make a comeback.

Under nature's cover, he eased down another foot or so and was prepared to make the last shift that would put him just below the door's edge, when the muffled cough of a silenced gun echoed and startled a couple of nesting birds. They tore their way out of the shaft as a bone-curdling scream chased their tail feathers.

Fuck! Mercy!

His heart froze but his body moved on instinct and scrambled the last bit, lunging for the dubious opening.

thirty

Mercy flinched at Felix's pained scream as he hit the ground and clutched at the bloody hole now perforating his thigh. *Oh, that's going to hurt.*

The guard behind Felix's rocking body held his position but his lip curled in disgust. The woman crouched and pressed the barrel to Felix's forehead. "Shut up."

Felix's pained screams gurgled to harsh gasps.

"You better start praying to your Virgin Mary that the Vulture shows up for his bitch or the next bullet ends up in your skull. *Comprende?*"

Felix managed a panicked nod.

She rose and turned away, dismissing the wounded man. As she crossed the floor, she slipped her gun back into its holster. She stopped in front of Mercy, and lowered to a crouch, wrists on her knees, hands hanging down, their eyes level. "Do you know who I am?"

Pinned by the motionless guards, Mercy held her pitiless gaze with stony deliberation. "Should I?"

The woman cocked her head. "The name Greer ring a bell?"

Terrifying fury surged through Mercy as recognition struck with poisonous fangs. *Michael's right-hand bitch*. The same one who led Michael's forces the night the Strix were killed. Mercy jerked against the unforgiving hold of her captors before she could stop.

"Ah." Cruel delight lit Greer's cold eyes as she deliberately patted Mercy's bruised cheek. "I see it does."

A guard came to a halt off to the side and drew both Mercy and Greer's attention. "Sir, everything's in place."

"Good." Greer put her hands to her knees and pushed upright. "Wrap the bitch up, and don't forget to gag her. Time to see what our bait will nab us."

Mercy's guards yanked her to her feet and the sudden movement left her vision swimming with black dots as the banked agony in her feet reignited. They quickly shifted positions, one locked her hands high and tight, the other used his grip on her hair to wrench her head back. Then he dug in in hard fingers on the pressure points on her jaw and forced her mouth to open wide enough to shove in a cloth gag.

She managed a couple of solid kicks but battered bare feet couldn't inflict damage. They slammed her back into the unforgiving pillar and the bruising impact generated a muffled groan. In seconds, she found herself gagged and bound, and not for anything remotely fun. When they stepped back, she looked up to find Greer watching the entire thing go down with a tiny superior smile. *Bitch!*

As if reading her mind, Greer's smile widened.

The guard next to her dug into his pocket and handed over a small black object. "Timer's set at thirty, press when ready."

Greer took it with a sharp nod.

Was that—oh my God, it's a detonator.

Ice filled Mercy's veins and a cold, sickening sweat broke over her skin. The crazy ass bitch had rigged the place to blow.

With a tinge of hysteria Mercy thanked all that was holy that neither Havoc nor Math was riding to her rescue, since she wasn't sure she could survive the guilt that would come with their deaths. Of course, with the way things were going, she might not have to worry about much of anything soon.

"Sir, what about this one?" The question came from the guard who stood over a softly moaning Felix and snapped Mercy out of her dismal thoughts.

Greer turned and eyed her former partner with a dispassionate coldness. "Dump his ass down the shaft."

The guard went to grab Felix only to discover that the wounded man had other ideas. In an impressive display of speed, Felix nailed the guard's balls with a wicked kick of his uninjured leg. Off balance and probably trying to relearn to breathe, the guard doubled over, which put his face in Felix's reach. Felix wrapped his thick hands around the guard's skull. The guard's shriek as Felix drove his thumbs into the guard's eye sockets made Mercy flinch.

"Shoot him!" Greer's order was drowned out by Felix's enraged roar as he twisted and used his hold on the guard's skull to flip the guard until his body was between Felix and the incoming bullets.

Mercy had to admit it was a brilliant move, especially coming from Felix. She didn't get much time to admire it because while the guard's body danced under the lead rain, her guards left her and ran to get in on the action.

She used the unexpected distraction to test her bindings when a movement at the back of the edges of the room caught her attention. As Greer and her men remained focused on Felix, Mercy turned her head. The last man she ever expected to see poofed into existence directly behind the guard at the far end. Her pulse began to pound. *Holy shit was that?*

Yep, that was Havoc.

A buoying mix of terrified joy and anxious relief turned

her muscles to the consistency of jelly. She stared as Havoc wrapped a hand around the guard's mouth, yanked his head back, and shoved a blade into the base of his skull. The guard jerked, then went limp. Havoc wasted no time dragging the corpse back into shadowed depths of the hall.

Havoc's entire takedown lasted mere seconds and she was trying to process what his appearance meant, when her brain kicked back in. *Havoc was here and Greer had the fucking place wired to blow.*

She clamped down on the panic that threatened to leave her screaming and jerked her head away from him so not to reveal his presence. Thankfully the guards were still trying to get to Felix, with Greer in their midst, and not one of them was paying Mercy any attention, thank Christ. She tracked Havoc's progress from the corner of her eye as he inched closer, sticking to shadows and the dubious cover of half standing walls.

In front of her, Felix was now pinned behind a wall, armed with his former human shield's gun and returning fire. Unfortunately, his aim was for shit. Then it ceased to matter because his gun clicked empty.

The deafening blasts of gunfire faded leaving her ears ringing and her nose stuffed with spent ammo, but under her feet the floor vibrated. Her heart rate kicked up as Havoc dove behind what must have once been a planter and she lost sight of him just as three more of Greer's goon squad emerged from the stairwell by the front door and ran past her.

She spared a rushed prayer of thanks they didn't come from the same direction where Havoc hid. With Greer distracted and Havoc nearby, she needed to move her ass. She tested the ropes again and discovered her two bookends knew their shit, because her arms weren't going anywhere. The best she could do was slide around the pillar like some warped May Pole.

She gritted her teeth, shuffled her abused feet, and wrenched her arms, feeling the pillar's cracked surface scraping her back. Maybe she could find a jagged edge on the pillar to saw the rope so she could get free and warn Havoc about the timer.

She started to move again, only to freeze as a warm hand squeezed her arm. *Havoc.*

Then the rope went tight as a cool kiss of metal brushed her skin. Tears of relief pressed for freedom, but she forced them back. With the gag stuffed in her dry mouth, the last thing she wanted was to choke to death on her own snot.

Seconds ticked by as he worked the thick rope. She silently urged him to hurry because at any minute Greer could turn and then they'd be screwed. Frustration rose and settled in with grim determination. Before it could get a crushing hold, the bark of a rifle echoed through the room and one of Greer's men hit the floor with a neat hole in his forehead.

"Cover!" Greer dove behind the collapsed remains of a pillar as her men scattered for whatever dubious protection they could find. Another rifle report and another guard dropped. That fast Greer went from a seven men team to four.

Mercy did a quick assessment of the dead guards' positions and gauged the angles of the kill shots. She didn't dare turn her head towards where she thought the shooter was (up and to the left behind her) because from her trussed-up position, she clocked the moment Greer sighted Havoc. Malicious delight lit her face and Mercy didn't need to be a mind reader to guess how Greer intended to play out this scenario. Mercy yanked against the fraying bonds and felt them snap just as Greer lifted her gun.

Mercy dove for Havoc, her scream of warning muffled by the damn gag. Her move had nothing to do with survival and everything to do with her bruised heart. She couldn't watch the man she loved be gunned down. She barreled into Havoc and knocked him back.

A gun fired.

A whip of agonizing pain sliced across her back as Havoc's arms curled around her to pull her with him. Another shot sounded and fire chewed along her hip. Then the world spun as Havoc rolled her back behind the protection of the planter. He crouched above her and kept his head down.

Greer barked out an order and someone moved.

Mercy's fingers dug into Havoc's shoulders as a deep cough of a rifle sounded. It was followed by a body hitting the floor and Greer's curse. Above her, Havoc flashed a fierce grin and lifted just enough to peek over the edge.

Okay, guess Greer was down to three men.

"Anyone else want a try?" When Math's familiar growl rolled through the air, Mercy's eyes widened, and she started to claw at her gag.

Greer's dark chuckle filtered through the room. "Is this the part where we negotiate?"

"Is that what you call this?" When Math's voice drifted down from a different direction, Mercy knew he was on the move.

She kept tearing at the gag, her nails breaking down to the quick before she finally ripped it free. Her lips stung as the gag took skin with it, and spit was a distant dream. Her mouth was bone dry but she managed a whispered croak, "Bomb!" But Havoc was too busy watching the show to hear, so she reached up, absently noting her hands were shaking, and cupped his face. His attention came to her and her back seized as she lifted her head, but she gritted out again, "Bomb! Greer has timer."

So focused on warning Havoc, Mercy missed whatever Greer said but caught Math's harsh, "Bullshit."

Havoc's face darkened and he warned Math. "She's not lying! Place is wired to blow."

Mercy guessed the part she missed, and needing to see what was happening, she stayed under Havoc and shifted to her stomach. She stifled her groan as her body protested and got to her elbows, each movement creating a violent protest from her back. She breathed through the nerve shredding pain and inched so she could peer around the end of the planter.

Greer was hunkered down behind the other planter with one of her guards. Another guard was trying to take cover behind an overturned desk.

"Since I'm not keen on dying today," Greer called out, "let's deal. You let me walk away with my men, I don't blow your asses sky high."

"Got a better deal," Math shot back, his voice hard. "You let the man and woman walk, I make your death quick."

Mercy's breath stalled as she saw Greer palm the timer. *Shit! Shit! Shit!* This wasn't going to end well.

Sure enough, Greer drawled, "Yeah, no."

Then shot to her feet, firing at Mercy and Havoc as her guards aimed high for Math. Bullets hit the brick planter and created stone shrapnel that kept Havoc and Mercy pinned. Mercy made out the rough bark of Math's rifle and couldn't help her silent cheer when he successfully winged Greer.

Unfortunately, the bullet's strike knocked the timer from her hand. With a snarl, she brought a booted heel down on the timer and smashed it to pieces before she and her two men crashed through the entrance and disappeared.

Mercy tried to lurch to her feet, but her body failed to respond.

Then Havoc was there, lifting her up. "How long?"

"Thirty seconds." It came out in a wheezing gasp.

He tossed her over his shoulder, wrapped one arm around her thighs, being careful to avoid the bleeding wound, and headed for the door.

She braced her hands on his back and managed a hoarse yell. "Math, get out!" She prayed he heard her.

Havoc gave her ass a sharp smack. "Settle. He'll be fine."

Her arms gave out and she dropped her head. She gripped his waist as he cleared the door. With nothing to do but hold on and pray, she pressed her face into his back and did exactly that.

He picked up speed and each pounding step sent his shoulder slamming into her already sore diaphragm. Salt-tinged air hit her nose and she lifted her face as a gust of wind swept over them, tangling her hair over her face.

She shoved her hair out of the way and noticed someone limping behind them. "Havoc, behind you!"

She felt him twist his torso without slowing down. "Fuck me, it's Felix."

She didn't get a chance to respond because a muffled boom sounded, and Havoc quickly changed direction, tearing her from his shoulder to cradle her against his chest. A series of progressively louder booms quickly followed. There was a breathless moment of silence as Havoc slid behind an ancient satellite dish, then the Railway building exploded.

thirty-one

Heart pounding, Havoc curled over Mercy as the concussion cloud threw dust, grit, and debris against the satellite dish. The force of the blast shifted the heavy object against the ground, but thankfully it didn't go far. Bits and pieces continued to pelt his shoulders and back with annoying stings. He tightened his hold as he cradled Mercy's head against his chest, her body shaking like a leaf. He closed his eyes and buried his nose into her hair, silently thanking all that was holy that they were both still breathing.

That was too fucking close for comfort.

Sound gradually began to filter through the clogged pressure of his ears. First came the high pitch ringing he knew from previous experience he'd be hearing for days. Then came the harsh sounds of breathing—his and Mercy's. Finally, the creaks and groans as broken stone, metal, and wood wailed their destruction and settled.

He needed to sit up so he could check out Mercy, so he started to shift only to bite back a curse as fire licked along his leg. He looked down and discovered that when he slid across the ground, he managed to leave a layer of pants and skin behind.

He shoved the inconsequential pain aside, ignored the various bodily protests, and finally made it upright. He took a moment to breathe through the aches, then adjusted his hold on Mercy.

She lifted her face from his chest, and he wanted to go back and beat the shit out of that bitch and gut Felix. Despite the gray layer of dust (the same he was he wore) the damage she sustained was painfully obvious. Her eye was puffy as hell, dried blood rimmed her mouth, her lips were torn, there was another cut was up near her hairline, and her eyes were sunk deep into her skull, the surrounding skin dark and bruised.

And that was just her face.

Maybe it was a good thing that was all he could see, because he wasn't sure he could handle the rest of what he would find. He carefully cupped her face. "Jesus, babe, they did a fucking number on you."

Her lips quirked, then quickly grimaced as some of the cuts reopened. Her hand lifted and brushed at something above his eye. When she brought it back and showed him a smear of blood, she croaked, "You too."

He caught her hand, turned it over to expose the torn knuckles and even more ragged nails, and helped her sit up. He wrapped an arm around her back. She jerked away with a hiss as a telltale wetness hit his arm. He shifted so he could see. "Son of a bitch!"

Blood painted the bottom half of her grimy shirt in rust. Cold sweat broke out as brain kicked into hellish overdrive. He braced her with a hand on her shoulder and used his other to gently raise her shirt. The tremble in his heart steadied. "It's a graze." Unfortunately, it spanned from one side to the other, nasty as all get out, which meant she'd find moving a bitch.

She shifted to her side and revealed the dust coated, blood-tinged tear along the back of her thigh. Then a harsh cough doubled her over. When it passed, her head hung down, and her hands were braced on the ground, arms trembling as a shudder worked its way down her back. After a moment or two, she raised her head, shoved the tangled mass of her hair out of her face, and gingerly rolled until she was sitting up on her own. Her tongue came out, touched her lips and she winced. "Don't suppose you have any water?"

"Wish to fuck I did." He hated the helplessness that cruised through him as he took in her pale face and the tight line of her lips. "You good while I see what we're dealing with?"

She put her hand to the ground to get up. "I'll come with."

He held her in place with a hand on her shoulder. "Not with those raw feet you aren't."

She opened her mouth to argue (Christ, the woman would argue with the devil), when a shout rang out. Havoc popped out of his crouch, spun around, and palmed his blade as he faced whatever in the hell was coming next.

"Havoc!" Dog's familiar voice bellowed. "Get your ass over here."

Havoc stepped around the edge of the dish to find Dog with his booted foot on Felix's chest and his gun pointed at a lean, dark stranger. Havoc heard movement behind him and turned his head to find Mercy struggling to her feet. "Dammit, woman."

She ignored him, a habit of hers, and shuffled over until she was at his side. She leaned into him, using his arm for balance, and stared at the scene. "Shit, that's Suárez's son, Xavier."

Of fucking course it was, because they didn't have enough shit to deal with.

Infuriated, Havoc flexed his fingers against the hilt of his blade and tried for some semblance of control. He shot her a narrow-eyed glare. "Any use in telling you to hang back?"

Her jaw jutted out and she started to limp her way to Dog.

He shook his head and followed in her wake, muttering under his breath, "Yeah, that's what I thought."

As they moved closer, he studied Suárez's heir apparent. Xavier wasn't a man you wanted to cross because you'd never see him coming. It was there in the cold-eyed perusal and the way he held his lean frame.

When they got close, Havoc took Mercy's back as she stopped next to Dog. "Xavier."

Xavier's gaze dropped to her, his face impassive, his voice flat. "Mercedes."

Undaunted, she motioned to the whimpering man who laid pale and wide-eyed between them. "I'm guessing you're here as Suárez's witness?"

Xavier flicked a glance to Felix who was trying to pry Dog's boot from his throat. "Yes."

Felix's whimpers gained strength, but everyone ignored him.

Not comfortable with Xavier's disturbingly timely presence, Havoc snapped, "How'd you find us?"

Xavier met his gaze and his lips curved into a condescending smile. But it was Mercy who answered. "You've been following us. I'm guessing since Page."

Xavier tilted his head in acknowledgement. "My father was quite enraged at Tavi's death and did not trust his vengeance to anyone but *la familia*." He sneered at Felix. "And he is no longer family." He lifted his head and aimed a telling look at Mercy. "But he is useful."

Mercy proved there was much more to her than most women, when she remained unmoved at the dark promise in Xavier's eyes. "Since you're not trying to kill me, I'm assuming you know that Tavi died at Felix's hand?"

Xavier granted her a stiff nod, confirming that he managed to witness whatever went down in the pile of rubble behind them.

Now it was Mercy's voice that went cold. "Good, that saves me the hassle of dragging his ass back to your father."

Xavier quirked an eyebrow. "You were planning on returning south?"

She went to shrug but stopped. "If it meant giving your father what I promised, yeah, I was."

A curious look passed over Xavier's face. "You are a strange woman."

"I've been called worse."

"No doubt," he murmured.

Havoc played the silent guard and refrained from taking this conversation to an abrupt end by reminding himself this was Mercy's game.

She rewarded his waning patience by asking Xavier, "The bounty?"

"Will be removed permanently," Xavier confirmed. "However, I suggest staying out of sight for a few days until the word spreads."

She nodded, and Havoc was fairly certain he was the only one who caught the slight sag in her posture.

Xavier shot a look to Havoc. "You will be informing Istaqa that our family had no part in the attempt on the dam?"

Havoc dipped his chin. "I will."

"Good." Xavier looked at Felix and dark anticipation shadowed his face. "Then, if you don't mind, I have a few things I'd like to discuss with Felix."

From his position, Havoc couldn't see Mercy's face, but there was no missing the hard edge in her voice. "Make it hurt."

Xavier gave her a chilling smile. "I intend to."

Havoc exchanged a look with Dog as Mercy nodded.

When she turned, he shifted aside, and let her move between them. He gave Dog a chin lift and turned to follow. He made it a couple of steps before a torrent of panicked Spanish erupted and then was cut off by a short scream. Havoc didn't bother looking back and neither did Mercy.

Dog fell in step beside him. Havoc slid a glance at the gun dangling from Dog's hand. "That thing have any bullets?"

Ignoring the nightmarish noises coming from behind them, Dog shot Havoc a wild grin. "Nope."

Havoc shook his head. "Crazy motherfucker."

"Yep."

Before he could say anything else, Xavier called out, "*El Verdugo.*"

Havoc rocked to a halt and turned back to find Xavier watching him, his blade buried in Felix's gut.

Xavier's attention slid past him to Mercy, who was still limping away, and came back. "Is she yours?"

Even knowing she could hear him, Havoc didn't hesitate to answer. "Yeah."

"If you plan on keeping her, keep her away from our territory." A world of warning sat behind his words.

It was time to remind the bastard exactly who he was dealing with. "The first time you and yours took my woman, I spent years wading through Cartel blood. Anyone tries for a repeat, and I'll ensure the only things standing down south are the bleached bones of the dead." He held Xavier's gaze. "*Entiendes?*"

He waited for Xavier's nod before he turned away and found Mercy standing still, staring at him, her expression hard to read. Her attention shifted when the sounds of Xavier getting back to work rode the air.

Next to him, Dog chuckled softly. "Balls of fucking steel, my man."

Havoc didn't answer and deliberately stopped in front of Mercy, blocking her view.

Her bruised eyes came to his. "We need to find Math."

"Good luck with that," Dog said as he tucked the empty gun into the back of his pants. "Saw him making tracks after that crazy ass bitch." He ran a critical eye over Mercy before adding, "Hate to break it to you, girly, but you're in no shape to go chasing after him either."

For a moment Havoc thought she'd argue, which would leave him no choice but to drag her kicking and screaming back into town.

Instead, she surprised him. "Fine, if we're done here, can we go?" She plucked at her shirt. "I want a shower, some food and a damn bed. Not necessarily in that order."

He caught the slight tremor on the last half of her statement. Whatever hold she had on her emotions was starting to fray, so he stepped in. "You won't make it far on those feet, so..." He gave her his back and, thanks to his ripped-up leg, stiffly dropped into a crouch. "Hop up."

Dog grinned as she heaved a put-upon sigh before she closed in, looped her arms over Havoc's shoulders and linked them in front of his chest. She hitched her uninjured leg over one hip, and then sucked in a breath before doing the same, with much more care to her injury, on the other side.

Once her weight settled, he reached back, slid his hands under her ass, and gave her a gentle boost as he stood up. Her face dropped to where his neck and shoulder met, her breath soft and warm against his skin. He tilted his head, touching his jaw to her head. "Ready?"

Her 'yeah' came out choked.

He turned to Dog and jerked his chin for the other man to take point as they headed back to their bikes.

thirty-two

Mercy clung to Havoc's back and did her damnedest not to fall apart. The fact that various body parts took turns vigorously protesting helped. The haze of discomfort was joined by a fog of numbness and by the time they hit where the men had stashed their bikes, the fact that Math's was busy chasing Greer barely made a blip on her radar.

Havoc's soft, "Babe" dragged her back.

It took monumental effort to lift her head. "What?"

A warm hand curled over hers and tugged. "Need you to let go." He sank into a crouch.

She forced stiff muscles to move, slid down his back, and was unable to stifle a whimper when her sore feet touched the ground. She grabbed the arm Havoc threw out so she wouldn't face plant and swayed in place. When she was certain she wouldn't tip over, she let him go. "I'm good."

"You sure?"

She nodded.

He took her at her word and walked to his bike. After digging around in one of the saddle bags, he came back with a canteen. He curled an arm above her waist, steering clear of the long stinging graze, and lifted it to her lips. "Take it slow."

She leaned into Havoc, her hands shaking as she covered his on the canteen, and then she almost sobbed as water hit her dry mouth. It was difficult not to gulp, but she managed to restrain herself to sips. When she finished, he put it away and got on his bike. Once he kicked it to life, he reached out. She took his hand and hobbled over. Together they got her up and in place behind him. She wrapped her arms around his waist, unable to hide the full body tremor that set up shop.

He covered her hands with his and squeezed. "Just a little longer, yeah?"

Her answering, 'yeah' was faint but solid. Then she dropped her head to Havoc's back, closed her eyes, and for the first time in ever, let someone else take over for a while.

LATE AFTERNOON SUNLIGHT danced across Mercy's closed lids, but she didn't bother opening them. She was lying on her less injured side, her head nestled on a pillow. Awareness crept in as her body caught up with her mind. First was the dull throb from the soles of her feet. It was soon joined by the mumblings of aching muscles, sore ribs, a low-grade headache, and topped off by the twitchy stings from two bullet grazes and multitude cuts and scrapes.

Despite all that, she let her lashes lift and managed a small smile when she discovered the mouth-watering expanse of skin in front of her. Unable to resist the temptation, she untucked one hand and placed her palm over Havoc's heart. Her lashes dropped as his heart beat a steady pulse under her palm.

The trip back to the Royal was vague but she did remember Havoc carrying her back to their room. As for what happened after he closed the door, those were just snippets as he treated her various injuries. She thought there might have been an argument about a shower but gave up trying to remember. Instead, she lay still and enjoyed the moment out of time.

A feather light brush against her temple was followed by a soft trail of kisses down the side of her face. When they stopped, she lifted her lashes and stared into Havoc's dark eyes. The hand at his chest went to his jaw, her thumb brushing over his lower lip. "Hey."

"Hey." Under her touch his lips twitched. He stroked her spine as his coffee dark gaze roamed over her with a visceral touch, leaving chills in its wake. "How are you feeling?"

"Sore, stiff," she admitted, as she dropped her hand back to his chest before adding a quiet, "stunned."

The hand at her back stilled and the heat of his palm seared through the thin material of the t-shirt covering her. "Stunned?"

She aimed her gaze at his chest as her fingers idly played with the thin dividing line of hair. "Wasn't expecting..." she trailed off as she realized what she would reveal if she finished.

It didn't stop Havoc. "Wasn't expecting what?" He tucked a finger under her chin and lifted her face to his. "Me to show?'

Her face heated as she tried to draw back only to find she was pretty much stuck in place. "You made it pretty clear you weren't planning on sticking around," she muttered.

A growl rumbled in his chest and then, before she could blink, she found herself flat on her back, arms trapped between them, as he caged her under his body. The protest from her back disappeared as Havoc dominated her attention. "That's a selective memory you've got there, darlin'."

Caught as she was, there was no way to escape his shrewd gaze. Something she refused to name slipped into his eyes and made her heart ache. Off balance and uncomfortable with the unfamiliar emotions churning inside her, feminine pride came to her rescue, and she arched a brow. "You have a strange definition for selective because I clearly remember you telling me I was on my own."

He dipped his head, nipped her chin, and against her lips said, "No, I told you to get your ass back to me once you found your balance." He dipped his head and took her lips in a soft seductive kiss that took her under and swept away her flimsy walls.

Maybe it was because she never expected to be here, in his arms or breathing, or maybe it was just because it was Havoc, but she didn't fight it. Instead, she dove in and let it flood her world. When he finally lifted his head, she was fighting for breath and a way to assuage the ache burning through her, so it took a few seconds for Havoc's question to penetrate. "What?"

The glow of humor edged the seriousness in his face. "I asked, did you find your balance?"

Since talking was proving difficult, she managed a nod.

"Were you going to come back to me?" There was a hint of vulnerability in his question that cut through everything and arrowed straight to her core.

It hit her then that she wasn't the only one on shaky ground. But when she went to answer, her insecurities rallied and forced different words from her mouth. "Did you want me to?"

The muscles in his arms flexed and something close to pain flashed over his face. "I waited, like some pansy assed idiot, for you to come back. When you didn't, I was beyond pissed." His gaze shifted and then came back. "Pissed and hurt," he admitted. "When you didn't show, thought you bailed."

The depth of emotion behind his admission sank past her worries and insecurities, to settle solid and sure against her heart. She wiggled until he lifted enough to release her arms. Then she brought her hands to his face and took pleasure in tracing his features. "I was going to come back, it's just Felix found me first." His jaw flexed, but she ignored it and kept going. "Found my balance before I went to see Math, but I owed it to him to let him know my plans, especially since they included helping you. Then, when I got back..."

"I jumped down your throat," he growled. "Shit."

She cupped his jaw and gave him a small shake. "You had a right to be pissed, Havoc, but they weren't my secrets to share."

He dropped his head to hers. "Yeah, got that when Math laid it out."

She brushed a fingertip over the cut on his cheek. "I'm guessing this was Math's doing?"

"Yeah, bastard wears too many damn rings."

She choked back an unexpected giggle at the disgruntled note in his voice and bit her lip, wincing when she hit a sore spot. "Since he was covering our asses with Greer, I'm assuming you two worked it out?"

He lifted his head and nuzzled her. "We came to an understanding." He lifted his head and held her gaze. "He knows I'm giving Reaper his name, and he's expecting you to be at my side."

She caught the question under his statement, held his gaze, and opened her heart. "Grew up thinking there were no such things as knights in shining armor. Until you came along, I figured I was just fine taking the dragons on my own." Being this honest scared the shit out of her, but there was no going back, not now, not when there was a chance at claiming something beautiful.

The big body surrounding hers froze and he narrowed his eyes. "You still thinking of going it alone?"

She arched a brow and tried not to let her nerves get the

better of her. "Actually, I've been thinking it might be in my best interest to take on a partner. You know, someone to watch my back." She met his gaze and made her offer. "And maybe help keep my heart in one piece. You up for the position?"

His 'hell yeah,' got lost as he took her mouth with a toe-curling possessiveness, she never thought she wanted and set a match to the ever ready fire blazing between them.

SHORTLY AFTER HAVOC left to get them something to eat, Mercy was startled awake by a knock. Not at the door, but at the window behind her. She grabbed the blade tucked under Havoc's pillow, ignored her body's protests, and rolled off the side of the bed, putting it between her and her window visitor. She fought not to wince as her bandaged feet hit the rug.

When she realized it was Math's face staring at her through the glass, she muttered, "Are you kidding me?"

Not wanting to walk, she crawled over the bed to the other side, grateful she'd put Havoc's t-shirt back on. She shuffled to the window and shoved it open. "What the hell, Math? There's a perfectly good door over there."

Math threw a leg over the sill, and she backed up as he climbed in. When the bed's edge hit the back of her thighs, she sat.

Math dropped into the chair. "You okay?"

"You care?"

He frowned. "That's a stupid ass question."

"Is it?" She tucked her lingering hurt away because emotion would get her nowhere with him. "Last time we spoke you made it crystal clear we were done."

"Don't be such a stubborn bitch, Mercy."

"Hello kettle, I'm pot."

He grimaced and blew out a hard breath. "Look, I get that you've gone and claimed the Vulture as yours, but I'm not ready to get all buddy-buddy with them."

"And why is that?"

He leaned forward and braced his elbows on his knees. "Ask Reaper."

She canted her head to the side and wondered yet again if her boss—ex-boss—was psychic. "You sound certain I'll be talking to him."

"Won't you?" When she didn't answer, he smiled. "Known you a long time, darling. Watched you spend years convincing yourself you don't deserve it, but now..."

When he trailed off, she couldn't help but urge softly, "What?"

His face gentled and something wistful drifted through it. "You're finally happy."

Stunned at his unexpected insight, she could only look at him her mouth hanging open.

His momentary softness disappeared under his normal stoic mask as he continued, "Don't know how he managed to convince you, but I've got to give the bastard credit, he did the impossible."

"Math, I—"

He held up a hand and cut her off. "Look, don't have much time, but I wanted to make sure you were okay before I head out."

And didn't that statement stoke all sorts of worries. "Where are you going?"

Math's face was grim but determined. "I'm going to follow that bitch back to her master."

Yeah, that was the answer she figured he'd give. Knowing there would be no talking him out of it, and besides, she wasn't sure she wanted to, she asked, "Then what?"

There was nothing pleasant in his smile. "Then we'll find out if we all really are on the same side." He got to his feet and brushed a hand over her cheek. "Tell Reaper whatever you feel you need to share. But fair warning, be prepared to duck when he loses his shit, and when he calms down, let me know."

And just like that, he truly let her go.

She stood up, wrapped her arms around Math, and whispered around the lump in her throat, "Be careful, Math."

His arms came around her and she felt him drop a kiss on her head. "You too, Mercy." He gave her one final, gentle squeeze, and stepped back.

She followed him to the window, watched as he swung out, and then leaned out the opening. "Math."

With one hand on the fire escape, he turned.

"Good hunting."

He gave her a fierce smile and slipped away.

She watched him disappear into the night and only turned away when the door behind her opened and the man who held her heart walked in. "You okay, babe?"

She crawled over the bed and met Havoc as he came to a stop by the edge of the bed. He dumped the food on the bed as she got to her knees, wrapped her arms around him, and took his lips in a fierce kiss. When she drew back, they were both breathing heavy.

"What was that for?"

"Math just left, he's going after Greer."

Havoc's arms tightened as his gaze went to the window and then came back to her. "Alone?"

"For now." When lingering doubts gathered in his gorgeous eyes, she was quick to add, "If he needs help, he'll let us know, but I think we need to get to Pebble Creek and get your friends up to speed before he gets in too much trouble."

He pulled her close. "You stayed."

There was a burgeoning hope in his voice, and it triggered

an unexpected lump in her throat that made her voice husky. "Of course I did, we're partners now, right?"

Something bright and beautiful crossed his face and erased the shadows in his eyes. "Yeah, we are."

"Good." She pressed in and put her mouth up to his ear. "Just so you know, Havoc, I love you."

He buried his hand in her hair and pulled her head and took her mouth in a searing kiss. When he lifted his head and whispered, "Love you too, babe," she found her balance was rock steady even as he stood by, arms at the ready.

THANK you for reading BEG FOR MERCY. Crave another hit? Then get ready for fireworks when Math catches the intriguing and attractive Vex in his wicked web of secrets in **CAUGHT IN THE AFTERMATH.**

Curious about Jami's other worlds? Then don't miss out on exclusive short stories & new release information by subscribing to Jami's newsletter at:
https://www.subscribepage.com/Jami-Subscription-Books

Do you want to share your exciting discovery of a new read?
Then leave a review!

Or you're welcome to swing by and visit Jami's website at:
http://jamigray.com

If you're looking for more titles to feed your reading fix, turn the
page and explore Jami's other series.

the collapse: fate's vultures

Meet a new breed of warriors, Fate's Vultures, a mercenary band who live by a code in a world gone to hell — loyalty to each other, but for the right price, they'll be the shield for those without. In the ravaged aftermath of the post-apocalyptic these evocative couples will stop at nothing to claim their future.

Binge your way through the world of The Collapse today!

LYING IN RUINS

Charity & Ruin

On a shared mission of vengeance, what will destroy them first—their suspicions or their enemies?

BEG FOR MERCY

Havoc & Mercy

Will an assassin and a mercenary find their balance on the thin line of loyalty, or will it snap under the weight of their wary hearts?

CAUGHT IN THE AFTERMATH

Vex & Math

Caught between a looming conflict and the fallout of a brutal betrayal, will they survive vengeance's aftermath?

FEAR THE REAPER

Reaper & Lilith

Two adversaries must navigate a minefield of past betrayals and broken promises to defeat a common enemy before it all turns to hell.

arcane transporter
books
Urban Fantasy Series

Race into this complete urban fantasy series thrill-ride today!

Need to ensure you delivery, magical or otherwise, makes it to its destination? For guaranteed delivery, hire the best in the west, Rory Costas, Arcane Transporter. (Independent contractor - not responsible for damage incurred in transit.)

GRAVE CARGO

When a questionable, but lucrative delivery job takes an unexpected turn, will Rory survive the collision or crash and burn?

RISKY GOODS

A dead mage, a missing friend, and an unpredictable alliance merge into a volatile package sending Rory careening through the Arcane elite's deadly secrets.

LETHAL CONTENTS

A failed assassination, a kidnapped ally, and a treasonous scheme pit Rory and Zev against a devious enemy determined to watch Arcane society crash and burn.

Meet Rory and Zev and grab your copy of *IGNITION POINT* by signing up for Jami's monthly newsletter at:

psy - iv teams books

Welcome to a world where facing danger requires the unique skill set of the men and women of Jami Gray's PSY-IV Teams. As sparks, and bullets fly, love, action, and adventure will target these unique couples as they race through each breath-stealing operation.

Binge the series today wherever books are sold!

HUNTED BY THE PAST

Cyn & Kayden

To escape a killer from their past, can a reluctant psychic trust the man who walked away?

TOUCHED BY FATE

Risia & Tag

A seer's secrets become her only bargaining chip in a high-stakes game of lies and loyalty determining her fate.

MARKED BY OBSESSION

Meli & Wolf

A woman in hiding. A telepath who sees deeper than her scars. Can they forge a bond stronger than the obsession stalking them before time runs out?

FRACTURED BY DECEIT

Megan & Bishop

After a brutal attack by a telepath, Megan turns to Bishop for help, but how does he keep her safe when she's threat?

LINKED BY DECEPTION

Jinx & Rabbit

Forced to play intimate criminal partners, will Rabbit & Jinx risk turning illusion to truth as they race to untangle a web of conspiracies and lies?

kyn kronicles series
Urban Fantasy/Paranormal Romance Series

Welcome to a world where the supernatural walks alongside humans, their existence kept secret behind the thinnest of veils. Now modern man's scientific curiosity is determined to rip that curtain aside, revealing the nightmares in the shadows.

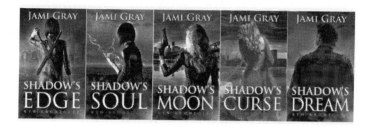

SHADOW'S EDGE

Raine's spent a lifetime hunting monsters, but can she stop her prey from exposing the supernatural community one bloody corpse at a time?

SHADOW'S SOUL

When a simple assignment turns into a nightmare, can Raine and Gavin unravel old vendettas before they both pay the ultimate price?

SHADOW'S MOON

Compromise isn't in Warrick's vocabulary and Xander won't abandon the hunt. As the line between instinct and intellect blurs, will they survive the fallout?

SHADOW'S CURSE

When the queen of chaos locks horns with death's justice, Natasha and Darius set a dangerous game in motion, leading two predators into a lethal dance of secrets.

SHADOW'S DREAM

Tala can't forget the past. Cheveyo can't change it. As the dreams they shared linger, can they escape the encroaching nightmare before it's too late?

Stay tuned for the final installment, SHADOW'S FALL arriving July 2021

about the author

Jami Gray is the coffee addicted, music junkie, Queen Nerd of her personal Geek Squad, Alpha Mom of the Fur Minxes, who writes to soothe the voices crammed in her head. You don't want to miss out on her multiple series that combine magical intrigue and fearless romance into one wild ride – with the worlds of the Arcane Transporter, The Kyn, PSY-IV Teams, or The Collapse.

amazon.com/author/jamigray

facebook.com/jamigray.author

bookbub.com/authors/jami-gray

goodreads.com/JamiGray

twitter.com/JamiGrayAuthor

instagram.com/jamigrayauthor

Made in the USA
Middletown, DE
07 March 2022

62183953R00189